Dead by Midnight

ALSO BY CAROLYN HART

Death on Demand

Death on Demand

Design for Murder

Something Wicked

Honeymoon with Murder

A Little Class on Murder

Deadly Valentine

The Christie Caper

Southern Ghost

Mint Julep Murder

Yankee Doodle Dead

White Elephant Dead

Sugarplum Dead

April Fool Dead

Engaged to Die

Murder Walks the Plank

Death of the Party

Dead Days of Summer

Death Walked In

Dare to Die

Laughed 'Til He Died

Dead by Midnight

A Death on Demand Mystery

Carolyn Hart

HARPER **LUXE**

An Imprint of HarperCollinsPublishers

HarperCollins books may be purchased for educational, business, or sales promotional use. For information please write: Special Markets Department, HarperCollins Publishers, 10 East 53rd Street, New York, NY 10022.

FIRST HARPERLUXE EDITION

HarperLuxe™ is a trademark of HarperCollins Publishers

Library of Congress Cataloging-in-Publication Data is available upon request.

ISBN: 978-0-06-201784-0

11 12 13 14 ID/OPM 10 9 8 7 6 5 4 3 2 1

To Deborah Schneider with love

One

Glen Jamison looked every one of his fifty-two years, his fair hair flecked with silver, his aristocratic face mournful, his six-foot-two frame too thin. He hunched at the desk in his study and felt a sense of panic, like the beginnings of a fire flickering at his feet then billowing to an inferno. How much longer could the firm go on?

There wasn't enough money coming in. The appointment book had too many empty spots. Maybe they shouldn't dump Kirk even though cutting him should save at least a hundred thousand a year. He hated looking into Kirk's blue eyes, which held the hurt puzzlement of a kicked dog. Of course, Kirk was young. Not yet thirty. He was a brilliant lawyer. He'd find a job. But he wouldn't find a job on the island.

There were only two other firms and neither intended to expand. Not in times like these. Kirk needed to stay on Broward's Rock. Glen tried not to think how desperately Kirk needed to be here.

Glen wondered if it would do any good to talk to Cleo again. If Kirk stayed, Laura wouldn't be so angry with him, either. It was a misery to go to the office and see Kirk, tight-lipped and grim. Then he shook his head. He knew in his heart that Cleo wouldn't agree to keep Kirk. Maybe it had been another mistake to give Kirk a couple of months to wind down his cases. But that had seemed the decent thing to do and Cleo had agreed.

Glen had been a little surprised at her acquiescence but grateful he didn't have to face her disapproval. He was getting enough disapproval around town. A couple of times at the Men's Grill, he was sure he'd been avoided by clients. In fact, Ted Toomey had canceled an appointment a few days after word got around that the firm was letting Kirk go. Ted had said evasively that he was still giving the matter that they had intended to discuss some thought. One more empty slot in the appointment book. The money wasn't coming in and Cleo wanted . . . Cleo wanted many things. He'd given in over the trip to Paris for Christmas.

When the kids were little, he and Maddy and the kids came home from the midnight service and put the baby Jesus in the crèche. Now the crèche was in the attic with the other Christmas decorations that had been in his family for generations. The decorations Maddy and the kids had made together were boxed up, too.

Cleo had wanted all new decorations for their first Christmas together. He'd hated the tree. Shiny white with all blue balls, the tree reminded him of a department store. The kids hated the tree, too. They hated everything Cleo did. This year she had waved away the idea of decorating. After all, they'd be in Paris . . .

The kids had been unhappy ever since he married Cleo. He used to be excited to have his children home. Not anymore. Maddy had been gone so long now. He still felt the clutch of emptiness in his gut when he thought of her and the night the police came to the door to tell him about the accident. The first few years he'd been in a daze, working, trying not to think, hurting. He owed everything to Elaine. She'd given up her job in Atlanta and come to help and be there for the kids. The kids loved their aunt.

He felt guilty every time he passed the first bedroom on the second floor that had been Elaine's room.

Now she lived in the cottage not far from the gazebo. She'd acted as if the new quarters were fine. Maybe she liked the cottage, but she didn't like Cleo any more than the kids did. Cleo had insisted Elaine needed a life of her own. After all, she'd done a good job with the kids. Maybe she'd like to go back to Atlanta. But Elaine had been on the island for so many years now. She had her friends, a life she'd built, and of course Tommy was still in high school. That was another problem. Well, Tommy had acted up. He had to find out who was boss. The matter was settled.

Anger was everywhere around him. Pat Merridew had worked for the firm for so many years, but Cleo had insisted Pat was frumpy and they needed a young and charming receptionist. Firing Pat hadn't saved money. Cleo was paying the new girl even more. Glen hated to remember the ugly look on Pat's face when he saw her yesterday on the street. And then there was Kirk . . .

Glen shied away from thinking about Kirk. It would be a relief not to have to face him every day. They'd given him two months to close down his cases. Three more weeks and he'd be gone.

Cleo told him to buck up. Everything would get better.

The money flow would have to get better soon.

Richard Jamison parked his rust-streaked 2004 Pontiac in the shade of a live oak. He left the windows down and pulled a stained duffel from the trunk. The house looked just as he remembered it, a gracious Lowcountry antebellum home, tabby exterior moss green in the June sunshine. Wicker furniture on the shaded verandah looked inviting. He'd like to settle in a rocker with a rum collins. He and Glen could talk over old times. He'd have to go cautiously with Glen. It would never do for Glen to realize that Richard had come to the island to seek financial backing. If he presented everything just right, he could persuade Glen that he was giving him a good investment opportunity.

Richard hefted the duffel. He was curious to meet his hostess. He'd been in Singapore when Glen remarried. Maddy had been dead for six years now, maybe seven. He wondered how the kids felt about a stepmother. Especially a stepmother who was only a few years older than Laura. And how did Glen's sister, who had since then served as chatelaine of the antebellum home, feel about the new Mrs. Jamison?

Kids . . . As he climbed the front steps, he gave a slight shake of his head. Not kids anymore. Laura must be about twenty-four. Kit was in graduate school. Tommy was in high school.

An old friend had written him about Glen's second wife. "Cleo's hot, a tall brunette, sultry brown eyes, leggy but stacked. Cleo's one lucky lady. Whatever she does succeeds. High school beauty queen. Top grades in law school. Bowls over guys with one glance. Her favorite game's roulette. The ball always seems to fall in her pocket. Don't know what she saw in Glen except he's top drawer when it comes to an old Southern family and her roots are middle class. She grew up in Hardeeville, mom a teacher, dad a fireman. They lived in a modest frame house on an unpaved road. Plus, Glen used to have a lot more cash till the meltdown in '08. Cleo came to work at the firm, made partner in a year, married Glen the next year."

Richard shifted the duffel, punched the doorbell. He'd selected his wardrobe with care, a boring blue oxford-cloth shirt, poplin slacks, and cordovan loafers, a far cry from his usual frayed tee, baggy shorts, and flip-flops. He'd shaved the stubble that he preferred, even sported a short haircut. He hoped the preppy look would reassure Glen that his wild cousin Richard could, with the proper financial backing, become a pillar of the community.

When the white door opened, Cleo Jamison pushed the screen, held it wide for him. Dark brown hair cupped a long face with deep-set brown eyes, a straight nose, and full lips. A summery blouse emphasized the curve of her breasts. Sleek jade slacks molded to her legs. She smiled. "You must be Richard." Her throaty voice made him think of cast-aside pillows and rumpled sheets. She reached out a perfectly manicured hand, the fingers long, slim, and warm, to take his hand.

Richard felt a flood of desire. His response was immediate and instinctual. For an instant, a hot current sizzled between them.

Cleo relinquished his hand. Her gaze was abruptly remote. Her lips curved in a conventional, polite smile.

He stepped inside, once again under control. But she'd responded for a flicker of an instant. Hadn't she?

A door opened toward the end of the hall. A tall man walked wearily toward Richard and Cleo.

Richard felt an instant of shock. Glen's fair hair was silvered, his face drawn and tired; his clothes hung too loosely on his body. "Hey, Glen." Richard forced a robust shout.

Glen's slightly reedy voice was raised in welcome. "Hey, little buddy, welcome home."

Cleo was well aware that Kit Jamison had been in her father's study for almost fifteen minutes. She felt a surge of triumph. It had taken all her cleverness to delicately maneuver Glen into a state of acute dissatisfaction with his daughter. He'd almost proved intractable, but Cleo's will had prevailed. Funny that he should be so devoted to unstylish, awkward, socially graceless Kit. Of course, she looked like her father, fair-haired, fair-skinned, slender, but her pale blue eyes were humorless, her thin face ascetic. Sure, Kit was academically brilliant, but she didn't have the smarts to go after a well-paying career. Kit's plan to go to the Serengeti to help catalog declining lion populations as a volunteer biologist might be admirable, but let her manage on somebody else's dollar. Asking Glen to support her intellectual and nonpaying lifestyle would have been all right a few years ago, but Glen not only lost half of his savings in the crash, he'd been panicked enough to sell when the Dow was plunging down toward seven thousand. Cleo's lips thinned. He should have asked her. But he hadn't.

Despite the thickness of the walls between Glen's study and hers, the sounds of acrimony penetrated.

Cleo rose from her chair. She paused in the sunlight that poured through the large, wide window to admire the glitter of the emerald bracelet on her wrist, a gift from Glen, then strolled toward the hallway. She knocked briskly on Glen's study door, swung it wide.

Kit jerked to face the door, her narrow face folded in a furious frown. Without makeup, her fair skin was pallid, though marred now by red patches of anger.

Cleo's voice was pleasant. "Kit, won't you stay for lunch?"

Kit flung out one hand. Her hands were graceful and elegant despite chipped nails. "I'd rather eat with hyenas." Head down, she rushed toward the door.

Glen pushed up from his chair. "Kit, come back here. Apologize to Cleo."

The only answer was the clatter of steps in the hallway and the slam of the front door.

Darwyn Jack straightened the collar of the green polo. His fingers luxuriated in the crinkly feel of the cotton mesh. His thick, sensuous lips curled in the half smile that made women his for the taking. Women couldn't resist his tangle of thick chestnut curls and sloe-brown eyes that held a reckless glint. He felt on top of the world, invincible.

He looked around the dim, small room, seeing only its cramped lack of space and shabby furnishings, blind to its scrubbed cleanliness and the lovingly hand-pieced quilt on the bed.

He gave a final approving glance at the mirror and moved into the hall. He was tall, muscular, and well built, but he walked with a slight limp. He'd been the best running back in the state when he was a junior and there was already talk of how he'd have his pick of colleges when he graduated. An accident while mowing a hayfield ended his football dreams and his college hopes. He'd never bothered much about grades. Who needed them if you could run like the wind?

In the kitchen, he walked to the old oak table, pulled out a chair. This room, too, was clean and bright with daffodil-yellow curtains at the windows.

Bella Mae Jack's cotton housedress was crisp and starched. A big woman, she moved slowly now that she'd reached her seventies. She no longer cleaned homes for a living but she baked and cooked for the weekly farmers' market that was held every Saturday in the park near the harbor. She was careful with her money, always frugal, unfailingly honest. She turned, a plate in her hand. "Sausage patties and dilly bread." She stopped, peered nearsightedly, her pale worn face folding into a frown. "You march back to your room and take that nice shirt off. You have work clothes. Wear them." Her voice was stern.

Darwyn hesitated for only a fraction, then, with a shrug, he came to his feet. When he'd played football, he liked to hurt opposing players. Darwyn had a cold, dark core, the product of abusive years before his drug-ridden parents died and he came, a withdrawn and wary seven-year-old, to live with his grandmother. Only for Bella Mae would he ever be meek.

In his room, he shrugged and carefully pulled off the polo. Soon he would wear fine clothes whenever he liked.

Pat Merridew walked back and forth across her small living room, too angry to sit and try to relax. Finally she stopped at the closet, reached for her light jacket. Even though it was summer, the nights were cool in the woods. She slid a small flashlight into her pocket and retrieved her BlackBerry from her purse. She didn't need a BlackBerry now, not since she'd lost her job. But she always carried a phone in the woods in case of an accident.

She edged out of the back door, careful to keep Gertrude from following. "Not safe for you, sweetie." Gertrude was only permitted outside on a leash and their walks avoided the lagoon with its leathery black king, a nine-foot alligator who would see Gertrude as an hors d'oeuvre. "You stay inside." The door shut, muffling the disappointed whine of the elderly dachshund. Pat walked swiftly, the way familiar now. She'd begun her late-night forays when she found it hard to sleep after she was fired.

Pushed by hatred, she walked the half mile to the Jamison property and stood in the shadows of an old live oak, glaring at the dark windows. Long ago, the land had been home to one of the island plantations. There were stories of a ghostly little girl wandering on summer nights, looking for her father, who had been killed in the Battle of Honey Hill. What if a ghost began to haunt the house? Or maybe a poltergeist might make its presence known by little destructive acts.

She stood in the shadows and hugged ideas of revenge.

Oyster shells crackled. She was alert, wary. It was past midnight. Pat watched a dimly seen figure slip through the moonlit garden to the gazebo. Footsteps sounded on the gazebo steps. A flashlight flared, illuminating the interior. The beam settled on a wooden bench. The shadow behind the light knelt for a few minutes, then rose. The light was turned off. Footsteps again thudded softly on the wooden steps. Pat watched the swift, confident return toward the house until the visitor to the gazebo was out of sight behind shrubbery.

Pat waited a few minutes. No one stirred in the garden. She walked swiftly to the gazebo and edged up the steps. She bent and used her pencil flash for a quick flicker. A rolled-up brown towel was taped beneath the bench. She knelt and touched the towel. Oh. She took a quick breath. She didn't need to remove and unroll the lumpy towel to know what it covered. She thought for a moment, then smiled grimly as she reached in her other pocket.

A moment later she moved swiftly along the path in the woods, using the pocket flash to light her way. A thought darted as swiftly as a minnow: knowledge was power.

Henny Brawley sat on her verandah overlooking the marsh. The spartina grass glimmered gold in the morning sun, rippling in a light breeze. Fiddler crabs skittered on the mudflats as the tide ebbed. She took a sip of rich, black Sumatra coffee and breathed deeply of the distinctive marsh scent. All would be well in her sea island world except, of course, for the challenge of personalities. But Henny wasn't irritated. Detecting motives, choosing the right word at the right time to achieve a desired effect, provided a never-ending challenge in her role as a volunteer, and was almost as much fun as reading clever, multilayered mysteries.

Henny laughed aloud. As soon as she identified one more of the paintings hanging this month in the Death on Demand mystery bookstore, she would break a current tie with Emma Clyde. Emma, the island's famed mystery author, was also—Henny was willing to give credit where credit was due—an omnivorous mystery reader and a worthy opponent in the contest. Each painting represented a particular mystery novel. The first viewer to identify titles and authors would win free coffee for a month and a new book. She would choose the latest by either Jasper Fforde or Rosemary Harris.

Henny could almost recall the book depicted in the third painting, but not quite. Browsing the store's shelves this afternoon, she was certain something would nudge her memory. However, first she needed to help her old friend Pat Merridew, who had applied for the paid manager's job at the Helping Hands Center, a private charity that threw out lifelines to the sick, the old, the troubled.

There was a fly in the ointment. One of the board members was a stickler for checking references, which seemed a trifle absurd on an island the size of Broward's Rock. All of them knew Pat Merridew, admittedly a bit quirky and sometimes fractious, but whatever her shortcomings, Pat exuded energy and she knew everyone in town.

Of course, there had to be a reason why Pat had lost her job at the law firm. That was the point made by Rachel Thompson in her brusque way. "Depend on it, Henny, there's a story there. We can't hire Pat until we know what's what."

Henny had made no headway when she'd suggested that Pat was simply another casualty of Cleo Jamison's remake of her husband's life and office. Rachel had insisted, "We must know the truth of the matter."

Henny flipped open her cell, punched a number.

"Jamison, Jamison, and Brewster." The unfamiliar feminine voice was obviously young. The new receptionist, no doubt.

Henny raised an eyebrow. Kirk Brewster's name was still included in the firm name. But not for long. Glen should be ashamed. Of course, everyone had been struggling with hard times. "This is Henny Brawley calling for Mr. Jamison." She and Glen had worked together on fund-raising for the island youth center.

"May I ask the subject of your call?" The voice was chirpy.

Henny felt as if a door had slammed in her face. If Pat had answered, the call would have been put through without question if Glen was in the office and available. It would take the new receptionist time to learn the ropes. "I'm calling in regard to a recommendation for Pat Merridew."

"How is that spelled, please?"

Henny responded politely, though she was annoyed. Pat had worked at the firm for more than twenty years. Was she already completely forgotten?

"Thank you. One moment, please."

Henny understood that Kirk had started looking for a job on the mainland, but law firms had cut back on hiring in the face of the economic downturn. Kirk's record was amazing. He'd been number one in his law class and made junior partner in a mainline Atlanta firm in four years, instead of the usual seven. He would likely still be on the fast track to an equity partnership except for his sister's serious illness. Both parents were dead and he was the only family she had. Henny felt sure Kirk would eventually receive an offer, but that didn't change the fact that his single-mom sister had leukemia and depended upon Kirk to help with her two little boys. The grim news had come only a few months after he made partner at the Atlanta law firm, but he'd immediately resigned and returned to the island. If he had to leave Broward's Rock, his nephews would suffer.

The chirrupy voice returned. "Mr. Jamison is in conference, but Mrs. Jamison is available."

Henny hesitated. She could call Glen at home tonight. But she'd promised Rachel she'd check this morning. Before she could answer, Cleo came on the line. "Cleo Jamison."

Henny raised a disdainful eyebrow. Cleo dismissed niceties such as hello. Implicit in her tone was the conviction that she, Cleo, was due homage. Cleo had succeeded in conveying her sense of self-worth to the community of Broward's Rock. Since her arrival on the island a few years ago, she'd excelled as a rising young lawyer, married the widowed senior partner, and now she dominated the island's social scene, young, beautiful, and joyously self-confident.

Henny spoke pleasantly. "Hi, Cleo. Henny Brawley. I need a rec for Pat. She's applied to work at Helping Hands. Of course, the job isn't on a level with her work at the firm. She'll be overqualified but we'll be glad to have someone to sort and arrange the clothes and household goods." *And you screwed her royally, so now's the time to pony up some help, lady.*

"Pat?" A sigh of regret. "I wish I could be helpful, but as I told Rachel this morning—"

Henny's eyes narrowed. Rachel was humorless, didactic, pompous, and perhaps the wealthiest member of the Helping Hands board. Rachel was pleased to provide support, but only if people and proposals met with her approval. Had she called Cleo?

"—I'm afraid Pat's become a bit unbalanced. She wasn't the right face for the firm now. The firm wants to project an up-to-the-minute image, youthful, forward-looking. Glen explained it to her as kindly as possible—"

"Pat doesn't need a youthful image at Helping Hands." Henny's tone was sharp, but she knew it was a stiletto flick at an opponent who wore emotional chain mail.

"Of course not." Cleo sounded amused. "But Rachel agreed that it wouldn't do to hire someone who is emotionally unstable." Now Cleo's voice was metallic. "Last weekend she slipped into the house and accused Glen of ruining her life. There was a dreadful scene. She refused to leave until I threatened to call the police. Of course, she's old—"

Henny was icy. "Not quite fifty." Cleo knew full well that Henny was a septuagenarian. Cleo was arrogantly on the sunny side of thirty.

"Oh, perhaps it's hot flashes." Cleo was dismissive. "In any event, you'd better check with Rachel. I gave her a ring when I heard Pat had applied to Helping Hands. I thought she should know the truth. But I suggested a charming young woman who's working on her certification for home health. Ciao."

Henny listened to the buzzing line, clicked off the handset. Was Cleo's tale of Pat's behavior true? Whether it was or not, Pat wouldn't get the job. It was too late to try to talk to Glen.

Henny sipped coffee. She watched a majestic blue heron poised to capture a fish. The heron's beak darted into the murky green water, lofted its prey. The great bird swallowed and the fish was gone, plucked from its summer moment in the warm water just as Pat had been ousted from her once secure job.

Annie Darling looked out at the teeming marina as she hurried toward the boardwalk that fronted the shops. She took a deep breath of the sea-scented on-shore breeze. It was a perfect June day, the sky a soft blue without a trace of clouds. Herring gulls bobbed in pea-green water. Fishermen dotted the pier that jutted into the sound. Boaters hosed down decks or maneuvered their crafts, everything from sunfish to sloops to catamarans to yachts. She shaded her eyes to search the marina. She felt, as always, a quick thrill when she saw Max, blond hair glinting in the sunlight. He was on his way out into the sound to take a run in his new fiberglass powerboat. He'd excused his absence from his office on the grounds that having a new powerboat and not taking it out the first day qualified as cruel and unusual punishment. It would have been fun to join him, but the bookstore needed all hands at the ready on a sunny summer day.

In fact, she needed extra help. She and Ingrid, her loyal clerk, were working long hours. Too long, according to Max. This morning when she attempted to slip from bed an hour early, the better to take care of needed orders, he'd caught her hand and tugged her back to his side, murmuring that early birds surely deserved a playful launch.

A smile touched her lips. How could she resist Max, his blond hair tousled, his stubbled cheeks bristly, his lips seeking. So she not only wasn't early, she was a few minutes late. She walked faster, passing his office with a smile. Jaunty letters announced: CONFIDENTIAL COMMISSIONS. Max specialized in solving problems. He always made his status clear to prospective employers. He was not a private detective. The state of South Carolina had particular and specific requirements for the licensing of private detectives. There was no law that a man couldn't offer advice and assistance to those in a spot of trouble.

Annie reached Death on Demand. As always, she was pleased and proud to see her storefront. A new cream-colored wooden sign hung above the front door. DEATH ON DEMAND gleamed in gold letters. A dagger dripping bright red drops pointed to the legend: *The Lowcountry's Finest Mystery Bookstore*.

Annie took an instant to glance in approval at the display behind the plate glass of the front window. Ranged on a beach chair were brightly jacketed books sure to please summer sun worshippers: *Our Lady of*

Immaculate Deception by Nancy Martin, *Cemetery Road* by Gar Anthony Haywood, *The Puzzle Lady vs. The Sudoku Lady* by Parnell Hall, *A Night Too Dark* by Dana Stabenow, *The Bone Chamber* by Robin Burcell, and *Revenge for Old Times' Sake* by Kris Neri.

The bell jangled as she pushed open the door. She eyed the recently hung poster at the end of the thriller section. She loved to tell the story of its discovery. Last month she and Max had wandered around a flea market in Savannah. Next to a particularly eclectic booth sat a worn old trunk adorned with this sign:

MYSTERY CONTENTS, YOURS FOR TEN BUCKS

She'd grabbed Max's arm. "Mystery contents!"

"To you and me, maybe. Not to the shopkeeper."

"Cynicism does not become you." Annie had always loved mystery packages with unknown contents. She remembered with delight *The Iron Clew* by Phoebe Atwood Taylor writing as Alice Tilton in which three brown packages powered the plot. Thriller writer Robert L. Duncan advised authors when they were stuck to have a package of unknown provenance left at a hotel desk for the hero.

All the way home Max speculated about what she would find, possibly old *National Geographics* (the trunk was heavy), maybe discarded cowboy boots, or Kewpie dolls from a carnival. At Death on Demand, Max had hefted the trunk on a table. He found a chisel in the back room. As he pried open the lid, his suggestions continued, " . . . stuffed moose heads . . . old Pittsburgh phone books . . . hand-knitted purple tea cozies . . ."

The lid popped up, as if snapped by an invisible hand.

"Oh." Annie's spirits had drooped at the sight of a dun-colored worn army-issue blanket, likely 1940s vintage. She'd lifted out one and a second and a third.

Max had taken pity at seeing her crestfallen expression. "Hey, they'll make a great gift for animal rescue. Put those back and I'll take the trunk over."

But maybe . . . just maybe . . . She kept on pulling out blankets. At the very bottom of the trunk, there was a rectangle covered by brown butcher paper. Annie lifted out the thin, stiff package and eased open the sealed wrapping. She had turned to Max and held up a poster and her smile was at a thousand watts.

Now customers shared her joy with the vintage movie poster for *Murder, My Sweet,* starring Dick Powell and Claire Trevor in the 1944 film version of Raymond Chandler's *Farewell, My Lovely.* The yellow letters of the title were as bright as the day the poster was created. Annie could almost smell buttered popcorn.

Agatha, Death on Demand's elegant and imperious black cat, shot past, batting at a small plastic ball with a wobbly feather.

"It just goes to show," Annie called after her, but Agatha was too engrossed to respond and disappeared around the end of a bookcase. Annie wasn't altogether sure of the cosmic significance of her fondness for mysterious packages and boxes, but she was certain they made life more interesting.

Maybe today there would be a new surprise awaiting her.

"Annie, is that you?" Footsteps sounded in the central aisle. Slender, quick moving, and efficient, Ingrid was, beneath her crusty exterior, kind to the core. Ingrid planted herself in front of Annie. Graying brown hair drawn back in a bun, her sharp-featured face looked harried. "Glad you're here." There was just the tiniest hint of rebuke for Annie's tardy arrival. "A book club from Bluffton is due in half an hour, Henny's waiting for you in the coffee area, and Laurel put a portfolio on your desk." Ingrid looked puzzled. "On the outside of the portfolio—I couldn't help seeing it as I went by—there's an inscription in straggling pink letters and a funny splotch."

Annie was well aware of the portfolio's contents, which Laurel had exhibited to her and Max over dinner one evening. "I'll deal with Laurel's portfolio later." Annie wished her reply didn't sound as strained as if she'd found a copperhead wrapped around the coffee machine. After all, her mother-in-law's enthusiasms were nothing new, from Laurel's flirtation with harmonic convergences when they'd first met to her fascination with saints and now . . . This time Max would have to corral Laurel. There were limits.

An inner voice hooted: *Sez who?*

Ingrid looked sympathetic and changed the subject. "Anyway, I'm on the phone with the Harper rep about the Mary Daheim titles. That bed-and-breakfast in Bluffton wants fifty copies by tonight." She whirled and rushed toward the storeroom.

A distant whir indicated that Henny, no stranger to the store, was making cappuccino. Annie hurried down the central aisle to the coffee bar. Readers sat at several tables, all with mugs and biscotti.

Annie reached the coffee bar. "Thanks for taking care of everyone." She gestured toward the contented coffee hounds and smiled at Death on Demand's best customer and her cherished friend. As always, Henny was fashionably dressed, the terra-cotta of her linen top flattering to her silvered dark hair and dark eyes.

Henny pushed a mug toward Annie. "Lots of caramel. Hey, I like your sundress."

Annie glanced in the mirror at the far end of the coffee bar that added illusory depth to the café area. She hadn't been sure about the color, a dusty plum. The mirror reflected her honey-blond hair and gray eyes and the loose-fitting A-line dress decorated with appliqués of silvery fern fronds. "I thought maybe the color was too cool."

"Perfect for you." Henny spoke with fashion authority.

Annie took a sip of the scrumptious foam. She was glad Henny liked the dress, but still felt a bit unsure of the shade. Though she knew she needed to get to work, she slid onto a stool at the coffee bar. She would take a moment to visit with Henny and admire the collection of coffee mugs behind the coffee bar, each with the name of a mystery author and title. Annie glanced at her mug. *Knocked for a Loop* by Craig Rice.

Henny followed her glance. "I know how you like surprises."

Annie noted the lively, determined intelligence in Henny's dark eyes and felt a tingle of alarm. "That depends."

Henny's smile was quick. "Nice surprises, like the *Murder, My Sweet* poster."

Annie, of course, had shared the story of her well-rewarded curiosity far and wide.

Henny finished a latte with an extra dollop of almond slivers and came around the bar to settle on a stool next to Annie. She held up her mug (*Taken at the Flood* by Agatha Christie) in a toast. "As you pointed out after you so wisely persevered despite initial disappointment, treasures can be found in the most unlikely places. Darling, do I ever have a treasure for you!" Henny's beautifully modulated voice was confident, but her dark eyes held a plea.

Two

"Did you read Nancy Drew when you were growing up?" Annie heard the discouragement in her voice. As far as she had been able to determine, Pat Merridew had never read a single Agatha Christie.

Pat pushed back a sprig of graying auburn hair. Her pale blue eyes slid away from Annie, then back. "I always watch *CSI*. I'll catch up. I'm a quick study."

Annie saw bravado and embarrassment.

Pat slid her fingers together in a tight grip. "I know it's important to be knowledgeable for customers. But Henny said you really needed help at the store. If you'll give me a chance, I'll do my best. Maybe let me try out for a couple of weeks." Her mouth twisted in a wry almost-smile. "I'll go nuts if I sit around the house much longer. I've always worked." She tugged at the collar of her blouse. She'd obviously dressed with care for the interview, a crisp white cotton blouse, a tropical bright skirt with cheerful splashes of indigo and rose, light blue leather loafers.

Annie knew it wasn't the money that prompted Pat's plea, certainly not the modest salary Death on Demand offered. It was the sense of worth conferred by holding a job. Jobs on a small island could be few and far between. It was the height of the tourist season, but those jobs had been snapped up before the end of May, primarily by college students. The handful of year-round shops near the marina or the island's small downtown belonged to people who had owned them for years, and openings were quickly filled by someone who knew someone.

Henny knew Annie. Death on Demand needed a clerk. But Pat obviously didn't know cozy from noir or thriller from police procedural.

Pat's gaze fell. She looked resigned and began to turn away.

Annie reached out, touched her arm. "I'm sure you'd like mysteries."

Pat faced Annie, her eyes brightening with hope. "I know I would. I'll read as many as I can as soon I can."

Annie forced a bright smile. "You can be a great help with unpacking and shelving and ordering. Let me show you around."

By the time they reached the coffee bar, Annie was berating herself internally. She was beginning to suspect that Pat not only didn't read mysteries, she didn't read, a state of being Annie equated with abandonment on an ice floe without a Kindle, Sony, or Nook, much less a book.

Annie gestured toward the watercolors hanging above the mantel. "Every month I hang fresh paintings for our mystery contest. Each represents a particular title. The first person to identify the book and author receives a month of coffee and a free book."

Annie admired the bright splashes of color.

In the first painting, moonlight beamed through tall windows, illuminating a staircase and great hall. Hanging banners appeared shadowy and gray in the cool radiance. A man in a soft bathrobe lay limply on the checkered floor. An awkward figure scrambling unsteadily to his feet reached out, crashing a suit of armor to the floor.

In the second painting, a fresh-faced teenager, eyes bright, held his cell phone up, but three women in a sunroom were oblivious. Seated with one foot on a hassock, a heavily made-up woman in a filmy dress and matching turban gazed in dismay at a small, older woman. The smaller woman also wore a turban. Gray hair poked from beneath purple cloth. Scowling, she held a bent cookie sheet. On the sheet rested a plate of cookies. Observing the turbaned women was a graceful, middle-aged woman whose expressive face reflected breeding, intelligence, and wisdom.

In the third painting, roiling smoke and shooting flames were shocking in the pale moonlight. Smoke darker than the night billowed through the front door of a three-story building as an obviously injured man hobbled across a porch toward the front steps, helped by a stocky figure wearing a bandanna that covered the lower part of his face.

In the fourth painting, a tall young woman with auburn hair stood in a radio studio. Her eyes wide, she stared out the window into the palm-tree-rimmed parking lot at a platinum-haired, voluptuous blonde in a shocking-pink halter dress and Jackie O sunglasses as she navigated forward in stiletto slingbacks.

In the fifth painting, shock was obvious in the moonlight-illuminated faces of two young women lugging a tarp-wrapped body. A Pomeranian, with its mouth open wide to bark, rode on the corpse's chest. Looking haunted were a tall, olive-skinned brunette and a plus-size Rita Hayworth lookalike with long red hair.

"Oooh." Pat looked impressed. "Do they get any book they want?" She had exclaimed at the $310 price tag for the three-volume leather-bound set of Sherlock Holmes.

Annie's reply was swift and firm. "Only a noncollectible."

"Noncollectible?"

Annie took a deep breath. Maybe Pat would be a whiz at the coffee bar.

Annie's cell rang. She stared at the computer. Online ordering might be easier for the publishers, but the lines to fill in and boxes to click made her feel as if she were negotiating a maze in a deep fog. Let's see . . . She needed to return the unsold Dan Brown hardcovers, but not the paperbacks. She answered absently, "Death on Demand, the finest mystery—"

"Hey, Annie. Has anybody figured out the paintings yet?" Henny's resonant voice, which easily reached the last row in island little-theater productions, was just this side of strident.

Annie tossed aside her usual tact. "Nope, but don't you sometimes feel like it's shooting fish in a barrel? Where's your sportsman's blood? Why don't you give ordinary readers a chance?"

"When Democrats embrace Sarah Palin or when you bar Emma from the contest."

Since Annie would rather sunbathe nestled next to an alligator than in any way challenge the island's rock-visaged queen of crime, she changed the subject. "Can you think of any way I can divert Laurel from hanging that stuff in the bookstore?"

A throaty chuckle was an answer. Of sorts. "I'm taking bets on whether Laurel prevails. And I wouldn't call those lovely matted photos *stuff.* I thought you loved cats."

Annie felt her spine stiffen. "I do love cats. And I know the posters are fetching." It was a grudging admission. "But Death on Demand isn't the place for Laurel to display them. I don't care how clever they are." Annie determinedly ignored the portfolio, only inches from her hand.

"Odds are running eight to one."

Annie didn't have to ask in whose favor.

"On a happier note—I hope—how is Pat doing?"

Annie smiled. "A much happier note. She's a live wire. She's trying so hard." Through the open door into the office, she heard Pat's eager voice. "Certainly if you enjoy Earlene Fowler, you'll love Diana Killian and Emilie Richards. Over here we have . . ." Of course, Pat was cribbing from the staff recommendations list at the end of the romantic suspense aisle, but she'd taken the time to learn. "I gave her some Christies and, no surprise, she was enchanted. She read those and now she has another batch. She's started quoting Christie."

"A quotable lady." Quick as a rapier thrust, Henny demanded, "Which character said: 'I had the firm conviction that, if I went about looking for adventure, adventure would meet me halfway. It is a theory of mine that one always gets what one wants.'"

"Anne Beddingfield in *The Man in the Brown Suit*."

Again that throaty chuckle. "Of course you know that one. I'll bet your copy is dog-eared. You have a dash of Anne Beddingfield. I like this game. We'll play it again."

Annie was smiling as she clicked off the phone. There were no clouds on her horizon this sunny summer Friday.

Except, of course, Laurel's latest project. And tomorrow.

Annie glanced at the portfolio, the better not to think about tomorrow. She reached out slowly, then yanked back her hand. No. Double, triple, quadruple no. She would not look and be charmed. Right was right. Death on Demand was a mystery bookstore, not a venue for highly original philosophical . . . She grasped for the proper word. Philosophical treatises? Too weighty. Philosophical exercises? Better. Philosophical nonsense? Too harsh.

As if on cue, Agatha bounded onto the desk. Before Annie could grasp the silky-haired creature, one black paw poked the keyboard.

The book order vanished.

"Did you do that on purpose?" Annie stared into cool green eyes that appeared both amused and questioning.

She suppressed the quivering thought that somehow Laurel had engineered the cat's action. She mustn't succumb to hysteria.

Annie grabbed the portfolio. Didn't self-help gurus counsel confronting fears? She reached in, pulled out the first cardboard-mounted photograph. She looked from the photo to Agatha. "When did you pose for her?" And since when did cats pose? Of course, the cat wasn't Agatha, although the resemblance was startling. There was no denying that the pictured cat had sleek black fur, glittering green eyes, and an uplifted (to swat) paw. The caption read: "British Black Shorthair. *My way or the highway.*"

Annie shoved the picture back into the portfolio and concentrated on breathing evenly. Was Laurel hoping to win Annie over by including a poster with Agatha's double? Possibly. Possibly not. Who knew what Laurel was thinking? That question had mystified all who had ever known the woman, especially her daughter-in-law. It was time to go home, relax, forget Laurel and her posters. In any event, Annie couldn't spare the emotional energy.

She needed every ounce of calm to survive tomorrow, which was a double feature for Death on Demand, Emma Clyde appearing at the Author Luncheon at the library at the same time as the Savannah Captivating Crimes Book Club arrived at Death on Demand for a light lunch and discussion of suspense novels from Eric Ambler to Suzanne Brockman. A recently departed (not from this life, but from the island) employee had blithely approved the date for both events. By the time Annie discovered the conflict, the schedules of the library and book club were set.

Somehow Annie had to sell books at the library while convincing Emma that, of course, the crowd was wonderful and not the least bit smaller because of the meeting at the store or the competition from several other luncheons occurring in various venues that the interim help also had not checked. Ingrid, meanwhile, would host the book club. Normally such an event required Annie's presence as well as a summer clerk. Henny often helped out but she was presiding at a Red Cross luncheon at the Sea Side Inn. Laurel loved to sub at Death on Demand, but Annie had no intention of calling on her.

Thank heaven for Pat.

Saturday wouldn't be doable without her.

Annie rushed into the kitchen. She'd changed into a short-sleeved knit top that matched a bright orange stripe in flamboyant cropped pants that shouted summer with pink, grape, white, lime, and orange stripes.

Max, muscular and tanned in a T-shirt, khaki shorts, and espadrilles, shredded carrots at the central workstation. Not only was he a gorgeous hunk, he was a super chef. He looked over his shoulder. "Sangria's made."

Annie felt bubbly without a sip. She moved toward the refrigerator. "What kind tonight?"

"Max's Coolest Ever. Chardonnay with fruit, lemonade, and two shots of peach brandy. You can add the ginger ale."

Annie fixed two glasses, placed one near Max, then perched on a stool to watch as catfish sizzled in the skillet. She cradled the cool glass in her hands. "If I ever needed a pick-me-up, it's tonight." She hesitated, then asked obliquely, "Have you talked to your mother?"

Max ladled rice from the cooker. "She looked cheerful when I saw her." He carried their plates to the table. "If you'll zap the corn bread in the microwave, everything's ready."

Annie put down her glass. "You saw her?"

"Why don't we eat and then—"

Annie folded her arms. "Where are they?"

Max's blue eyes shifted away. He moved fast as Dorothy L, his plump white cat, jumped onto the table. "Not when we're eating, D.L." He retrieved the fluffy cat and carried her to the kitchen door.

Annie was still waiting when the door clicked shut.

Max studied Annie's face and placed the plates in the microwave for later reheating. "In the living room."

Annie stalked from the kitchen and strode to the living room, her sandals clicking on the heart-pine floor. Just inside the wide double doors, she stopped and took a deep breath. She spotted a portfolio, twin to the one in her office, pink letters and black splotch straggling across the stiff plastic over. The inscription was burned into her consciousness:

PAWS THAT REFRESH: Cat Truth

She wanted to snarl that the black splotch following the title, obviously a paw print, was just too cute. Actually, the paw print was cute, even though Annie loathed cuteness. She didn't turn when Max came up behind her and slipped an arm around her rigid shoulders.

His voice was conciliatory. "Don't you think they're clever?"

"Of course they're clever. But they don't have anything to do with mysteries. Displaying them at Death on Demand would distract from the books." Not to mention the watercolor contest. She had no doubt Laurel coveted the expanse above the fireplace as a space to display the cats.

Laurel had discovered free online pictures of exotic cat breeds and never looked back. She printed photos on glossy paper and mounted them on acid-free mat board. In printed letters beneath the photos, each cat was identified by breed, and a caption expressed a "Cat Truth." The classy, high-end posters were everywhere, propped against the sofa and several chairs, ranged along the mantel, and spread across the coffee table.

A smile tugged at Annie's lips. She honestly couldn't look at pictures of cats, all kinds of cats, Maltese, Abyssinian, Siamese, Scottish Fold, domestic short hair, tabbies, and not be enchanted by their beauty. The coup de grâce was the legend beneath each picture. A Sphynx, its hairless gray skin wrinkled, stared with obvious reproof. Uneven pink letters inquired: *Who you lookin' at, dude?* A multicolored Manx, mostly white with a black half mask and black back with a dash of orange, stood with his head twisted staring over raised haunches: *Nobody sneaks up on me!*

Annie counted twenty admittedly fetching photographs of gorgeous cats, each mounted on poster board with the announcement of breed and an inscription. "Cat Truth," she mused. "Okay, the pix are great, the comments priceless." If Max quoted her to Laurel, maybe this sop to TV ads would soften the blow. "However"—she was emphatic—"a Philosophy of Life according to cats has no place in a mystery bookstore." She turned and realized she was in Max's embrace, a very nice place to be. She smiled up at him. "I have a great idea." She wriggled one arm free and made an inclusive gesture. "We'll leave the posters just the way they are and have a cocktail party here to celebrate Laurel's"—she paused for inspiration—"trenchant philosophical triumph."

Annie's cell rang. She glanced at the clock. A quarter to eleven. She felt beleaguered, irritated, pressed, and ill-treated. She needed to get to the library and set up the book table. Emma Clyde wanted books on sale both before and after an event. What Emma wanted, Emma got, Annie having long ago decided the better part of valor was never to rouse a quiescent literary lioness. She checked her caller ID and frowned. "Hi,

Henny." She tried to sound pleasant, but if she hadn't listened to Henny, she'd probably have found someone other than Pat to hire and today would not be a disaster waiting to happen.

"You sound stressed."

"That sums everything up nicely. I have the library Author Luncheon for Emma and"—she heard the high twitter of feminine voices through the open door of her office—"the Savannah book club's here and Pat's a no-show, which puts Ingrid in a deep, deep pit. I need to get to the library. I'll talk to you later."

Annie put more copies of Emma's new paperback, *The Case of the Curious Cat,* into a box. She moved too quickly and a stack of the books tilted from the worktable and slapped to the floor. As she scrambled to pick them up, she glanced at the cover art and glared into the almond-shaped blue eyes of a white, long-haired Siamese with an inscrutable expression. "Cats," she muttered. "Everywhere I go, cats."

A black paw snaked through the air, leaving a mark on the back of her right hand.

"Agatha, I'm not playing now. I don't have time." When the books were safely in the box and Agatha distracted with a moist treat, Annie pressed a Kleenex against the scratch and poked her head out of the storeroom.

"Has Pat shown up?"

Ingrid slid her hand over the portable phone's mouthpiece. "No. I called Laurel and she's going to help out."

Annie opened her mouth, closed it. Pat Merridew had picked a lousy day to be late for work. Obviously, Ingrid couldn't handle the book club by herself. Henny was committed for a luncheon. Emma would be wearing her author hat. That left Laurel.

"What did she say?"

Ingrid blinked uncertainly. "Kind of a funny answer. She said: 'He who asks shall be rewarded.'"

Annie whirled back into the office and snatched up Laurel's portfolio, thumbed through the contents. She found the proper poster, a large, sleek, muscular Bengal cat with a dense marbled coat—and a hugely satisfied expression: *He who asks shall be rewarded.* So Laurel was quite willing to help out. No doubt, radiating charm, she would expect Annie to hang cat posters in Death on Demand as a reward.

Annie gripped the portfolio. Could she hide the thick manila folder?

Her cell rang again. She fumbled in her pocket, lifted the phone, saw the caller ID, tried not to squeak when she answered. "I'm on my way, Emma." She tossed the portfolio on the worktable. *Que sera,*

sera. She grabbed the box of books. "I'll be there in a jiffy."

Annie whistled a jaunty tune as she toted a single box with no more than a half-dozen unsold titles up the steps to the back door of Death on Demand. Even Emma had been pleased by the sales and it took a lot of *ka-chings* to bring a smile to her redoubtable square face. She had even offered a grudging compliment. "Better than I expected. Of course, everyone loves Marigold."

Annie loathed Emma's sleuth, Marigold Rembrandt. Annie considered her a carping harpy with all the charm of a molting mongoose, but since she enjoyed *ka-chings*, too, she had warbled happily to Emma, "Marigold knocked 'em dead." A flash in Emma's frosty blue eyes reminded Annie that the author's insatiable hunger for praise must be fed. "You were wonderful, Emma. Splendid. Brilliant." Annie paused.

Emma had nodded, looking expectant.

Annie had almost rebelled. How much attention did the old warhorse need? She knew the answer. She took a deep breath. "Cogent. Compelling. Charismatic." When they'd parted in the library parking lot, Emma had been at her most congenial.

Annie laughed as she opened the back door, the box on one hip. All's well that ends well. Now, if only

Ingrid had weathered the book club. Annie put aside any thoughts about Laurel and Cat Truth. Time would, unfortunately, tell.

She stepped into the storeroom. The door to the coffee area was ajar.

". . . and what am I bid for the Chestnut Oriental Shorthair?"

Annie would know that husky voice anywhere. Adrift on a space station. In a Deadwood saloon. Behind a Venetian mask. From the depths of a cavern. Riding in an alpine cable car.

Annie stopped in the doorway.

Her slender blond mother-in law, her patrician features quite lovely and perfect, her pale blue linen dress elegantly styled, stood in stocking feet on the coffee bar. She held up a poster. A rectangular-muzzled, green-eyed, chocolate-colored cat appeared as brooding as a gothic hero. The legend read: *Always say yes to adventure.*

A lantern-jawed woman in the front row thundered, "Two hundred dollars."

A plump matron with untidy brown curls jumped to her feet. "Three hundred."

"Three hundred dollars." Laurel repeated the sum twice. "Do I hear three-fifty?"

After a beat, she clapped her hands together. "Sold for three hundred dollars. That completes my offering of *Paws That Refresh: Cat Truth.* I thank you for your wonderful support today for our animal rescue center. The sum raised by the auction—"

Annie took a step into the coffee area.

Laurel continued smoothly, "—will help provide shelter and treatment for abandoned and abused dogs and cats. We would also like to thank Death on Demand for offering to host the auction. And here is the wonderful proprietor of Death on Demand, eager to welcome you lovely ladies from the Captivating Crimes Book Club. Perhaps Annie would like to share a tribute to Mississippi Delta author Carolyn Haines, who writes wonderful books and helps rescue abused and abandoned horses, dogs, and cats, and to Mary Kennedy of *Dead Air* and *Reel Murder* fame, who rescues cats and supports all efforts to protect animals."

Annie remembered one of the posters now residing in her and Max's living room, a silky-furred, mitted, and bicolored Ragdoll stretched out on a red silk cushion, looking as comfy as Eva Longoria in a Hanes ad: *Go with the flow.*

Annie's smile was genuine. "Thank you, Laurel, for your support for animals and for sharing news of Carolyn Haines's Sarah Booth Delaney series and Mary Kennedy's talk-radio series. Animal lovers"—she swept her arm in an all-inclusive gesture—"will enjoy visiting Carolyn Haines's online animal rescue page, www.goodfortunefarmrefuge.org."

Immediately, several ladies lifted their iPhones and fingers flew as they typed in the link.

Annie beamed at Laurel. The best outcome, in addition to sales, was that the dreaded posters were no longer on her worktable, though Annie well knew there were more where these came from. However, there was no point in borrowing trouble. Moreover, a worthy cause had profited.

Annie mingled and was charming. But if Pat Merridew dared enter Death on Demand, it would be the shortest stay in history.

As soon as Henny reached her car at the Sea Side Inn parking lot, she flipped open her cell.

"Death on Demand, the finest—"

Henny interrupted. "Hey, Ingrid, did Pat show up?"

"No. Laurel helped out. We made it through." Ingrid described the auction.

Henny grinned. "If you can't beat 'em, maybe you need to join 'em."

"I don't think that's what Annie wants to hear. Oh, got to go. Some tourists . . ."

Henny sat behind her wheel, tapped Pat's number. No answer. She had called twice before going to the luncheon. Pat wasn't at the store. She wasn't home. Where was she? Maybe she had a call from a friend who needed to go to a doctor's appointment in Savannah. Maybe she forgot to call the bookshop. Maybe a lot of things.

Henny tried to maintain a positive outlook, but she felt both irritated and disappointed. She had helped Pat find a job and now Pat had let Annie down. Henny pressed her lips together. Her words might be sharp when she found Pat. With a decided nod, she turned on the motor and headed for Pat's house instead of home.

Henny drove with her windows down, enjoying the pleasant June heat. In July the island would swelter and cooling the car with air-conditioning would be automatic. She turned on a dusty narrow road north of downtown. Palmettos, live oaks, red cedars, and yellow pines crowded the road. The burgeoning woods were interrupted by occasional houses. She enjoyed the variety: shacks perched on pilings; late-nineteenth-century, two-story frame or tabby homes; and new multistoried mansions of stucco or stone.

The road swung around a lagoon. On the wooded side of the road, Henny turned into a driveway. Pat's modest home was an early Colonial clapboard cottage. It was well maintained, the white paint fresh. Henny pulled up behind Pat's blue Chevy. Had she returned home shortly before Henny's arrival? Henny's eyes glinted. Had she chosen not to answer the phone?

On the porch, Henny admired some crimson begonias in a glazed blue vase. A light cotton sweater lay on the green swing. Letters and magazines protruded from the mailbox. Before she could ring, frenzied barking erupted beyond the front door. Gertrude sounded frantic. That was unusual. She was a good-natured dog.

A frown touched Henny's narrow face. There had been enough time for Pat to answer the door. The dachshund's yelps continued, faster and faster.

Henny glanced out at the drive. That was Pat's car. Of course, someone might have picked her up . . .

Dog claws scrabbled on the other side of the door.

Henny pulled open the screen. She turned the front knob and pushed. She wasn't surprised to find the door open. Many islanders only locked up at bedtime. "Pat?" The door swung slowly inward. Henny stepped into the small foyer. A grandfather clock ticked to her left.

Gertrude twisted in a circle, her claws clicking on the wooden floor, then bolted to the living room. She skidded to a stop, lifted her sleek head, and howled, the pitiable cry high and mournful.

Henny felt a tightness in her chest. She crossed the hall, stopped in the doorway.

Sun spilled across the room, illuminating the rose sofa and the cream chintz easy chair and the pinewood coffee table. A crystal mug with dark sludge in its bottom sat on the table. Pat slumped to one side of the easy chair, her auburn-gray head resting against the upholstered side, her face slack. One arm dangled over the side of the chair.

Annie loved the long sweep of the garden behind their house, azaleas bright in spring afternoons, dusky roses damp with dew in summer, billowy white blossoms of sea myrtle in late fall. Tall pines and Spanish-moss-draped live oaks framed the view down to the pond with its resident alligator. Tonight the beauty was dimmed.

"I feel awful. I was so mad at Pat. And she was dead." Annie's voice was shaky.

Max lounged against the railing, his back to the garden. "Hey, you didn't know." He looked at Henny in the red wooden rocking chair next to Annie. "Do they have any idea what caused her death?"

Henny shook her head. "So far as I know she didn't have heart trouble, but that's always possible. They're doing an autopsy." She stroked the fluffy white fur of Dorothy L, who snuggled in her lap.

Annie nodded. That was the law when cause of death could not be certified by an attending physician.

"She had finished supper. The dishes were done and draining in a rack. She was fully dressed." The purring cat rose and placed her paws on Henny's shoulder, butted Henny's cheek gently with her head. Henny smiled. "Dorothy L is offering comfort. Now, if she could only steer us in the right direction, like her namesake."

Annie squeezed her eyes in remembrance, seeing clearly Pat's uneven features and pale blue eyes and straggling auburn curls. "That last day Pat wore a bandanna-print navy-blue dress with a white seashell necklace."

Henny nodded. "Apparently, she came home from work, fixed her dinner, then sat in the living room to drink coffee. I suppose the illness was sudden and she wasn't able to call for help."

Annie felt a wash of sadness. Not sorrow, for she hadn't known Pat well or long, but sadness. She admired those who landed on their feet and kept on slugging even when life landed a hard blow. Annie had sensed residual anger beneath Pat's cheery appearance at the bookstore, but her efforts to master her new job had been evident and sincere. She'd carried yet another Christie home that last night. A cynic might suggest that Pat had merely played to her audience when she talked about the books to Annie, but Pat had plucked meaningful bits and pieces from each book. They had last talked about *The Secret of Chimneys* and Pat had quoted Virginia Revel: " 'It's just as exciting to buy a new experience as it is to buy a new dress—more so, in fact.' " Pat's cheeks had flushed and she'd blurted, "Until now I never thought about doing anything out of the ordinary."

At that moment, Annie had a strong sense that Pat had in mind doing something she considered daring. She repeated the quote to Henny.

"Virginia Revel." Henny looked intrigued. "I wish we knew what Pat wanted to do. I don't suppose we'll ever know."

Three

Annie admired the watercolors above the mantel, then stepped behind the coffee bar at Death on Demand. "Amaretto in your mocha?"

Laurel beamed at her daughter-in-law. "Such a lovely idea, my dear."

Annie added chocolate sprinkles to mounded whipping cream, then placed the mug to one side of the artist's portfolio Laurel had casually placed atop the counter. Laurel's mug read: *You Can't Trust Duchesses.*

Laurel glanced at the title and made no comment. Her golden hair shirred short, blue eyes sparkling, face radiant, Laurel looked young and vibrant in a scoop-neck pale blue sweater and knee-length frilly polka-dot-print silk skirt. She crossed her legs. The delicate blue of butterfly-bow denim slides matched her blouse.

Annie fixed an iced latte with a shot of raspberry syrup for herself. Her mug read: *Stalemate*.

Laurel looked amused.

Not, Annie thought, a good sign.

A sip and Laurel patted the familiar portfolio. "You always work so hard, my dear." Her tone was admiring.

Annie was instantly on alert. The smiling comment, though ostensibly a compliment, was a subtle reminder that Laurel had stepped into the breach when Pat failed to show up. Annie gave a modest shrug. "Same old, same old."

"It was such a pleasure for me to be able to help out last week when you were busy at the library and dear Ingrid had the book club all by herself." Almost as if inadvertently, though Annie knew better, Laurel pushed the portfolio nearer Annie. "I know you didn't mind my taking advantage of that lovely group of women to raise money for animal rescue. Now I feel in my heart"—a graceful hand was delicately placed— "that I must repay that debt and so"—the words came in a rush as swift as the flutter of mallards honing in on a lagoon—"I'm giving you at no charge, of course, your very own collection of the *Paws That Refresh* to

share with Death on Demand's wonderful readers."
She picked up the portfolio and held it out to Annie as
if presenting her firstborn.

Annie's mouth opened. Closed. To refuse a gift was
rude. She limply took the manila folder.

Laurel beamed and plucked the folder back. "Since
you are always busy, I will take care of all the details."

Laurel twirled in her seat to drop lightly to the
heart-pine floor. She dashed another smile. "I use
masking tape to mount them and that will make it easy
to change them out when I have new ones."

Annie gripped the edge of the coffee bar. New ones?
Was the collection intended for permanent display?
Would cat photos cover every inch of free wall space,
spreading like kudzu? There had to be some way of
deflecting her mother-in-law, short of a lasso.

Annie's cell rang. She plucked it from the pocket of
her skirt and glanced at the caller ID. Maybe Henny
would have an idea. "Hey, Henny—"

"Annie, I need help." Henny's tone was grim. "I just
talked to Billy."

Billy Cameron, Broward's Rock's stalwart police
chief, was a good friend and a fine policeman, devoted
to his community, hardworking, fair.

"He says I'm too close to Pat's death to be objective." Henny's tone was brusque. "He might listen to

you. After all, you scarcely knew her, but you saw quite a bit of her in the days before she died. You can describe her state of mind. What upsets me the most is that the report will be released and there will be a story in the *Gazette*."

A chair scraped. Laurel popped up to stand on the seat and survey the rectangle of space on the left side of the fireplace. She stood on tiptoe to tape a photograph of a thick-furred, piebald Siberian Forest cat, its white front a brilliant contrast to a charcoal head and back. In a side view, the cat's broad face appeared almost angelic. *Always try a smile first.*

If Laurel poached on the space for the mystery paintings, there would be a line drawn in the sand. "A story about what?"

"The official pronouncement of cause of death: suicide."

Annie gripped the cell. "Suicide?" Pat's days at Death on Demand whirled through her mind. In particular, she remembered Wednesday afternoon when they'd visited over coffee about mysteries. "I don't think that's possible. I'll talk to Billy."

Billy Cameron, tall, sturdy, and muscular, pushed back his office chair and stood. "Hey, Annie. What can I do for you?" His thick sandy hair held traces of white. His strong face was genial, but it was ever and always a cop's face, with an underlying toughness, eyes that had seen the worst of pain and injury and death, a mouth that could tighten into a hard line of confrontation.

Annie sat on one of two hard wooden chairs that faced his desk.

Billy settled in his chair, looking large and official.

She began without preamble. "Pat Merridew worked at Death on Demand."

He glanced at her, his blue eyes thoughtful, then pulled a green folder from a stack, flipped it open. "She was fired from the law firm. She started to work at the bookstore two weeks later. She was in your employ for four days."

Annie knew that Billy always did his homework. His dispassionate tone suggested Pat Merridew's file was complete.

Annie scooted to the edge of the hard wooden seat. "Billy, I think it is very unlikely that Pat Merridew committed suicide."

Billy arched one eyebrow. "You knew her well?"

Annie made an impatient gesture. "I scarcely knew her. I'm not here as a friend. I'm here with specific information that, to my mind, suggests she didn't end her own life."

Billy folded his arms, but asked politely, "What information do you have?"

Annie could read body language. Billy's mind was closed. He was asking politely, but his voice was distant. She spoke quietly. "Pat knew very little about mysteries. I gave her some Agatha Christies to read. Billy, two days before she died, we sat at the coffee bar." Pat had made the drinks under Annie's tutelage, two iced lattes. "Pat thumbed through her copy of *Towards Zero* and found the passage where Superintendent Battle figured out the truth about his daughter's confession. Pat thought that was really clever on his part. I told her my favorite passage was when a young nurse spoke with a would-be suicide bitter at having been saved. The nurse said, 'It may be just by being somewhere—not doing anything—oh, I can't say what I mean, but you might just—just walk along a street someday and just by doing that accomplish something terribly important—perhaps without even knowing what it was.'"

"Good book," Billy said mildly.

Annie nodded in agreement. "One of Christie's best. But that's not the point. Pat said, 'I wouldn't make a guy a hero who tried to commit suicide. He should have sucked up his guts, gotten on with life.' That sure doesn't sound like someone who's thinking about suicide. I don't know anything about how Pat died. But if she didn't die from natural causes, then I think her death had to be an accident. Or murder." She threw out the last without conviction. Who would want to kill Pat Merridew?

Billy picked up the file, found a page. "This is part of the public record now." He slid a sheet across the desk. "You can look at the toxicology report. She died as the result of ingesting four hundred milligrams of OxyContin, which had been dissolved in Irish coffee."

Annie scanned the sheet. The damning information was there. Four hundred milligrams. No one took four hundred milligrams of an opiate by mistake. "Did she have a prescription?" OxyContin was exceedingly strong and one of many prescription painkillers that were commonly abused.

"Not a current one. She had a prescription a year ago, but it wasn't renewable. She fell last year, shattered her wrist, had a plate and six screws. The painkiller was prescribed then."

"Did you find the container for the OxyContin?"

Billy nodded. "The last thing thrown in the trash. Empty. Only her fingerprints on the vial."

Annie knew that people often didn't use all of a prescribed med. In fact, she had a plastic vial in a kitchen cabinet that contained pills left over from a prescription she'd been given following a root canal.

Billy was calm. "No surprise she kept the stuff. People do. In any event, the dregs in her crystal coffee mug contained OxyContin. Her fingerprints were on the mug and only hers. There was no disarray in the room, no evidence anyone else had been present." His face softened. "Look, Annie, she was distraught after she lost her job—"

Annie interrupted. "She had a new job. She didn't skulk around acting upset. She was eager and cheerful and she did everything she could to learn as much as she could as fast as she could."

He lifted a hand in negation. "Of course she acted positive at the store. I get your point and"—a bemused head shake—"Henny is adamant she didn't kill herself because of her dog. Apparently the dog has special medication for a heart problem. Henny claims Pat would never have put the dog in jeopardy." He paused. "Henny took the dog home with her. But suicides aren't thinking straight. They're depressed. They can't see any hope in their lives."

Annie was no psychologist. She couldn't swear to Pat's mental stability, but she remembered with clarity Pat's disdain for the would-be suicide in *Towards Zero*.

"If she ground up the pills"—once Annie had read that OxyContin was even more lethal if the pills were broken or mashed—"and put them in her coffee, then you're right, she was deeply depressed and not herself. But, Billy, if she didn't put the drug in her coffee, someone else did."

Billy slowly shook his head. "It doesn't play, Annie. I know my job. I don't take anything for granted. I checked out Pat Merridew upside down and sideways. She was kind of a live wire. She liked to play cards, go bowling." For an instant, there was a shadow in his eyes. "She bowled the night before she died. She paid her bills. Her only relative was a sister, who lives in California. The sister was at a baseball game in Anaheim the night Pat died. Pat's estate goes to her sister but it's modest: the house, a bank account with three thousand dollars, some stocks amounting to about seventy-five thousand, which shows she was thrifty and prudent. Everybody I contacted spoke well of her. The only blot in a happy-days life was losing her job at the law firm. She was upset and angry with Glen Jamison and with his wife-slash-partner, Cleo. If I'd found Glen bashed over the head or a stiletto in Cleo Jamison's back, I'd have looked at Pat Merridew. Plenty of bad feelings there. But they're fine and Pat's dead. So, nobody wanted Pat dead. What does that leave? Accident or suicide? No way it was an accident. Besides, OxyContin is bitter and she'd made Irish coffee. The whiskey and the sugar hid the taste and, of course, the whiskey intensified the effect of the opiate."

He didn't say "case closed," but he might as well have.

Annie knew Billy had years of experience and a thorough investigation to back up his conclusion. All she had was the memory of Pat's conclusion about the would-be suicide: *He should have sucked up his guts, gotten on with his life.*

Suicide or murder.

"Billy, will you do me a favor?"

He straightened the papers in the folder, flipped the cover shut. "Such as?"

"I'd like to see Pat's house. Please." Maybe there would be something there that would bolster her argument.

Billy's mouth turned down in a wry half smile. "I swear to God, when a woman gets an idea in her head . . ." But his voice was genial. His big shoulders rose and fell. "Henny's handling everything for the sister. I was going to turn the keys over to her. I suppose it wouldn't do any harm to meet her at the house. There may be some things she wants to take care of."

Annie easily pictured Pat Merridew in the small, cheerful living room. White flowers with yellow centers formed bouquets in light blue wallpaper. Pale yellow drapes were drawn at two side windows and the wide front window. A braided oval rug lay smooth in the center of the wooden floor. Not a trace of dust marred the room.

Henny pointed at the chintz-covered chair on one side of the coffee table. "Pat was there." A faint frown. "The chair is out of line. She kept the chairs turned the same way next to the coffee table."

Billy took a step forward. "Probably the techs moved the chair when they came for the body."

"Everything seems to be in order." Henny sounded weary. Then her head came up and she gave Billy a combative look. "Pat did not commit suicide."

Annie looked at the coffee table. "The drug was in her coffee."

Billy was brisk. "Found in the dregs in a ten-ounce crystal coffee mug. The coffee in a carafe was free of drugs."

"Only in the mug." Henny's dark eyes narrowed in thought. "Let me check." She whirled and hurried to the kitchen.

Annie and Billy followed.

The kitchen was narrow and small. A wooden chair sat at each end of a Formica-topped table. A newspaper, carefully folded, lay to the left of a single, woven red cloth place mat. An old-fashioned six-cup metal percolator sat on the tiled counter next to an avocado-green fifties-era stove. A bottle of Irish whiskey sat on the counter next to a sugar canister.

Henny didn't pick up the coffeemaker. Instead, she bent near. "It hasn't been washed." She turned and faced Annie and Billy. "Pat ate dinner. She washed her dishes." Henny nodded toward the drainer, which held a plate, glass, cutlery, saucepan, and skillet. "She made the coffee. So why six cups if she didn't expect company? Look next to the row of canisters on the counter." She pointed. "A single-cup French press. That's what she would use to make a cup for herself. Irish coffee was one of her specialties, with a hefty slug of whiskey and lots of brown sugar." Now she faced Billy. "How much coffee was left in the carafe?"

"I can find out, but the amount left in the carafe proves nothing." His voice was patient. "You're trying to make the case that she served coffee to someone else, that she wouldn't have made six cups for herself. We can't know that for a fact. Maybe she drank one mug of the coffee, then tossed the OxyContin in her second serving."

Annie twisted to look back into the living room. What if Henny was right? What if Pat had a guest? Then there would be two crystal mugs.

Annie felt a rush of excitement. "Billy, you said the mugs were crystal."

He nodded. "Pretty pricey stuff. I got four of them for Mavis for her birthday."

A Southern woman of Pat's age would put out her best for company.

"Let's find where she kept her crystal ware."

Henny gestured toward the hallway. "In a breakfront in the dining room." She led the way.

Billy looked through the glass pane. "Yeah. The stuff was in one of those mugs." He reached out to open the breakfront.

"Wait." Annie's command was quick.

He looked at her.

She lifted a hand in supplication. "Billy, please do me one more favor."

At the first peal of the phone, Annie glanced at her caller ID. She looked across the coffee bar at Henny. "Billy." Now they would know. She clicked the speakerphone. "Annie here."

There was an instant of silence. The police chief cleared his throat.

Henny leaned forward, her face intent, her posture tense.

"A technician—"

Annie mouthed silently, "Mavis." Billy's wife doubled as dispatcher and crime technician. She was careful, methodical, and meticulous.

"—checked the entire set of crystal mugs for fingerprints as well as the sugar bowl and cream pitcher. One mug yielded no fingerprints." His voice gave no hint to his thoughts.

"None?" Henny's demand was sharp.

"None."

Henny slapped a hand on the counter. "You see what that means, Billy." It was a statement, not a question.

"Someone washed the mug and replaced it in the breakfront without leaving any fingerprints." His tone was neutral.

"A murderer." Henny was firm.

"Or someone who was very tidy."

"Please." Henny sounded incredulous.

Billy spoke with equal firmness. "The evidence is open to interpretation. Conceivably, the last time she washed the mugs, she managed to dry one without leaving any fingerprints, perhaps holding the mug with one cloth, drying it with another. Alternatively, as you suggest, someone else carefully washed and dried a mug to remove fingerprints and placed the mug in the breakfront."

Annie asked quickly, "How about the other chair?" Could fingerprints be taken from cloth?

"The chair arms yielded no prints."

Henny was quick. "Not even Pat's?"

"No prints."

"Murder." Henny was forceful.

Billy's question was quick and sharp. "Who had reason to kill Pat Merridew?"

Henny's reply was slow in coming, but honest. "So far as I know, no one."

"At this point"—Billy sounded somewhat ponderous—"the file remains open. We will pursue inquiries." A pause. "You knew her well. If you hear of anything that could assist us, please be in contact." He ended the call.

Annie clicked off the phone.

Henny lifted her coffee mug (*Devious Design* by D. B. Olsen) in a salute. "You asked Billy to have the mugs fingerprinted." Her tone was admiring. "If it weren't for you, a perfect murder would have been committed. Now Pat's death will be labeled possible homicide instead of suicide."

Annie didn't feel triumphant. "Billy said he would pursue inquiries. Like what? I suppose he'll check with neighbors, but if no one saw Pat's visitor, where does he go from there?"

Henny frowned. "No one will have seen the visitor. I think we can count on that. Anyone smart enough to set up her death to appear as a suicide is too smart to be seen. But"—she was emphatic—"that's a lead right there."

Annie brought her mug around the coffee bar and sat down next to Henny. "How so?"

Henny lightly touched fingertips to each temple. Eyes narrowed, she stared into the distance.

Annie wondered if Henny was channeling Madame Arcati, the ebullient psychic in Noël Coward's *Blithe Spirit*, a role Henny had recently played with élan in the local little theater.

"I see a close connection," she intoned.

Definitely Madame Arcati.

Henny swiveled to face Annie. "The OxyContin! That's the tip-off. Only someone who knew Pat well, someone who spent time around her, would be aware that she had broken her wrist and taken pain pills. All right. Who knew? Certainly the people she worked with—Glen Jamison, Cleo Jamison, Kirk Brewster. In fact, all of the Jamisons. Pat was close to Maddy and later to Glen's sister, Elaine. Through the years, Pat took the kids to doctor appointments, all that sort of thing."

Annie shook her head. "Maybe she talked to her postman about her pain pills. Henny, we don't have anywhere to start."

Henny looked stubborn. "All right. Forget the pain pills for now. Instead, I'll call mutual friends who knew Pat, see if I can turn up anything odd or unusual in the last week or so."

Annie refrained from pointing out that Pat's final two weeks had been very different, fired from her job of more than twenty years, hired into a retail position for which she had no background. What else was Henny likely to hear about from Pat's friends? Henny was unlikely to discover why Pat brewed coffee for a killer. "Good idea." She knew her lack of enthusiasm was evident.

Henny's gaze was searching. "Do you have a better idea?"

Annie turned her hands palms up.

After the front bell signaled Henny's departure, Annie walked slowly toward her office. She heard Ingrid suggesting titles to a thriller fan, the latest titles by Michael Connelly, Daniel Silva, Laura Bynum, Kayla Perrin, Judith Cutler, and Steven Hamilton. She needed to unpack boxes of books by Robert Crais, Parnell Hall, Janet Evanovich, Diane Mott Davidson, and Joanne Fluke. Hilton Head mystery writer Kathryn Wall was coming over for a signing next week.

Annie reached for the box cutter. What would Wall's sleuth, Bay Tanner, do in these circumstances? Bay would make her choice on the basis of honor and execute any plan with tenacity. Annie understood that inner compulsion to follow where conscience led. She had felt compelled to approach Billy Cameron because of her conversation with Pat about suicide.

Annie slid the tempered steel blade down the center of the box lid, careful to avoid damage to book jackets. *Yeah, yeah, yeah,* a small inner voice sneered. *You didn't believe Pat committed suicide. You pointed the way for an investigation. Big deal. But now you know Billy's best efforts won't lead anywhere. He's already found out that no one local profited from her small estate, that she had no known enemies, that she was well regarded in the community.*

Impatiently, Annie lifted out five books and another five. The cover of the Hamilton thriller, *The Lock Artist*, featured a shiny steel padlock with the shackle unfastened. That lock was open.

Was there a way to unlock the truth about Pat?

Maybe, just maybe . . . She reached for her cell phone. "Max, meet me at Parotti's. I need help."

Four

Annie stepped inside Parotti's Bar and Grill, the island's oldest and most successful café and bait shop. She welcomed the air-conditioning, augmented by ceiling fans. In winter, she ordered a fried oyster sandwich. In summer, she opted for fried flounder. Despite Ben's transformation from grizzled leprechaun to snazzy proprietor after his marriage to tea-shop–genteel Miss Jolene, Parotti's maintained its rakish atmosphere, sawdust on the floor in the adjoining bait shop, battered old Burma Shave signs as decor, and a 1940s jukebox that worked. Maybe she'd play Frankie Carle's "Rumors Are Flying." Of course, Miss Jolene's influence was unmistakable, quiche on the menu and red-and-white-checked cloths on the tables.

Annie slid into her favorite booth. In a moment, Ben brought iced tea for her and lemonade for Max, left menus and a breadbasket. She sipped the tea and absently scanned the Burma Shave signs. Her favorite sequence read: *Don't stick / Your elbow / Out so far / It might go home / In another car.*

She looked across the room as the heavy oak door opened.

Max swerved around a group of sunburned tourists, moved purposefully toward her. As always when she saw his blue eyes looking for her and his generous mouth widening in a smile for her, she felt a familiar thrill. Tall and blond, he was the handsomest man there. Or, as far as she was concerned, the handsomest man anywhere.

He slid into the booth, reached out to touch her hand. His touch was warm and she felt, as always, a surge of happiness.

Ben was there to take their orders, fried flounder for Annie, grilled for Max, fries for her, coleslaw for him.

As Ben turned away, Max buttered a slice of jalapeño corn bread. "You sounded grim."

"I feel grim. Pat was murdered." She described her visit to the police station, her trip to Pat's house, Henny finding the six-cup percolator, Billy agreeing to check the crystal mugs for fingerprints. " . . . so it seems obvious. Someone washed that mug and dried it without leaving any trace."

Max added sugar to his lemonade. "I get your reasoning, but it's hard to prove anything just because there aren't fingerprints. Besides, why would anyone kill Pat Merridew? You said Billy checked and Pat didn't have enemies and nobody here profited from her death."

"There has to be a reason." Annie added another huge splash of tartar sauce to her sandwich.

Max professed deep concern. "Careful with that tartar sauce. You might choke."

Annie finished the bite, smiled sweetly. "The better to slide down my throat." She recalled one of Laurel's Cat Truth posters, a European Brown Tabby with elegant markings delicately chewing blades of grass: *Don't knock it till you try it.*

Max reached across the table, used his thumb to brush between Annie's eyebrows. "Ease up, Annie. You look like you have the weight of the world on your shoulders. Billy will investigate."

She looked at him soberly. "Of course he will. He'll check with neighbors, see whether anyone was seen going into Pat's house that night. I don't think a clever murderer would take a chance of being seen. Besides, sometimes people don't want to talk to police."

Max started to speak, stopped, then said mildly, "Honey, if Billy can't find anything, I don't think anyone else will either."

She understood. Gently, kindly, he meant that if Billy couldn't find a lead, neither could she. "Maybe not. But I can try."

His gaze was curious and a little puzzled. "Why?"

Annie almost felt as if she were having a Madame Arcati moment. Everything seemed crystal clear. "When Billy called, he said the investigation would continue and then he asked Henny and me to let him know if we found out anything. Don't you see? He knows that whatever led to Pat's death is hidden in pieces of her life that a police investigation will never uncover. I'm sure he wants us to help. He was saying the truth won't come out unless we find out what Pat had done that made someone want her dead."

Max scooped coleslaw. "There aren't that many reasons for murder. Anger. Jealousy. Fear. Greed. Revenge."

Annie glanced at the bowl containing tartar sauce, decided to honor Max's sensibilities. Instead, she added a dollop of cocktail sauce. "Her estate goes to a sister in California. That knocks out greed. You don't invite someone for coffee if you are furious with each other. As for jealousy, why would anyone be jealous of Pat?

She wasn't young, beautiful, or, so far as we know, involved in an affair. Revenge implies some kind of estrangement, so again an invitation for coffee is out. That leaves fear."

Max forked a piece of flounder. "If she wouldn't invite someone for coffee because she was angry with them, she certainly wouldn't invite someone she feared."

Annie put down her fork. "Max, that's brilliant."

"Really?" A blond eyebrow quirked.

"Don't you see; Pat wasn't afraid. She invited someone over for coffee. She wouldn't ask someone if she felt she was in any danger." Annie's voice was hushed. "The other person was afraid."

Max didn't appear overwhelmed with her sagacity. "Why did someone fear Pat?"

"She must have posed a threat." Annie frowned, thinking out loud. "Maybe she knew something someone was determined to keep secret. Maybe Pat knew about something illegal or embarrassing or compromising in some way. Maybe Pat called the person, suggested they visit over a cup of coffee, maybe she dropped enough of a hint that it was clear what she was talking about."

Max forked coleslaw. "What was her point?"

Annie recalled another mystery discussion with Pat and her admiration for Christie's Virginia Revel, who looked for new experiences. "Maybe she wanted to see how the person would react. Or maybe Pat thought she could profit if she kept silent."

Max lifted his tea glass. "In less polite circles, that's called blackmail." He looked more interested. "She could have picked up some damaging information at the law firm. Maybe that's why she was fired."

Annie pressed fingertips against her temples. Possibly channeling Madame Arcati was habit-forming. "That doesn't work. If she threatened someone at the law firm, she wouldn't have been fired."

Max objected. "Wait a minute. What's the best way to get fired? Pose a threat to someone you work with."

Annie was thoughtful. "She lost her job a couple of weeks ago. Henny says she was furious. If she'd known anything, she would already have caused trouble. I think something happened after she lost her job. We have to find out everything we can about the last two weeks. What Pat did, who she saw, where she went."

Max took a moment in his stroll toward his desk to select a putter from a green ceramic vase shaped like an elephant's huge foot and a ball from a soft purple velvet bag hanging from a bronze hook next to the vase. An indoor putting green of synthetic bent grass graced one corner of the room. Today the hole was placed in a far corner beyond a challenging contour.

Max placed the ball at the edge of the green, assumed a putting stance. He drew the club back, making sure the putter face was square to the line. He stroked, smooth as butter. The ball rolled true, quivered for an instant, plopped into the cup. Max hoisted the club in triumph, then returned it to the vase.

He was smiling as he settled in the red leather chair behind the gleaming Renaissance refectory table that served as a desk. The surface was bare except for a matching red leather desk pad and the ornate silver frame that held his favorite photograph of Annie. He stared into her steady gray eyes. Flyaway sandy hair framed her open eager face. "Okay, babe. You want info on people around Pat Merridew. Maybe losing her job at the law firm doesn't have anything to do with her murder, if it was murder, but that's the place to start. For sure, they knew her well."

He turned to his computer, went online, Googled Jamison, Jamison, and Brewster + Broward's Rock. The Web page came up, reading: *Jamison, Jamison, and Brewster, LLC.* Max pulled a legal pad close, made notes. When he concluded, he printed bios for Glen Jamison, Cleo Jamison, and Kirk Brewster. His brow furrowed. There was no indication on the Web site that Kirk was leaving the firm. Maybe they were waiting to update after his departure.

Max read the bios, then looked again at the Web site, which listed office personnel. His eyes settled on a familiar name. He reached for the phone. When he was connected, he spoke quickly, " . . . I don't want to interrupt your workday. I saw one of your watercolors at the library and I wondered if you would be interested in doing a painting for my office." The law-firm building was a half block from the island's newest business, a frozen yogurt shop. "Could I buy you a yogurt on your break?" He smiled. "See you there."

Annie had scarcely noticed the neighborhood when she came to Pat Merridew's house with Billy. Now she studied her surroundings. Pat's house was on the wooded side of the road with no neighbors on either side. However, across the unpaved street several houses backed up to a lagoon. Two houses faced Pat's cottage.

Annie pulled into Pat's driveway, parked next to the blue Chevy. She glanced at the printout she'd made with the addresses and names of Pat's near neighbors.

Annie slipped out of the car, shaded her eyes to look directly across the street. The one-story, pale lemon stucco house belonged to Mrs. Charlene Croft. About a hundred yards away was a gray stone ranch house. She glanced at her sheet. The owner was Mark McGrath. Pat's drive and front porch were visible on an oblique line from the McGrath home.

She walked across the dusty unpaved road to the Croft home. Squirrels chittered and blue jays scolded as she knocked on the screen door. It popped open and a tiny, rail-thin woman with a mass of white curls and curious brown eyes peered at her.

Annie smiled. "Mrs. Croft?"

"You aren't the nurse's aide." There was a quick frown. "Well, I'm not buying anything."

As the door started to close, Annie said quickly, "I'm here because of Pat Merridew."

The door was pushed wide. "Oh." Her soft voice was quavery. "Such a shame. She was the nicest neighbor. When I broke my hip, she brought me casseroles and stayed to visit. She kept up with everyone in the neighborhood. The McGraths"—Mrs. Croft gestured to her left—"go to Minnesota every summer and Pat kept an eye on everything for them."

"Are they gone now?"

Mrs. Croft nodded. "They left two weeks ago." She cocked her head like an eager bird. "Are you family?"

"No, ma'am. I'm Annie Darling. I own the bookstore on the marina and Pat had just started to work for me."

She nodded, the white curls quivering. "Pat told me she had a new job." The wrinkled face drooped. "She was so excited. And now she's gone. Are you taking up a memorial? I'll get my purse."

"Oh, no. I'm hoping to find out who visited her the night she died. You know, it would be helpful to the family to know if she had begun to feel ill."

"Why, that's the oddest thing. A police lady came by just a few minutes ago and asked me the same thing. I think it's very nice of everyone to want to know what happened. But no one came to see her that night."

Annie felt an instant of shock. "We were sure someone came."

Mrs. Croft's head shake was decided. "I sat on my front porch from supper time on in my swing. I was reading Ann Ross's new book and I tell you I laughed until I almost cried and I didn't move until it was almost ten, and the police lady said that a friend talked to Pat and she was sitting down to eat at six o'clock and I know that's right because that's when she always ate, and the police lady said that meant she died sometime between eight and nine o'clock."

Annie understood. Time of death had been esti-mated on the basis of the state of digestion of her final meal.

Mrs. Croft looked regretful. "I should have known something was wrong when I looked out about two-thirty in the morning—I got up to rub some liniment on my hip—and her lights were still on. But I didn't go check again because her lights had been on late ever since she lost her job at the law firm."

Annie almost ended the conversation there. She was ready to speak when one word registered. "You 'didn't go check again'?"

Mrs. Croft nodded energetically. "Pat used to go to bed at ten every night after the evening news. You must think I am the world's nosiest neighbor"—her smile was quick—"but I have bursitis and some nights I can't sleep because of the pain. I get up and walk around and I was used to seeing Pat's lights go off. Well, more than a week ago, the lights were on and it was past mid-night. I was worried that maybe she was sick, so I put on my robe and shoes and went across and knocked on the door. And you know what?"

Annie shook her head.

"She didn't answer the door." Mrs. Croft's tone was portentous.

Annie tried not to reveal her disappointment.

"That worried me, so I tried the door. Pat never bothered to lock up until right before she went to bed. I stepped inside and called out. No answer. I started looking around. Gertrude came up to me in a minute, though I could tell she'd been asleep. Pat wasn't anywhere, not in the living room or the bedroom or little den or kitchen or bathroom. I was puzzled because her car was outside. Gertrude followed me all around. I went right through the house and out into the backyard thinking maybe she'd fallen and"—Mrs. Croft clapped her hands together—"here she came up the boardwalk. I told her I was so glad she was all right, that I'd come to check because her lights were on so late. She gave me a hug and said she had trouble sleeping and she'd gone for a walk." Mrs. Croft's animation fled. "After that I noticed her lights were on late every night. I didn't worry about her Friday night. I thought she'd gone for another late walk."

Max took a half spoon of raspberry and a half spoon of chocolate. ". . . love to have a watercolor of the pier, a summer scene with people fishing." His expression was enthusiastic.

Edna Graham smiled, easing the severity of an angular face with heavy dark eyebrows and strong nose and square chin. "I have several new watercolors of the pier." Her eyes shone with eagerness. "I could bring some to your office tomorrow over my lunch hour."

"That would be great." His tone was hearty. Edna was reputed to be a superb legal secretary. He'd seen several of her paintings at the local artists' community show at the library and they were pale and subdued for his taste. But a man in search of information did what a man had to do. "It's outstanding that you have a successful career and find time to paint as well. Do you find painting a relief from the stress of your job?"

Max found Edna's expression uncannily similar to one of his mother's Cat Truth posters: a thick-furred, brown rosette-tabby Pixie-Bob, its wide rounded head held in a pose of supreme satisfaction: *Tell me again how fine I am.*

"Oh"—her sigh was heartfelt—"you can't imagine how stressful work can be. Everything has to be right when you are a legal secretary. No mistakes." Her chin jutted. "I don't make mistakes."

"I suppose it's been even harder since Pat Merridew left the firm."

Edna looked offended. "Pat wasn't a legal secretary. Believe me, no one would have trusted her with substantive work. She was a receptionist. She didn't have anything to do with legal matters." Her tone indicated disdain. Then her angular face softened. "Poor

Pat. Such a shock about her death. Everyone's awfully sorry. I can't imagine anyone dying at her age." There was a flicker in her eyes, the recognition of mortality sparked by unexpected death.

Max gave it one last try. "So Pat wasn't privy to confidential information that would burden her."

"No." Edna's reply was unconcerned. She glanced at her watch. "I must get back. I have a contract to finish. I'll come to your office at noon tomorrow."

Annie stopped at her car, tossed her purse in the trunk, then hurried around the side of Pat's cottage. The backyard was shallow. Spanish moss and resurrection ferns dotted the live oaks. A slight breeze stirred dangling willow fronds. Patches of grass spread in irregular clumps on the dusty gray ground. A boardwalk led from the back steps of the cottage to an opening in the pine woods. Annie recalled the geography. She thought much of the wooded area behind Pat's house was part of a nature preserve.

Lights gleaming late at night had drawn Mrs. Croft across the street. She had found Pat's house empty and found Pat in the backyard coming up the boardwalk.

Annie looked at the woods. She had a healthy respect for island woods after dark when a fox might nose cautiously through undergrowth or a bobcat wait in ambush for an unwary deer. Yet Pat Merridew had been returning from the woods when Mrs. Croft came to check. Moreover, Mrs. Croft became accustomed to lights on late at night in Pat's house, which suggested her foray into the woods might have been repeated. Maybe the deep darkness with the rustle of night creatures had soothed Pat.

Annie almost turned away, then stopped, staring at the dim entrance into the woods. Something had occurred recently in Pat's life that had led to murder. Certainly late-night walks in the forest qualified as unusual. Annie walked swiftly across the yard.

In the woods, she studied a narrow path. With a shrug, she turned right. She followed a twisting, vine-shrouded path that grew ever fainter. The path finally ended at a murky lagoon with water as black as pitch. She'd not glimpsed a single house or offshoot trail. Hot and bug-nipped, she retraced her steps and paused at the opening into Pat's backyard. She spoke aloud. "She was some kind of nut if she went that way." With a sigh, Annie continued in the other direction. The path curved generally north and west. She waved away swarms of flies and no-see-'ums. Yaupon holly and ferns choked the ground beneath the canopy of live oaks, slash pine, and magnolias. A recent heavy summer rain had left puddles. She squished along the muddy trail, probably staining her cream leather loafers for all time. She was leaving a distinct set of tracks. A bicycle could have come this way, but she saw no tire prints.

Children's voices rose in chatter and shouts.

Finally, a sign of life.

Annie carefully eased apart saw-palmetto fronds to reveal an asphalt parking lot behind a playground. She stepped warily, after a careful survey of the ground. She was well aware that rattlesnakes and alligators inhabited the woods. She let out a small breath of relief as she reached the parking lot unscathed. A chain-link fence bounded the playground. Toddlers scooped sand into buckets. Four- and five-year-olds swung, clambered up and down ladders to a wooden fort, slid down slides, or maneuvered on a small plastic climbing wall.

Annie walked past the small gray structure. In the street, she saw the entrance and a sign hanging from an iron post: HAPPY DAYS CHILD CARE. She noted the hours. The day care closed at seven P.M. Owner or staff might have been there on Friday evening, but the path would only be visible to someone standing in the parking lot and pulling aside greenery.

Annie reentered the woods, snagging her blouse on a saw-palmetto frond. A hundred yards farther on, she heard the yipping of dogs. Again she pulled aside fronds and recognized the back parking area of the island's veterinary clinic. This time she didn't bother to struggle through the undergrowth. Obviously, the path wasn't usually accessed from either business site.

She almost retraced her steps, then, lips folded stubbornly, continued forward. The pines thinned to her left. Through the trees, she saw a gazebo, a garden with banks of azaleas, several plots filled with rosebushes, and the back of a three-story tabby home. The path at that point turned due east but a red-and-white barrier prohibited entry.

POSTED
RICE FIELD RECLAMATION
KEEP OUT

Very likely, the path beyond the barrier might be all but impassable. In the dark, Pat surely hadn't continued.

Annie felt discouraged. Mrs. Croft saw Pat emerge from the woods, so clearly she'd taken the path. She hadn't turned to the right unless she wanted to commune with a black lagoon. Clearly she'd traveled this way. But why? Moreover, she may have likely trekked into the woods not once, but several times. Mrs. Croft reported she'd continued to see lights late at night. Whatever Pat had done, wherever she had gone on the night Mrs. Croft came to check on her, she likely had gone again and again.

Where and why?

Annie stepped cautiously on slick pine straw. When she reached the base of the garden, a charming one-story gray wood cottage was in full view. Annie stared. She hadn't recognized the house from the backyard, but she immediately knew the cottage. Annie had been there last week for a committee meeting for the League of Women Voters. Elaine Jamison was the committee chair. Annie liked working with Elaine, who was crisp, kind, clever, and insightful. But much more important to Annie was the fact that the softly green tabby house was the home of Glen and Cleo Jamison.

Annie turned toward the cottage. Elaine's car was not in the drive. Annie walked back into the woods, thinking hard. She returned on the path to Pat Merridew's backyard. As soon as she reached her car, she retrieved her purse from the trunk and lifted out her cell phone. She called the police station, recognized the voice of the dispatcher—Billy's wife, Mavis. "Mavis, this is Annie Darling. May I speak to Billy?"

In a moment, Billy answered.

Annie plunged into her recital, stopping only when Billy interrupted. Finally, she concluded, ". . . and I think Pat went late at night to the Jamison house."

Billy was sharp. "Wait a minute. You don't have any basis for that conclusion."

Annie was fervent. "Why else would she go on that path?"

"There's no proof she turned left. Maybe she went toward the lagoon."

"Pat told Mrs. Croft she couldn't sleep after she lost her job. She was furious with Glen Jamison. I think she went on that path to the Jamison house."

"Why?" Billy sounded bewildered. "What possible reason would she have to go there late at night after everyone was asleep?"

"Because she was upset." It seemed eminently reasonable to Annie.

Billy drew a deep breath. "There's no point to it."

She had a quick memory of a Cat Truth poster: a small Brown Tabby, clearly a female, stalked a mesmerized rabbit while a Golden Shaded Persian male lolled back against a cushion, one leg raised for grooming. *She takes care of business. Maybe if the rabbit kicked him . . .*

Annie wasn't sure she could breach the divide between Venus and Mars. "Women take things personally."

"You got that right." Billy's agreement was fervent and obviously the product of experience.

Encouraged, she continued. "Pat was upset. I think she wanted to go and look at the house and think how much she hated them. Like sticking pins in a voodoo doll. Anyway, she went somewhere on that path late at night and not just once but several times. She wouldn't go to the child care or the vet's. They're closed in the middle of the night. The lagoon was a dead end. The only other place is the Jamison house. I don't believe in coincidence, and since it was the Jamison house, that had to be why she went." Annie realized her reasoning sounded a trifle inchoate, but she was sure of her conclusion. "I mean, think about it." Was she starting to sound like an eighties Valley Girl?

Billy was patient. "I see what you're getting at. Let's say you're right." He sounded dubious. "Let's say Pat Merridew went sneaking up that path to go think evil thoughts about the Jamisons. Annie, she's the one who's dead, not Glen or Cleo Jamison."

"That's the point. Pat's dead. She went up that path and she saw or heard something at the Jamison house that led her to try blackmail."

"Come on, Annie." He was clearly incredulous. "That's a leap too far."

Annie strove to be calm and reasonable. "Mrs. Croft didn't see anyone visit Pat's house Friday night. But someone came and washed up that crystal mug and didn't leave any fingerprints. Where did the murderer come from? Why not the path from the Jamison house? If the murderer came from the Jamison house, that proves Pat's death is linked to the Jamisons."

"A leap way, way, way too far." His tone was cautionary. "If we're going to create scenarios out of nothing, including the idea of murder, how about some enemy knew Mrs. Croft watched the neighborhood, so this person parked at either the vet's or the child care and took the path. Or maybe Mrs. Croft went in her house Friday night for a few minutes and that's when the visitor came. Or maybe Mrs. Croft and Pat were crossways and that's who came to visit. But, we have no proof"—he emphasized the noun—"that a visitor came or that the mug without fingerprints has anything to do with the night Merridew died. Or that she was murdered."

Annie thought that battle had been won. She spoke sharply, "Nothing else makes any sense."

"I'm talking about proof. As for linking the people in the Jamison house to the Merridew death, that's what I call imaginative reconstruction, like they do in political books these days. Of course, those writers claim to have deep background, they just don't ever cite a source. You don't have a source, deep or not." He took a deep breath. "But thanks, Annie, I'll add this information to the file."

Henny Brawley traced the red letters on her coffee mug: *Murderer's Mistake* by E.C.R. Lorac. Her fine dark eyes were troubled. "After we caught the mug without fingerprints, thanks to you"—she gave a nod to Annie—"I thought we'd easily discover a motive. I haven't had any luck. I've checked with everyone who knew Pat well. All of them tell the same story. She was upset about losing her job, mad as a hornet at Glen and Cleo, happy she'd found a job here"—Henny spread her hand to include the coffee area of Death on Demand—"but no one could suggest any reason anyone would want Pat dead. Not money"—she ticked off possibilities one by one— "not love, not hate, not revenge, not jealousy, not despair."

"Fear." Annie was emphatic. "Pat knew something or threatened to do something that endangered the murderer. The murderer came to Pat's house prepared to kill. That means a threat was made in advance."

"So"—Henny's smile was wry—"maybe the motive is money, after all. I had lunch with Pat after she was fired and she was worried about having enough income to keep going. She didn't want to touch her savings. She said that would be the last resort. That's why I helped her get in touch with you. So I know she was concerned about money. Yet I discovered she was planning a cruise to Alaska. Kathy Kilgore—"

Annie knew the travel agent. Travel More with Kilgore had planned several trips for Annie and Max.

"—said Pat came in on Friday—"

Annie's eyes widened. Pat went to the travel agency the day she died.

"—and picked up a bunch of brochures. If Billy's still thinking Pat committed suicide, Kathy can certainly say that Pat was excited about planning her trip."

"Let's call Billy and tell him," Annie suggested. She swiveled to retrieve the portable phone. She clicked speaker and handed the receiver to Henny. "You do the honors. You talked to Kathy, plus he may be a little tired of hearing from me."

Henny called and Mavis Cameron answered. Henny asked for the chief.

"Just a moment."

"Chief Cameron." His deep voice was pleasant.

"Henny Brawley. Billy, I have more evidence that Pat Merridew wasn't suicidal."

He listened as Henny reported Pat's interest in an Alaska cruise. "Yeah. It could indicate she was upbeat, looking forward to travel. It could also suggest she was trying to find something to dispel depression. We'll never know."

Henny was emphatic. "Pat didn't have the money to make that kind of trip. The fact that she planned the trip means money was available from some source. She told Kathy she'd be in this week to make the reservations. Where did she plan to get the money? If she was murdered, as I firmly believe, there had to be a compelling motive. We haven't found anyone here who profited from her death. We haven't found any apparent enemies. What does that leave? Maybe Pat made a big mistake. Maybe she knew something that threatened someone and she attempted blackmail."

Billy said calmly, "Maybe she was dreaming. People can plan trips and know they'll never take them. Maybe picking up those brochures and knowing she couldn't afford to go tipped her over to suicide. That seems more likely than the idea she blackmailed somebody. We have to have proof. We haven't found anything to support the idea that Pat Merridew was murdered." He was matter-of-fact, not defensive.

Annie leaned toward the speakerphone. "Did you find the Alaska brochures in her house?"

"Hey, Annie." Papers rustled. "No reason for the brochures to have been noted. I'll have Officer Harrison check. But if we find them, what does that prove?"

"If you don't find them, that will be odd, won't it?" Annie looked across the coffee area at a Cat Truth poster. A muscular Louisiana Creole Cat with a thick long coat, gold shading to brown on the face and back, white shoulders and paws, stood upright on his back feet, front paws pressed against a windowpane, and stared with unblinking intensity at a bullfinch: *Keep your eye on the prey.*

"As in?"

"If we're right about the crystal mug, Pat served Irish coffee to a guest. Let's say she'd already made it clear she knew something. She handed the brochures to her guest and said how nice it would be to go on the trip. Maybe there was talk of how much it might cost for the cruise package. Maybe the guest asked for another dash of whiskey for the coffee, and while Pat was in the kitchen, ground-up OxyContin pills were dropped in her cup and stirred to dissolve. When Pat came back, she drank the coffee and pretty soon she slipped into unconsciousness. The murderer had to take the brochures away because they held fingerprints. Maybe—"

"Maybe," Billy interrupted, "you can explain how this visitor got hold of leftover pills Pat Merridew probably kept in her medicine cabinet."

Annie blinked, but she didn't see the acquisition of the pills as a big problem. "People who knew Pat—like the Jamisons—were aware she broke her wrist. Oxy-Contin's a commonly prescribed pain pill. Pat could have mentioned what she was taking. Or maybe the visitor had an old leftover prescription at home. Anyway, I think this murderer is smart enough to know about the drug and get into Pat's house when she wasn't at home and take the pills. I'll bet Pat left her back door unlocked. Lots of people do. Or maybe—"

"Maybe," Billy interrupted again, "you have a future writing one of those tell-all books that don't cite any sources."

Annie felt hot. "It could have happened that way."

"Could have." He was pleasant. "But I'd like a source, even a deep one. Anyway, we'll check out the brochures." The call ended.

Henny handed the receiver to Annie. "If those brochures are missing, I think you hit the bull's-eye. She tried to blackmail the wrong person." Her animation ebbed. "But who and why?"

Annie well knew that scarcely anything of interest, much less scandal or confrontation, escaped the attention of island residents. The grapevine flourished. Moreover, no one had greater access to that kind of information than Henny, who was plugged into the social scene, charitable endeavors, and the church milieu. Whatever knowledge or act had led to Pat's death, it had escaped public notice.

Annie tapped her mug: *Night Encounter* by Anthony Gilbert. "Everything hinges on Pat's night walks. Billy may disagree, but I don't have any doubt that Pat took that path"—she dropped the words like a mallet striking a gong with measured force—"to the Jamison house. I want to find out everything about everyone in that house."

Five

Max lined up his putt. He bent his knees, steadied the club. The phone rang. He glanced at the clock. A quarter to four. He would not be a happy man if actual work raised its hairy head when he was ready to call the day done, retrieve Annie, and maybe go to the beach.

His secretary poked her head inside his office. Today Barb's bouffant hairdo was a brilliant red, shades of Reba McEntire. Was it a coincidence that she'd been belting out "I Keep On Lovin' You" while whipping up a chocolate cherry cake in the small back kitchen that doubled as a storeroom? "Annie on the line."

Max tapped the ball too quickly and it wobbled off the synthetic green and sped across the wood floor. On the way to his desk, he scooped it up with his putter.

He bounced the ball in his hand as he sat on the edge of his desk and picked up the receiver. He'd put off calling Annie because he knew she would be disappointed. He settled behind his desk and listened. He pulled a green folder close, flipped it open. "I have a file on the firm, but, Annie, there's nothing there. Pat didn't have access to anything confidential. I talked to Glen's secretary. I don't think there's any link to the law firm." His shoulders lifted and fell. "Sure, I'll talk to Glen if you want. I will leave no stone unturned." He hung up, popped to his feet, sheathed the putter.

On his way out of the office, he turned a thumbs-up to another stanza of "I Keep On Lovin' You." "Check it in for the day, Barb. Go to the beach and take a wave for me." The surf was usually mild on Broward's Rock unless a storm was coming, but this afternoon the tide would be high, so there might be some decent waves. Maybe he and Annie could take a picnic to the beach. Mmmm, Annie in a gold bikini, smooth soft skin glistening with SPF coconut oil, the best of both worlds, protection married to scent. He walked faster.

Elaine Jamison was fair like her brother with the same deep-set blue eyes and high-bridged nose and pointed chin. She welcomed Annie warmly, though there was sadness in her eyes. "You're wonderful to set up a memorial for Pat. I should have thought of it but I haven't been myself." Her voice trailed away as she led the way into the small living room of the cottage. The room was cheerful with a red upholstered sofa and easy chair and red curtains at the windows. A tall pottery vase on a side table held fresh red hollyhocks.

Elaine gestured at the easy chair. "I'm so glad you've come. Would you like iced tea? It's fresh."

In a moment, they sat opposite each other, a low stone coffee table between them. Annie squeezed lemon into the tumbler, enjoyed the scent of fresh mint. "I know Pat's death has been a shock. She hadn't been working at Death on Demand long but we liked her and I wanted to make a contribution in her name to the Red Cross. I understand she went down to Florida to be a volunteer after that last hurricane."

"Of course I'll help." Elaine rose and went to a small desk in the corner. She quickly wrote a check and brought it back to Annie. "Thank you for remembering me." She picked up her glass, then set it down without drinking. "I know it's silly, but I think it's even harder for me because I talked to her Friday evening. She called to ask if I found my present on my front porch. My birthday's next week. She had dropped off a Doreen Tovey book. Pat had been after me to get a new cat. Bongo died two months ago and I didn't think I was ready to get a new cat. But the Tovey books reminded me how much I love Siamese even though they are always impossible. Bongo"—she smiled and gestured at a strip of carpet installed on the wall next to a window—"spent most of his time climbing up to rest on the valance." Her smile faded. "Pat sounded upbeat, kind of excited. We planned on having lunch the next day. I settled in with the book and laughed and laughed. I had such a happy evening, thanks to Pat. I laughed and Pat was dying." Tears streamed down her face. "Excuse me." She jumped up and left the room for a moment, then came back, scrubbing her face. "I'm sorry."

Annie reached out, touched her arm. "She would be happy to know the book made you laugh." She looked inquiring. "Pat sounded excited? Do you know why?"

"She was going to take an Alaska cruise. She went on and on about how wonderful the cruise was going to be. I'm glad she was happy that last night." Elaine's voice was subdued. She reached for the pitcher. "Would you like more tea?"

"No, thank you." Annie opened her purse, dropped Elaine's check in a side pocket. "Pat would appreciate your remembering her. You'd been friends for a long time."

"She was a rock after Maddy died. Pat could be prickly, but she was loyal and kind. I think that's why she was so upset after Glen fired her." Elaine's eyes looked stricken. "I don't know how he could have done it. Oh well." Her tone was bitter. "I do know. It's that woman he married. She causes trouble for everyone, but Glen won't hear a word against her. Now his home is a cold and angry place. He's at odds with the children. Laura can't help it that she lost her job. Everybody's been getting fired. Unemployment's awful. All kinds of people with college degrees don't have jobs. Of course, Laura came home. Would Glen want her out on the street? That's where she'd be if Cleo had her way. Sure, Laura's unhappy. It's humiliating to lose your job and not be able to find one. She's sent out résumés everywhere. It doesn't help matters that she and Kirk Brewster were getting to be friends. Of course, he's stopped coming around now. Glen knew about them. That makes booting out Kirk even worse. So Laura's mad and Kirk is mad and Kit is mad, too. I'm just sick about Kit. Going to Africa means everything to her, but Cleo has poisoned Glen's mind, said Kit should have to pay her own way. If Kit can't turn in the money by next week, she'll lose the chance for the internship. Maybe it's worst of all about Tommy. He shouldn't have to go away to school. Everybody knows how boys can be hazed at military academies. He's on the high school football team and so excited about their chances next fall. Maddy would be heart-broken. When I try to talk to him, Glen looks beaten down. He won't meet my eyes. It reminds me of when he was little. Our dad was . . . stern. When Glen got in trouble, he'd promise anything to keep Dad from getting mad. Glen"—she looked at Annie with a plea in her eyes—"wants to do the right thing. He really does. But Cleo—" Elaine pressed the tips of long thin fingers against her temples. "Oh, I'm sorry. Please forgive me, Annie. You didn't come to hear all my troubles. I didn't mean to get started about the family, but everything's been difficult lately. And to have Pat die so unexpectedly is awful." Her eyes filled with tears. "I can't bear the thought that she killed herself because she lost her job. Glen's really upset."

Annie took an instant to answer. Billy hadn't enjoined her and Henny to silence. If Billy learned that Annie was saying Pat had been murdered, well, so be it. "I understand the question of how she died isn't settled. There's reason to think she didn't commit suicide."

Elaine clasped her hands together. "I'm relieved to hear that and Glen will be, too. I heard she died from a drug overdose. Was it an accident?"

Annie was firm. "That doesn't seem likely either."

Elaine looked puzzled. "What happened?"

Annie picked her words carefully. "Someone may have had coffee with her the night she died and put the drug in Pat's cup."

Elaine drew in a sharp breath. Her eyes widened. "On purpose?" Her voice was hushed. "Are you saying that Pat was murdered?"

"Yes."

Incredulity warred with shock. "That can't be true. Pat didn't have an enemy in the world."

"Mr. Darling." The pretty, dark-haired girl gave him a bright smile. "Mr. Jamison can see you now." She held open the swinging gate to the inner office and started to turn.

"Thanks. I know the way." Max moved past her and into a corridor. The law firm of Jamison, Jamison, and Brewster was quartered in a one-story building shaped like a T, the reception area in the crossbar, the offices and conference rooms in the vertical bar. He walked up the hall to the third door on the left, tapped, and pushed the door in.

Glen Jamison came around his desk, hand outstretched. His face, always pale, looked weary with bluish shadows beneath his eyes. Max wondered if he had been ill.

They shook hands and Glen waved Max toward a comfortable brown leather chair.

Glen dropped onto a matching couch. "Hell of a thing about Pat. She was always game for everything. I missed having her around. I hear she died from a drug overdose. Somebody told Cleo they thought it was suicide."

Max shook his head. "It turns out that was a mistake. I've heard the investigation is focused on murder."

Glen's eyes widened, his lips parted. He looked utterly stunned. "Pat murdered? That's crazy." His voice was shocked. "Why would anyone murder Pat?"

Why, indeed? Max thought. "I'm hoping to find out more for the family." There were, as Max well knew, many ways to tell the truth. Certainly he would be happy to share whatever he learned with Pat's sister in California. If Glen mistakenly assumed Max was working for the family, the interpretation was Glen's, not Max's. "I thought you were the best person to tell me about Pat's last few weeks."

Glen's aristocratic face drooped in unhappy lines. "Yeah. Well, I don't suppose you knew, but we had to let Pat go a couple of weeks ago."

Max kept his face interested and uncritical.

Glen's gaze slid away, fastened on a print of the Acropolis hanging on a sidewall. "Cleo was thinking about redecorating the office, make it more gray and chrome like the big-city firms. I'm afraid Pat wasn't very tactful. Anyway, Cleo said we should have a young, eager receptionist." He avoided looking at Max. "So I let her go. I'm afraid she got pretty upset with me. That's why when we heard she committed suicide, I felt really bad. But Cleo said people make their own choices."

Max could hear the voice of Glen's second wife, smooth and satisfied, as he spoke.

"Murder . . ." Glen sagged back against the couch. "God, I'm glad it wasn't suicide."

"Do you know anyone who was angry with Pat? Or anyone who feared her?"

Glen looked startled, eyes widening, lips parting. "Not that I ever knew about. It doesn't seem possible. I guess there's something we didn't know about Pat. But"—he looked at Max with a suddenly relieved expression—"I'm sure glad she didn't kill herself."

Annie always took pleasure in their back porch. Green wicker chairs with cream-colored cushions offered comfort and a gorgeous view of the garden. She plopped into a chair on one side of the wicker table, bright with daisy-yellow place mats and settings for breakfast. She took a deep breath of the sweet scent of pittosporum blooms. Hydrangeas, butterfly bushes, jessamine lantana, roses, and bougainvillea created a patchwork of colors. In the early-morning quiet, the caw of crows sounded cheerful. Glossy magnolia leaves rattled in a light breeze.

The screen door opened and Max stepped out of the kitchen, carrying a plate. His hair was still damp from the shower. "Hot, moist, and ready to devour."

Annie grinned. "You or the Danishes?"

Max laughed. Despite the shower, his face was still flushed from their prebreakfast jog. "Both. And the same to you, Mrs. Darling."

After an early-morning jog and shower, Annie enjoyed cooling down on the back porch. It was a lovely beginning to a lovely day except for her nagging sense of a task left undone. She took a sip of orange juice, frowned, and opened her mouth.

Before she could speak, Max broke off a piece of a raspberry Danish and popped it in her mouth. "You look like the Selkirk Rex."

The sweet roll was flaky with just the right amount of buttery richness. She reached up to touch her damp tangled hair. Surely she wasn't that frizzy, though it was flattering to be compared to the elegant long-haired cat with soft, plush, curly ringlets and amber eyes. The Selkirk Rex on Laurel's Cat Truth poster had its mouth agape: *Hey, listen to me.*

Annie grabbed her coffee mug. "I wish somebody would listen to me."

Dorothy L darted after a butterfly, then jumped onto the tabletop. Annie gently removed her. "Not during breakfast." She took a moment to smooth Dorothy L's fluffy fur, but she wasn't distracted from her worry. "Pat walked to the Jamison house. That has to mean something."

Max settled in the opposite chair, poured coffee into their red pottery mugs. He speared a piece of papaya. "Sometimes what you see is what you get. She walked to the Jamison house. Maybe that's all there was to it. I'm not saying she committed suicide. Maybe somebody dropped OxyContin in her coffee, but," and he flipped up one finger after another for emphasis, "we can't find any hint anywhere that anyone had any reason to kill her. At the law firm, a competent, hard-nosed legal secretary made it clear Pat knew nothing about the inner workings of the firm, plus Glen Jamison was pitifully glad to hear she didn't kill herself. Henny Brawley knows everybody on the island, but Henny can't come up with anything out of the ordinary about Pat. You talked to Elaine Jamison and she said Pat didn't have an enemy in the world."

Annie felt as isolated as if she were marooned on a desert island. "She had an enemy. And I think it was someone who lives in the Jamison house."

Annie enjoyed the quiet at Death on Demand before it opened. She'd left Max murmuring into his newspaper that people who went to work at eight-thirty when they didn't have to be there until nine were seriously deranged and in need of recreational counseling. She'd kissed the back of his neck, which caught his attention big-time, but she'd not been deflected from her departure. She was still smiling as she unlocked the door. She would catch up with paperwork, and though she hadn't told Max, she would continue to worry at the problem of Pat Merridew. There would only be a few early shoppers. Readers looking for hammock books would begin to drift in after lunch as the June day heated up.

Instead of heading straight to her office, she wandered aimlessly around the coffee area. Finding out what happened to Pat was like tugging at a ball of snarled yarn. She felt sure if she tugged at the right string, she would find some proof of her conviction that Pat had been murdered and that her murder was linked to the Jamisons.

She glanced at the Cat Truth poster with the gorgeous, wide-mouthed Selkirk Rex. "You tell 'em, honey." But her smile slipped away. Annie had told everyone, most especially Billy Cameron, and he wasn't listening. She reached down to straighten a poster hanging crookedly beside the fireplace. A red-brown Abyssinian, tail high, stepped through dew damp grass: *Come with me to the Casbah.* Shades of *Casablanca*, one of Laurel's favorite films. Annie imagined the muscular cat with a Humphrey Bogart face. Bogie never gave up. He was the quintessential American private eye in *The Maltese Falcon.* Annie didn't fancy herself as an incarnation of Sam Spade, but she could follow Spade's mantra: nothing and nobody kept him from finding out the truth.

Annie whirled and marched to the coffee bar, plucked the receiver from the phone, punched a number. Max claimed no one had found anything out of the ordinary during Pat's final days. That wasn't true. At least one night Pat's lights were on late and she was seen returning from the forest. Okay, what was in the forest? A path that led to the Jamison house. Billy could claim Annie was reaching too far to insist that Pat saw something at the Jamison house that caused her death. Maybe so. But there was no denying Pat's lights had continued to shine late at night. That was odd fact one. Odd fact two was Pat's trip to the travel agency on Friday, the very day she died. She'd taken travel brochures with her. Annie could imagine those brochures lying on the table and a guest picking them up. Or perhaps Pat handed a brochure to her guest, saying something lightly about a trip of a lifetime—if only she had the money.

When Billy Cameron came on the line, Annie plunged right to her point. "Have you found the travel brochures?"

"I'm sending Officer Harrison to the Merridew house to look for them." He sounded patient. "Since you are convinced the brochures are important, why don't you meet her there? Maybe you will have some good ideas. Be there in fifteen minutes."

The phone clicked off.

Annie would have been pleased, but she knew her presence was just another way of saying sayonara.

Officer Hyla Harrison had relocated to Broward's Rock after her patrol partner was gunned down in a Miami alley. She always moved fast, her narrow face often drawn in a frown of concentration. She was serious, responsible, and humorless. She took murder very seriously indeed and initially had found the idea of a mystery bookstore offensive. "There's nothing funny about murder," she'd told Annie not long after they first met. When Annie agreed and explained that murder is never funny, people are funny, Hyla reconsidered. Now she was a devoted reader of Tana French and Ed McBain.

Annie watched as the patrol car turned precisely into Pat Merridew's driveway. Perhaps only Officer Harrison could make the turn of a car appear as skillfully executed as a scalpel marking an incision.

Hyla, as always, looked crisp and fresh in her khaki uniform, her auburn hair drawn back into a sleek bun. She walked swiftly to the front steps, carrying a black case. Unsmiling, she looked up at Annie. "The chief said you were here to observe me." She jerked her head and marched past Annie to pull open the screen and unlock the door.

Annie hurried to catch up. "Hyla—"

The trim patrol woman turned. "Officer Harrison."

Annie reached out a hand in appeal. She wasn't going to lose the trust she'd slowly, very slowly, earned with Hyla if she could help it. "The chief knows I have great respect for you. You are careful and thorough and this is a situation that needs that kind of attention to detail. That's why he sent you. He knows you won't miss anything. He gave me permission to be here because I think Pat Merridew was murdered." Because she believed what she was saying, her tone was genuine.

Hyla's stiff shoulders relaxed. A slight frown tugged at her brows. "He told me you suggested the check for fingerprints in the china cabinet." She tilted her head to study Annie. "Why did you think of that?"

Quickly Annie described Pat's attitude toward the suicide in *Towards Zero*. ". . . so if she didn't commit suicide and it couldn't be an accident, that left murder. The drug was found in Pat's crystal coffee mug. It seemed to me the only answer was someone else sitting across from her and dropping the drug in her coffee. But—"

Hyla swung the door open, held it for Annie.

"—only the one mug was found"—Annie pointed at the coffee table—"so we looked for the other." She pointed toward the breakfront.

Hyla nodded. "Crystal."

Annie knew Hyla understood. Sitting alone in the evening for a cup of coffee, Pat would drink from her everyday pottery, not use crystal. Annie's eyes met Hyla's and saw a gleam of agreement.

"Okay." Hyla was crisp. "The victim picked up travel brochures the day she died."

Annie felt as if she'd climbed a steep cliff and emerged on top. To Hyla, Pat Merridew was now a victim.

Hyla's eyes narrowed. "So she was excited about the trip she wanted to take. She gets the brochures. She probably put them in her purse. She comes home after work." Hyla surveyed the small living room. "Let's check the purse first."

The slender patrol officer put down the case on the coffee table, flipped up the lid, pulled out two pairs of latex gloves, and handed one set to Annie. She picked up the purse, a nylon summer tote bag with a design of blue sailboats against a cream background. She opened the bag and, using pincers from the case, carefully lifted out the contents: lip gloss, compact, hand sanitizer, aspirin bottle, box of mints, hairbrush, comb, case with sunglasses, BlackBerry, small notebook, three ballpoint pens, crumpled bingo card, small packet of Kleenex, billfold, checkbook, change purse, car keys, package of red licorice. She shook her head and returned the items as carefully as she had removed them.

Annie moved slowly around the perimeter of the living room. Pat had been a tidy housekeeper. There were no papers or magazines tucked in the bookcase. She edged open the TV console. The remote lay atop the previous Sunday's TV guide.

Hyla jerked a thumb. "Let's try the kitchen. Maybe she wanted to study them while she ate dinner."

Once in the kitchen, Annie was struck by the supper dishes now bone-dry, the dog's empty water bowl. She looked at the kitchen table, empty except for one place mat and a pottery sugar bowl and salt and pepper shakers.

Hyla stepped to the white plastic wastebasket, used the foot press to lift the lid.

Annie moved near. "Billy said they found an empty pill bottle right on top of the trash."

Hyla spread a black plastic bag on the kitchen floor and painstakingly removed the contents of the wastebasket: an empty egg carton, used tea bags, rinsed-out cans, cellophane wrappers, assorted boxes and bags.

No travel brochures.

Annie was emphatic. "They should be here. She'd have no reason to hide them."

"We'll continue to look." Hyla sounded patient.

At the end of a half hour, they stood again in the small living room. Hyla shook her head.

Annie pointed at the coffee table. "Like I told Billy, I think someone else was here Friday night. Pat used her crystal for a guest, made her favorite specialty coffee drink. Pat handed the brochures to her visitor. Later, when Pat was dying, the murderer took the brochures away because the brochures held fingerprints."

Hyla Harrison looked at the empty chairs and the coffee table. "I don't know about that. I know there aren't any brochures in this house." Her glance at Annie was commiserating. "I get where you're coming from. But it's awfully hard to prove anything with nothing." She peeled off the gloves and started to turn toward the door then stopped. "I wonder . . ." She pulled the gloves back on and walked to the purse. Again she used the pincer, this time to retrieve the phone. She glanced at it in mild surprise. "I'd have thought the chief would have already retrieved it. Pirelli probably checked it out, didn't see any unusual calls or messages." Hyla held it carefully at the edges, opened it, tapped her finger. "No recent text messages." She moved her finger again. "Got some pix." She looked at the images. "Nice one of the raven. Guess she wanted to show somebody that the place where she worked had this molty-looking bird on a shelf."

Annie was touched that Pat had taken a photo at the store.

Abruptly, Hyla frowned. "Odd one here."

Annie moved to look over her thin shoulder. In a small circle of light bounded by darkness, a lumpy towel lay on wood. "A wooden bench?"

"Maybe." Hyla looked intent. "Taken at night obviously." She moved her thumb; the photo was followed by six more in quick succession. Several featured the dachshund. All were straightforward photographs of people or places. "There's only the one of the towel." Hyla returned to the photograph. She tapped Properties. "Taken at twelve-oh-nine A.M.

June thirteenth. I'd guess Pirelli didn't know the time might matter."

Annie was excited. "Pat took the picture late at night in the dark. It was late at night when she walked through the woods to the Jamison house." Quickly Annie described her conclusions about Pat's late-night excursions.

"I get you. Of course, Pirelli didn't know all that when he checked the phone." Hyla was calm. "However, there's no proof this picture was taken anywhere near the Jamison house. Or that the pix has anything to do with Merridew dying five days later. But"—she reached for a plastic bag in the tech case, dropped the BlackBerry inside, made a notation—"it sure isn't your everyday photo."

Six

Max fluffed red feathers on the end of the steel-tipped dart, raised his arm, threw. The dart quivered triumphantly in the center of the bull's-eye. His gaze dropped to his desk and a welter of papers, then swung to Annie's picture. "Sometimes you have to accept reality." He spoke conversationally, then his mouth spread in a wide grin. So, hey, Annie was fixated on a death that couldn't be proved to be murder or suicide or an accident. "Look, honey"—his tone was eminently reasonable—"Billy left the file open. That's an accomplishment. Pat's death will never officially be listed as suicide. Maybe you should settle for that." His eyes dropped to the papers. "Trying to connect the people who live in the Jamison house with Pat's death is like grabbing at no-see-'ums with your bare hands."

Max settled in his red leather desk chair. He had assembled the bare bones of lives, easily scoured from the Internet and from strategically placed phone calls. More important, perhaps, was an emerging sense of personalities, the attitudes and enthusiasms of six people who shared a name. He turned to the computer and opened the newly created Jamison file, which contained photos obtained online from the Web, the *Island Gazette*, or Facebook. His fingers moved fast over the keyboard.

GLEN JAMISON

Member of a leading island family. Parents Woodman and Caroline Jamison. One sister, Elaine. Father died after a stroke, mother died of complications of diabetes. Attended island schools. Graduate of The Citadel. Law degree from the University of South Carolina. Middle of his class. Married Madeleine Barrett upon graduation. Three children, Laura G., 24; Katherine L., 23; and Thomas A., 17. Madeleine died six years ago. Last year he married Cleo J. Baker, partner in the firm. Glen is patrician in appearance, narrow aristocratic face, blond hair, blue-eyed. Tall, slender, graceful. Serves on the boards of many island charities. Republican. Good golfer, mediocre tennis player.

Temperate in his approach to life, pleasant, undemanding though fairly feudal in expecting deference because he is a Jamison. The Jamisons have always been among the island elite.

Max spared one longing glance toward his indoor golf green, then focused on his task. He had called people who knew Glen on the pretext of gathering information for a profile for a Good Neighbor Award. The award had been handily created by Max for a nonexistent Atlanta-based foundation. He glanced at his notes, added the comments his questions had elicited:

"Good old Glen." "Nice guy." "Not very active in the bar." ". . . can't recall involvement in any leading cases . . ." ". . . wouldn't say he has any political clout." "Family man. Active in his church." "Not out in front on island issues." "Doesn't make waves." "Never had to hustle, so it doesn't come naturally."

The consensus: not a mover and shaker. Imbued with a healthy dose of entitlement. Ineffectual. Nothing discreditable either personally or professionally.

In the photograph, Glen looked distinguished but there was a hint of weakness in his mouth. In fact, he appeared to be what he was, a nice man with a mild, possibly malleable personality, but a man who was generally liked and respected. Max concluded:

This guy definitely can't be cast as first murderer.

CLEO BAKER JAMISON

Grew up in Hardeeville. Only child. Parents died young, mother of cancer, father in trucking accident. Attended Clemson on a scholarship. Majored in political science, minored in French. Phi Beta Kappa. Beauty queen. Class president. Used student loans to attend law school. Graduated third in her class. Came to Broward's Rock three years ago and joined Glen Jamison's law firm. Became a partner in one year. Married Glen Jamison last year.

Max used the ploy of writing a feature on success under thirty for an online magazine, promising anonymity to those with whom he spoke about Cleo.

"A pleasure to work with her on a project. You knew you had an A+ in the can." "Smart, ruthless,

but she can turn on the charm." "She's a law bitch if there ever was one." "Never turn your back on Cleo. She'll smile and always cheat just a little bit." "Nobody works harder or smarter. She's lucky but she makes her own luck." "She picked guys from upper-crust families, then loved 'em and left 'em. I wasn't surprised she married a geezer from an old South Carolina family. If you aren't an aristocrat, the next best thing is to marry one."

Cleo's photo was striking, a brunette with reddish highlights, confident brown eyes, magnolia-creamy skin, a winner-take-all expression. Coral lips curved in a smile with a hint of triumph. Cleo was a good-looking woman well aware of her attractiveness. She was smart, hardworking, willing to wield power, definitely not passive like her husband. If Annie was right and a Jamison killed Pat, Cleo was a possibility. She was clearly strong-willed and not overburdened with scruples. It seemed likely Cleo had arranged Pat's dismissal, but that didn't seem a lead-in to murder.

From Cleo Jamison to her sister-in-law, Elaine, was a study in contrasts. Max scanned an article that had appeared in the church newspaper about Elaine Jamison and extracted several facts:

ELAINE JAMISON

Graduate of Clemson, degree in marketing.
Worked in fashion design in Atlanta until she came
back to the island after her sister-in-law's death.
She ran the household and took care of her nieces
and nephew. She was active at their schools, took
them to sports practices, planned parties, hosted
sleepovers. She taught Sunday school and was a
past president of the Episcopal Church Women.
Member of the Friends of the Library. Volunteer at
the island charity store. After Laura and Kit left for
college, Elaine started working part-time at an
island dress shop. Graceful, charming, responsive,
devoted to her family.

Max felt a dim tingle of memory. Hadn't Elaine been
in the news for something? Not a story he'd followed,
but something . . . He reached for the phone.

"Coffee?" Billy Cameron looked at Annie.

Annie shook her head, dropped into a chair in the
snack room that opened off the main hall at the police
station. Wanted posters filled one bulletin board. Island
maps were mounted on another wall. Three windows
overlooked the picnic area that fronted on the harbor.

Billy settled on one side of the table with a chipped ceramic mug.

Annie carefully kept herself from shuddering as he stirred nondairy creamer into his coffee.

The BlackBerry lay on the table, the late-night photo on the screen.

Annie pointed at the picture. "Pat Merridew started going out late at night in the week or so before she was murdered—"

"Before she died."

Her stare met his.

Billy's didn't yield.

Annie took a deep breath. "She started going out late at night—"

"After she was fired," Billy interjected.

"—and then she died from an overdose of an opiate. That photograph was taken late at night. Maybe this is what Pat saw that caused her death."

She didn't say murder, so this time Billy let her statement ride.

She leaned forward. "We need to find out where this picture was taken."

Billy looked again at the photograph. "A bunched-up towel on a wooden bench doesn't give us much to go on." He lifted his mug, drank coffee. "I'll add the BlackBerry to the file."

"Yo, Max. You got an antidote for boredom?" The *Island Gazette*'s chief (and almost only) reporter, Marian Kenyon, was always brusque.

Max pictured her with the receiver cradled between ear and shoulder, eyes skipping in discontent around the newsroom.

She caroled, "You know what the big story is today? An alligator that ticks. Honest to God. They think he swallowed an alarm clock. I want to meet the fool that got close enough to hear the tick. Where do you suppose the creature found an old-fashioned, windup clock in a swamp? Hey, maybe it's a bomb?" She sounded brighter. "Maybe something will pop today."

Max grinned. "That's more exciting than my day." He glanced at the clock. "It's only a quarter after nine." He preferred amorous late nights and sleepy slow mornings, but his significant other embraced vigor and early rising. Vigor, properly directed, was fine. Early rising . . . "There's plenty of time for you to get a good story. While you're resting your creative juices, will you fill me in on Elaine Jamison? Annie wants to host a b-day fling for Elaine." He had discovered Elaine's birthday was next week and he had no doubt Annie would welcome the idea of a party. "Annie thinks I can always get the goods on everybody. She's put me in charge of rounding up tidbits for a toast. Can you help out?"

"Steel sheathed in charm, that's my take." Marian was admiring. "Did you keep up with the blow-by-blow in the school-board election a couple of years ago?"

Neurons clicked. Max remembered a series of stories about packed meetings when the chairman of the board proposed barring several award-winning books from the middle school library.

Marian's tone was admiring. "She ran for a seat, won, and no books were banned. She was a Southern lady to the hilt, but the iron will was on display. The campaign got pretty nasty. She never stopped smiling and never raised her voice. Now, Max, level with me. What's behind your innocent curiosity about Elaine Jamison?"

"You wrong me, Marian," he said lightly. "I'm just giving Annie a hand."

"Oh, sure." Her disbelief was patent. "Tell you what, when you decide to come clean, maybe I'll share an interesting tidbit about Elaine." The connection ended.

Max gave the phone a thoughtful glance. Marian might be pulling his string. But she might not. He added to Elaine's dossier:

Willing to fight. Unyielding when challenged. Marian knows something interesting?

He studied Elaine's photo. She was fair with the same fine bone structure and elegant appearance as her brother, but the line of the jaw was stronger, the fuller lips determined, the uplifted head imperious.

He clicked several times, arranging the photos of Glen Jamison's daughters and son in order of age. Laura Jamison didn't resemble her father. Curly dark hair framed a rounded face with a pug nose. It was a face made for laughter, but she stared into the camera unsmiling. The photo was from a party scene on Facebook. Wearing a flowered blouse and linen slacks, she stood a little apart from a picnic on the beach. She looked discontented and very much alone in a crowd.

Max glanced at his notes, began to keyboard:

LAURA JAMISON

Older daughter of Glen and Madeleine Jamison. Grew up on the island. Excellent sailor. A top junior tennis player. Graduate of Clemson. She began her career in finance in Atlanta, lost her job during the financial downturn, no success in obtaining a new position. Returned to the island six months ago, working as a lifeguard this summer. High school tennis coach said she was a good player, could have been better, but had trouble with her temper, otherwise a good kid.

In the next photo, Glen's younger daughter, Kit, looked a good deal like her father, fair-haired, fair-skinned, narrow face, but with an intensity of expression foreign to her father. Straight, unsmiling gaze and lips pressed firmly together suggested a humorless intensity.

KIT JAMISON

High school valedictorian. Phi Beta Kappa graduate of Carleton. Master's degree in biology from University of Pennsylvania, began work on PhD. Last several summers worked as intern on research projects on the effect of climate change on lions. Accepted for fellowship in Kenya, but must fund her own travel. High school principal: "One of the finer intellects I've encountered. She is totally focused on scholarship." Socially? Very independent. Pleasant, but distant. Not especially gregarious with her classmates.

Max reached out and picked up another dart. Bright geek and a social misfit would be his interpretation. Annie had learned that Kit was in danger of losing her chance to go to Africa. He threw the dart. This one struck at a slant and toppled to the floor. "What," he said aloud, "does Kit Jamison's angst have to do with Pat Merridew's death?" He turned dutifully back to the computer. He'd promised Annie he would find out what he could about the Jamisons. He was almost there.

Sandy-haired and blue-eyed Tommy Jamison had on his game face in a football photograph, unsmiling, gaze stern, helmet in hand, down on one knee. Tommy would be a senior in the fall and on the first team. On his Facebook page, he clowned with a bunch of guys, shirttails out, baggy shorts, throwing a Frisbee. He liked sports, girls, sports, girls, sports . . . Max grinned. There was a man with his head on straight. "And about as much connection to Pat Merridew's house as a late-night comedian."

Max swiftly entered a bio for Tommy, then leaned back in his chair. He glanced without enthusiasm at the last page of notes and the admittedly intriguing facts he'd gleaned about Glen Jamison's cousin Richard, who'd come for a visit and seemed settled in for the summer. Max punched his intercom. "Hey, Barb, anything tasty in your kitchen?" Since he often had little work to occupy Barb's energies, she spent free time whipping up delectable desserts. He deserved a break.

Annie shut the front door of the police station carefully behind her. If she'd allowed herself to relieve her feelings, she would have slammed the door with a bang. She stalked down the steps and walked fast to her car. She'd left the windows down, but the seat was hot. She started the car and stared through the windshield.

The prospect should have been pleasing. The police station sat on a slight rise. Beyond the one-story white building, the harbor glittered in the June sunlight. A red-sailed catamaran skimmed along the water. The ferry slip was empty, the *Miss Jolene* on a regular run to the mainland. A bright yellow hydroplane race boat skimmed the whitecaps. Pelicans dove for fish. Seagulls squalled.

And Billy Cameron wasn't stirring from his office with windows that overlooked the sound. Annie felt the tightness in her face. Okay, she was irritated. As she had now told Billy several times, they needed to look for something unusual that had occurred in the days before Pat died. Annie felt like she'd found information that fit that criteria: Pat's late-night meanderings and, thanks to Officer Harrison, the midnight photo on her BlackBerry.

Annie's insistence that the BlackBerry photo was important hadn't spurred Billy to action. Her suggestion that he survey the Jamison property and try for a match to the BlackBerry photo had brought a weary head shake. His reply had been succinct: What would that prove?

"Well"—she spoke aloud—"it would prove something peculiar was going on late at night near the Jamison house."

She brushed aside an inner voice saying calmly, *Pat Merridew sneaking around someone else's backyard and taking a photo of a bunched-up towel was darn sure odd.*

Annie's fingers tightened on the steering wheel. Wait a minute. Back up. Think. Pat had no reason to take the picture unless circumstances that night led her to believe something strange had occurred.

Think, Annie, think, she prompted herself. Was the towel itself important? Or had Pat seen someone act suspiciously? She wouldn't risk taking a picture of a person. A flash or click might reveal her presence and certainly she had no right to be on the Jamison grounds.

Or maybe the person's identity became important only after Pat discovered the contents of the towel, if indeed she did. But why take a picture unless something made the towel seem important to her? Whatever the contents, Pat had decided to make a record of what she'd seen.

Annie was convinced that the photo was linked to Pat's death and that her death had to be murder because ground-up OxyContin in Irish coffee could not be accidental, and a woman planning a grand cruise to Alaska didn't commit suicide.

Annie realized the trail was nebulous. No fingerprints on a crystal mug was a great deal less satisfactory than clearly observed prints of a suspect. A photo in a BlackBerry, even though it clearly was an anomaly, didn't qualify as a smoking gun. Missing travel brochures were suggestive, but not conclusive.

She turned the key, made a U-turn, and drove swiftly north of town to the dusty road where Pat Merridew's house sat silent and untenanted. She parked in the drive, skirted Pat's house, plunged into the woods. She stepped carefully over the web of an industrious spider, spinning silky strands between the fronds of a fern. She looked thoroughly on either side of the path. She reached the gap in the woods at the base of the Jamison garden. She could honestly report (if Billy cared) that there was nothing between Pat's house and the Jamison garden that could have served as the backdrop of the photograph.

The scream of a leaf blower blotted out birdcalls and the rustle of tree limbs in a light breeze. Glossy magnolia leaves quivered but the only sound came from the blower. Annie heard the noise, but the screech registered only peripherally. She stared through the strands of a weeping willow at a mahogany gazebo, gleaming bright in the morning sunlight.

The reddish wood matched the color of the wood in the BlackBerry photo.

She glanced around the garden, noting a young man with the blower at work about twenty feet away near a flower bed. He carried himself with the grace of an athlete. He gave her an unhurried glance and moved the nozzle to avoid scudding dust in her direction. She nodded her thanks. In five quick strides, she reached the steps and climbed up.

Annie gave a soft whoop of triumph when she saw the interior bench. She had found the site of the photograph. In the photograph, the rich color of the wood had been clearly revealed in the glow of a pencil flash.

Her quick elation subsided. Pat had taken a photograph of what appeared to be a rolled-up towel lying

on a seat within the gazebo. Billy would say, "So?"
So, Annie thought grimly, Pat had died five days later
and the photo could now be absolutely linked to the
Jamison property. The photo had been taken shortly
after midnight. She looked out into the garden, but
the house was screened by a row of palmetto palms.
Turning back, she saw Elaine's cottage.

If Elaine had been up late that night, perhaps she
might have seen or heard something.

The front door of the cottage opened.

Annie took a step, started to call out, then stopped.

Elaine Jamison stood on her front steps. Every line
of her body was taut, strained. Even at a distance,
the expression on her face was shocking, eyes wide,
jaw clenched. Elaine was upset, distraught, obviously
holding herself in check with a supreme effort of will.
She clutched what appeared to be balled-up blue cloth
tight against her chest, her left arm bent at the elbow,
her fist hard against her collarbone.

Elaine's gaze swept the garden, her face tense and
fearful. Her thin features were rigid.

Annie was hidden from sight behind a column of
the gazebo.

Elaine darted down the cottage steps, ran on the
path toward the marsh. She rounded a pittosporum
hedge and disappeared from Annie's view.

Annie hesitated. Elaine had surveyed the yard to be sure no one was about. If that were so, she wouldn't welcome Annie's presence. Yet it seemed wrong to turn and walk away. Uncertain of what she should do, she crossed the yard, ending up behind a thicket of cane. She bent stalks apart.

On the bank, Elaine faced murky water and golden green cordgrass rippling in the breeze. She lowered her right arm and whirled away from the marsh. Breathing jerkily, her gaze fell to the blue cloth bunched in her left hand. She shuddered, broke into a run. She followed the path, then veered out of sight around the side of the cottage.

Annie remained behind the cane, uncomfortable in her role of unseen observer. Elaine's actions were odd, strange, disquieting. Apparently, she had thrown something into the marsh, though she still held a bundle of blue cloth. Why had she run away?

The roar of a car motor drowned out the whine of the leaf blower. Elaine's yellow Corolla burst from behind the cottage and disappeared in a whirl of gray dust.

Annie absently took a bite of Barb's chocolate pudding pie, the base dark and rich, the pudding layer crunchy with pecans. But she scarcely took notice of one of her favorite desserts. "Elaine looked awful. I wish I had called out, tried to talk to her. But"—the words came slowly—"I don't think she would have wanted me to see her like that. I keep wondering if this has any connection to Pat."

Max's face was carefully bland.

Annie rushed ahead. "You think I'm trying to connect everything that happens at the Jamison house to Pat."

He was silent, but his blue eyes were understanding.

"Maybe I am." She felt forlorn. "But I know something was seriously wrong with Elaine this morning. And"—she was emphatic though she knew the link was obscure—"that midnight photo was definitely taken in the Jamison gazebo."

Max was patient. "I agree that Billy needs to look harder when you tell him about the gazebo. As for Elaine, maybe she quarreled with Glen. You said she was upset the other day because her nieces and nephew were angry with their dad. For all we know, Elaine and Glen had a real battle this morning. Anyway, speaking of personal information." He picked up the printout of the Jamison file. "Here's what I've rounded up. You can look it over while l finish up on Glen's cousin." He handed her several sheets and turned to his computer.

Annie read, her expression thoughtful.

Max finished typing and punched print. He handed another sheet to Annie.

She turned over the last of the bios about the immediate family and looked at Max's report on Glen's cousin:

RICHARD JAMISON

Island born, grew up in Columbia. Son of Percy Jamison, who had middling success as an artist, and Amanda Riley Jamison, a potter. Thirty-three. Single. Attended University of South Carolina for two years. Dropped out to work as a deckhand on a private yacht, *Pretty Girl*, out of Fort Lauderdale. Since college he's worked as a sailor, travel agent, gambler, and bartender in between several failed businesses. Recently he was on the cusp of success with a condominium project in Costa Rica, but financing disappeared in the stalled economy. He returned to the island six weeks ago and is staying at his cousin's home.

Richard's photograph was from a news story published in the Bahamas and showed him on the deck of a sloop, longish brown hair riffled by a breeze, angular face sunburned, muscular in a tee and baggy shorts. Annie studied the picture. She had no doubt that Richard was a party boy, a good-time Charlie, footloose and ready for fun. She scanned the comments made by people Max had contacted:

"Good hand. Be glad to sail with him anywhere." "Always thinks he's onto the next big thing." "Man, I wish I could attract chicks the way he does." "You've never partied till you party with Richard." "I can't imagine he'd hang long on Broward's Rock. He couldn't wait to shake the dust. It's either money or sex."

Annie finished reading and placed the sheets on his desk. "Nothing about Pat." It was not a complaint. It was an acceptance of fact.

Max pushed back his chair and came around the desk to place his hand gently beneath her chin. "We've done everything anyone could do."

She looked up into dark blue eyes that told her he was sorry, that he admired her for keeping on, that it was time to admit defeat.

His hand rose, touched her cheek. "Hey, I've got an idea." His tone was warm. He glanced at the clock. "It's twenty to eleven. I have to be here at twelve-thirty.

Edna Graham's bringing some watercolors over on her lunch hour. I'll buy one because that was my excuse for contacting her. But you and I have time to go home"— his eyes gleamed—"and—"

The phone rang.

Max turned to his desk, glanced at the caller ID. "Edna Graham. What are the odds she's canceling? I knew my good efforts would be rewarded." He grabbed the phone. "Max Darling." Abruptly his easy expression faded. His brows drew down. His face was grim. He held the receiver away from his ear.

Annie heard the sound of an agitated voice. She popped up and leaned across Max's desk to punch the speakerphone button.

" . . . so terrible." Edna Graham's voice wobbled. "I was able to contact Mrs. Jamison. She's in Savannah. She was taking a deposition. It was horrible to tell her that kind of news over the phone. They said Glen was murdered, that he was shot several times. I promised her I'd go out to the house and talk to the police, do what I can to help. Apparently he was killed sometime this morning. She's started home, but it's an hour's drive and then she has to catch the ferry. I'm on my way and I remembered I'd promised to come by your office. I can't come now."

The connection ended.

Max replaced the receiver. He turned to Annie. "Glen Jamison's been shot. His body was found by his cousin Richard."

Annie sank down on the chair by Max's desk. She felt as if the floor were rocking beneath her feet. "When was he killed?" It was an effort to squeeze the words from a throat tight with shock.

"I don't know." Max pushed up from his chair. "Come on, Annie."

Slowly she came to her feet.

Max moved around the desk, slipped an arm around her shoulders. "You have to tell Billy what you saw this morning."

She wanted to object, insist that Elaine Jamison's stricken face and desperate dart to the marsh had nothing to do with her brother's murder.

Max spoke quietly, but firmly. "If Elaine is innocent, she has nothing to fear."

Three police cars, the forensic van, an ambulance, and Billy Cameron's faded green Pontiac filled the Jamison drive. Marian Kenyon's battered old tan Beetle was parked out of the way beneath a magnolia. Across the street, the lane was blocked by a bucket truck. A telephone lineman peered down, watching the arrivals.

Annie pulled in at the curb, stopping short of the drive. An old sedan drew up behind her and Doc

Burford, the island medical examiner, slammed out of the car, carrying a black bag. His square, blunt face was dark with a scowl. Doc Burford hated death and most of all he hated untimely death. He moved like a charging bull, heavy shoulders hunched.

Once out of the car, Annie clutched Max's arm. Glen's death hadn't seemed real. Now that she saw Doc Burford, the reality made her feel sick. She stared at the house. It didn't seem appropriate to go to the front door and ring the bell.

Max gestured toward the backyard as Doc Burford swung around the corner of the house, out of sight. "We'll find Billy if we follow Doc."

At the end of the walk, they turned the corner and came face-to-face with Hyla Harrison.

Officer Harrison, her thin face set and intent, held up a hand. "Crime scene. No admittance."

Annie looked beyond her at the police, who were gathered in a semicircle on the verandah, and Doc Burford stepping inside an open French window. A few feet from the terrace, Marian Kenyon, Leica hanging from a neck strap, wrote furiously, then craned to see inside the open door.

Annie wished she could turn and walk away. In her heart, she didn't believe Elaine Jamison had any connection to her brother's death. Edna Graham said Glen had been shot several times, that he had been murdered. Of course, that was not official. Possibly Edna had misunderstood. With sudden death from a gunshot, there was always the possibility of suicide. Suicide. That had been the initial judgment after Pat Merridew died from an overdose. Pat dead . . . Glen dead . . .

"Please move on. Crime scene." Officer Harrison's voice was sharp. "No loitering."

Crime scene . . . Harrison's blunt comment indicated that Edna had not been mistaken. Glen Jamison was a murder victim, which made Elaine's demeanor in the garden disturbing.

Max spoke firmly. "Annie may have information Chief Cameron will want to receive."

Officer Harrison gave Annie a searching glance. "This way." Her tone was brusque.

Seven

We'll go in the main entrance." Officer Harrison gestured for them to follow. She strode swiftly along the drive to the front yard and shepherded them up the steps to the verandah of the Jamison house. She opened the door and held it wide.

In the hallway, Officer Coley Benson, lean and trim in his khaki uniform, greeted Annie and Max with a friendly hello, then assumed a stoic professional manner. His magnificent tenor voice was known across the island from his church choir and high school musicals. After college, he had returned to the island to become the youngest member of the Broward's Rock police force. "Everyone who may be able to help in the investigation is waiting in there." He gestured toward the open doors to the living room.

Annie gripped Max's hand as they stepped into a spacious room that contained period furniture. The silence was broken only by the resonant tick of an elaborate blue-and-gold Louis XV–style French clock that sat on the mantel between two blue Delft jars with iron lions on the lids. The soft cream of an American Chippendale sofa was echoed in the worn Tabriz carpet. Cypress paneling original to the house gleamed a soft russet.

Three people stared at Annie and Max without a flicker of recognition or understanding.

Annie knew them from the photographs in Max's Jamison file. A wan and trembling Kit Jamison huddled in a flower-patterned small Queen Anne wing chair on one side of the fireplace. Her dark-haired sister, Laura, stood, one hand gripping the mantel. Glen Jamison's cousin Richard was sprawled on a sofa. His sunburned face could have been hewn from a block of wood. Sitting a little distant from the family, Edna Graham nodded to Max. She looked doleful and shaken.

Their blank stares told Annie they were unwelcome intruders in a room heavy with grief and fear. She and Max were outsiders and had no place among those who were distraught over Glen Jamison's death.

"Who are you?" The emphasis was on the personal pronoun. Kit's voice was sharp with an undertone of hysteria. Her thin face was pale and drawn, her pale blue eyes strained.

Max was bland. "Max Darling. This is my wife, Annie. We were told to wait here to see Chief Cameron."

"Why do you want to talk to him? Do you know something about my dad?" Kit's voice was shrill.

"Miss, please." Officer Benson stepped into the drawing room. "Everyone is requested to remain silent until Chief Cameron speaks with you."

Kit came to her feet, stared at Annie and Max with her face working, her long, thin fingers clenching. "Do you know what happened to Dad? No one tells us anything. I want to see him."

Officer Benson moved toward her. "Police procedure forbids communication among witnesses."

Kit whirled toward Richard. "You have to tell us. You said Dad's dead and you called the police and locked the study door. You have to tell us what happened."

Coley Benson's face stiffened. "Miss, please be quiet."

Richard pushed up from the sofa and walked across the room to stand in front of Officer Benson. "Ask the police chief to come." He was polite, but his tone was firm. "The family needs information." He gestured at

Kit and the tears sliding down her pale face. "Her dad's dead. She has a right."

"So do I." Laura was too thin in a soft tee and a denim skirt. She glared at Richard. "You pounded on my door to tell me Dad was dead, that he'd been killed." She turned angrily toward the officer. "Now you won't let us know anything. We have a right to know what's happened."

Edna Graham nodded in agreement, her strong face grim.

Benson yanked his cell from his belt, punched. "Chief, the family's upset and wanting to know details."

"Now." Kit's voice rose in a wail. "I want to know now."

Laura clasped her hands tightly. "We have every right to know what happened."

The officer clicked off his phone. "Chief Cameron will be here shortly."

Kit took two quick strides to face Richard. "You found Dad. What did you see?"

Richard's face was suddenly haunted. "You don't want to know, Kit. Remember your dad alive."

Billy Cameron strode into the drawing room. The burly police chief brought with him a sense of solidity, order, and calm. A step behind him was Frank Saulter, the former police chief who often volunteered assistance when a major crime occurred. Saulter's bony face was more lined than when he and Annie had first met, his dark hair now peppered with gray. He still moved with authority. He looked gravely around the room.

Kit jerked away from Richard. She lunged toward Billy. "What happened to my dad? Why are you keeping us here? Where is Dad? Where's my aunt?" She jabbed a finger toward Officer Benson. "He won't let me use my cell. I need to find my aunt and my little brother."

Annie felt a quiver of apprehension. She'd seen Elaine's car leave. That must have been shortly before ten. But Elaine wasn't the only missing family member. Where was Tommy?

Billy spoke quietly. "I understand that you are upset, Miss Jamison. We are still trying to determine what occurred this morning. Mr. Jamison"—Billy nodded toward Richard—"placed a 911 call at ten-fifteen. We arrived on the scene to find the deceased in the study. The victim was identified as Glen Jamison by Mr. Richard Jamison. The medical examiner has now determined that death resulted from multiple gunshot wounds."

Kit lifted her hands to her face. Tears streamed down her ashen cheeks. "Somebody shot Daddy?"

Laura hurried to her sister and they clung to each other. Her face empty and sick, Laura looked at Billy. "Have you found anybody? Why would somebody shoot Dad?"

"Our investigation has just begun. We have very little knowledge——"

A door slammed and running feet sounded in the hallway. Tommy Jamison thudded into the living room. His sandy hair was tousled. A blondish stubble marked his face. He was breathing hard. He looked at his sister. "What's going on? Why are the police cars here?" His blue eyes were wide and staring. A too-tight green-and-orange-striped polo stretched across his husky shoulders and exposed his abdomen. Ragged khaki shorts sagged low on his hips. He wore worn leather sandals.

Kit moved toward him. "Tommy, Daddy's dead. Someone shot him."

The teenager stepped back as if he had been struck. He looked at Billy Cameron in his khaki uniform. "Dad?"

Billy's voice was gentle. "I'm sorry, son. Your father was found dead in his study shortly before ten-fifteen this morning. You are Tommy Jamison?"

"Yes, sir." The burly teenager struggled to answer, his voice shaking.

Billy gestured toward the sofa. "We've asked family members for their cooperation as we attempt to find out the circumstances. Were you at home this morning?" Billy spoke quietly, but his gaze at Tommy was searching.

Kit stood by her brother, faced Billy. "He spent the night with a friend."

Billy looked at the teenager. "Where were you?"

"At Buddy Crawford's house. He lives over on Heron Point."

"When did you leave the Crawford house?"

"I don't know exactly." Tommy's eyes shifted away. "A while ago. I went by the beach." He looked around the room. "Where's Elaine?"

Kit massaged one temple. "She isn't here. She doesn't know yet."

Tommy's face suddenly screwed up into misery. "Dad . . ." He turned and bolted toward the door. The pounding of his feet on the staircase was loud and sad.

Kit started for the hall.

Billy lifted a big hand. "Miss Jamison, we need for everyone to remain here until we can speak with you."

She stopped, glaring. "His father's dead. He's just a kid. I'm going up to him. You can come and see us upstairs when you want to." She moved swiftly into the hall.

Laura ran after them.

Billy's face folded in a frown.

Richard spoke quietly. "Chief, we all want to help. I'll get Kit and Laura and Tommy when you are ready for them."

Billy acquiesced. "We'll be as quick and brief as possible. Former police chief Frank Saulter"—he gestured toward the older man who looked authoritative despite his informal dress, a cream polo and khaki slacks—"has agreed to help us. He will take individual statements and share what information we have at this point. When the statements are done, I would appreciate all of you remaining in the house in case we need to speak with you further. However, once you have given your statement, you are free to go. The room where the crime occurred may not be entered until we have completed our preliminary investigation." Billy looked from face to face. His gaze stopped when it reached Annie. He glanced at Max, then back to Annie. "What," and his voice had all the warmth of cracked ice, "are you two doing here?"

Max gave her an encouraging nod.

Annie took a deep breath. "I was in the garden here this morning."

Billy waited for Annie and Max to precede him, then closed the swinging door.

The old-fashioned kitchen was an odd backdrop for a conference with Billy. The avocado-green electric range, white refrigerator, and green-tiled counters evoked the mid-twentieth century and under different circumstances might have seemed homey and comforting. Annie couldn't picture Cleo in that kitchen. Elaine, yes; Cleo, no.

Dishes were stacked in the sink. The scent of bacon and coffee hung in the air. On the white wooden kitchen table, a sports section of yesterday afternoon's *Gazette* lay next to a box of cornflakes. Soggy cereal remained in a bowl half filled with milk.

Billy frowned at Annie. "Why were you in the Jamison garden?"

Annie was defiant. "You wouldn't come and see about the picture in Pat's BlackBerry. That's why I drove straight here after I saw you. I found where Pat took that photograph—the gazebo. The color of the wood there matches the picture. A pattern on the left side of the picture turned out to be part of a lattice."

"I don't care about Pat Merridew and her Black-Berry right now." Billy was dismissive. "That photograph and Pat Merridew have no connection to Glen Jamison being shot to death. We will never be able to prove how Pat Merridew died, whether it was suicide, accident, or murder, but we know for sure she didn't die from a gunshot. Give her death a rest, Annie. Right now I'm dealing with a homicide. Tell me what you saw this morning."

Annie wished she hadn't hurried to the gazebo this morning. She wished she didn't have to speak now. But she had come to the Jamison yard and she had seen what she had seen. "I was in the gazebo. When I realized Pat took that odd photo there, I decided to ask Elaine if she happened to hear or see anything the night the picture was taken. Before I could reach the gazebo steps, Elaine came out of her cottage."

Billy looked intent. "The time?"

"A few minutes before ten."

Annie saw intense interest in his eyes. The 911 call had been made at ten-fifteen.

Billy pulled a notebook from his pocket, held a pen ready. "You arrived at the gazebo a few minutes before ten?"

"Yes." Her excitement at discovering the background for Pat's BlackBerry photo seemed several lifetimes ago.

"Did you look toward the house?"

"Yes, but the terrace was screened by palmettos." Annie felt a tightening in her throat. "When was he shot?"

Billy looked impatient. "Please answer my questions. What did you see when you arrived?"

"I wasn't thinking about the house. I went straight to the gazebo and found the place where the picture had been taken. Then I looked toward the house, but I couldn't see it. I saw a yardman. He was near a flower bed with a leaf blower. I turned toward Elaine Jamison's cottage. That's when she came outside."

"Did you talk to her?"

Annie's hands clenched. She didn't like the picture she had in her mind, Elaine with her face pale and strained, darting a hunted look around the garden, whirling to run to the path. "I didn't have a chance to call out to her. She rushed down the steps and took a path toward the marsh."

Billy's eyes narrowed. "What was her demeanor?"

Of all the questions he might have asked, this was the most deadly for Elaine, but Annie would not mislead Billy. He had been their friend, their champion, Max's rescuer when Max had been enmeshed in an ugly crime fashioned to incriminate him. "Elaine was upset."

Billy pounced. "How did you know she was upset?"

Annie spoke quietly, all the while feeling as if she personally were dropping a noose around Elaine's neck. "Her face was flattened, stiff. She was breathing fast. She looked around the yard, then hurried to the path to the marsh. She was carrying a lumpy blue cloth pressed against her chest. She went around a hedge, and I lost sight of her. I hesitated to follow her. I had no business being there and I didn't think she would want to see me. Still, I hated to go away without making sure she was all right. I cut across the yard and pulled apart some cane stalks. She was standing on the bank of the marsh." Annie's voice dropped. "I think she had thrown something into the marsh. Her upraised right arm was coming down. She held a blue cloth in her left hand. She turned and ran behind her cottage and in a moment her car left."

Annie stood to one side of the stand of cane. The late-morning sun felt warm on her face. On the bank of the marsh, a blue heron perched on one elegant leg, neck craned, ready to pounce on an unwary frog or lizard. From the swath of greenish waving grass, a clapper rail cackled. The sulfurish scent of the marsh was comforting and familiar in contrast to the scene on the bank.

Annie called out. "A little more to your left."

Officer Harrison obediently edged to her left.

"Stop there."

The slender policewoman stood still.

Annie nodded approval. "Turn toward that big hummock." A raccoon stood on a hump of greenery about forty feet out in the marsh. "The one with the raccoon."

Officer Harrison faced the marsh. She was very near the spot where Elaine Jamison had stood earlier that morning.

"That's it."

Billy lifted his voice. "Stay where you are, Officer." He nodded at Annie. "You didn't see what she threw?"

"I didn't see her throw anything." Annie emphasized the verb. "When I looked around the cane, her arm was coming down." Annie raised her arm above her head, began a downward sweep. "Her arm was here." Her elbow slightly bent, she lowered her arm until it was level with her shoulder. "As I watched, her arm came down to her side."

Billy's cell phone rang. He lifted it, spoke fast. "Right. Yellow Corolla. Check the ferry. Send Officer Portman to make sure the car doesn't leave the island. As soon as she's found, inform her that the police would like to speak with her." He clipped the phone to his belt, nodded at Annie. "Thank you for your assistance." Billy started to turn away.

Annie blurted, "Whoever killed Glen Jamison killed Pat Merridew."

The police chief stopped, looked toward her, his impatience scarcely concealed. "This investigation has just begun, but I might point out, even assuming the Merridew death was homicide, that there is no apparent connection between the two deaths, including the fact that the manner of death is different. However, I will keep your suggestion in mind." This time he moved purposefully away.

Clearly, she and Max had been dismissed. "Billy," she called after him. She asked what she knew must be asked: "Did you find a gun in the study?"

He paused, looked over his shoulder. "No weapon has been discovered. Now, if you'll excuse me." He strode swiftly toward the marsh.

Max touched Annie's arm. "Billy's finished with us."

Annie pointed toward the lagoon. "Let's see what they find." She knew what they were seeking, a missing murder weapon.

Billy reached the bank and spoke with Officer Harrison. Lou Pirelli, a stocky, baseball-loving police officer, swung down from the crime van and strode toward the marsh. He carried a pair of waders in one hand and a chunk of brick in the other. A cane fishing pole rode in the crook of one arm and a plastic-handled landing net dangled from a wrist strap. Dark-haired, handsome Lou was always good-humored. He helped coach baseball at the island youth center, where Max taught tennis and golf. Lou handed the chunk of brick to Hyla Harrison, then stepped a few feet away to pull on the black rubber hip waders.

Annie and Max joined Marian Kenyon behind crime-scene tape strung across the path between a live oak and a palmetto.

The classical round lens hood of the reporter's M8 Leica gleamed in the sunlight. Marian held a pen poised above a notepad. She practically quivered with excitement. "Fill me in. Why's Hyla standing on the bank after you choreographed her?"

Annie looked at the dark-haired reporter. Marian was as persistent as a Lowcountry mosquito and just as hard to evade. "Let's watch and find out."

Marian scowled. She spoke to Annie, though she didn't take her gaze away from police clustered on the bank of the lagoon. Lou pulled on plastic gloves. Marian's tone was cool. "Why the brush-off?"

Max was placating. "Give Annie a break. If she told you, you couldn't use it. Vince is pretty particular about libel."

"Oooh." Marian made a note on her pad. "Don't think I'm going to forget." She took a step nearer the tape and stared at the lagoon. "What's up now? Why's Hyla clutching that piece of brick?"

Billy Cameron's voice carried well. "Officer, pretend the brick's a gun. You want to get rid of it pronto. Heave it as hard as you can."

"I like that. Very cunning." Marian made quick notes. "For a little while there, I thought maybe our uniformed best planned to play skip-a-rock for a little R and R."

As they watched, Officer Harrison threw. The chunk of brick splashed into the marsh midway between the bank and the big hammock. The raccoon whirled and disappeared into a thicket of greenery.

Using a cane pole to test the squishy bottom, Lou slogged through marsh water. The tide was running out, exposing the mudflats. Fiddler crabs moved swiftly like small herds of thundering bison. Lou moved on a steady slant toward the big hummock, though his progress through the mushy mud was clearly an effort. Several times he stumbled, possibly hooking the toe of a boot into submerged roots.

Max shook his head. "Finding anything in that glop is as likely as picking a diamond out of broken glass mired in muck. And that would be if you could see what you're doing. Lou can't see a thing in the silt-filled water. The pole will strike either mud, reeds, or roots. If he bangs something hard, it could be a gun or a root. I'd say this is an exercise in futility."

"About there," Hyla shouted.

Lou poked the pole in delicate jabs, going a few inches at a time as he explored the brown water in front of him. *Tap, tap, tap. Tap, tap, tap.* Two steps forward. *Tap, tap . . .* Lou raised the pole, returned it toward the same spot with the same angle.

A car's motor sounded. Dust boiled up as a yellow Corolla jolted to a stop in the dusty drive near the cottage. The driver's door was flung open. Elaine Jamison rushed across the uneven ground with its clumps of wire grass amid open patches of sandy soil.

She came to the bank, stared at the uniformed police. "What's going on here?"

Billy eyed her thoughtfully. "Perhaps you can tell us, Miss Jamison."

She was abruptly wary, her narrow face intent, questioning. "Who are you?"

"Police Chief Billy Cameron."

"A little more to the left," Hyla called.

Elaine looked out at the marsh. She might have been a lovely woman in expensive casual summer wear, a terra-cotta linen blouse, white cropped slacks, rose-red sandals—except for the tautness of her body.

"Like she's up close and personal with Dracula," Marian breathed. She lifted her camera, adjusted the lens, clicked several times. The reporter's inelegant comment was utterly apt.

Elaine lifted a hand to the open throat of her blouse. "Chief Cameron, why are you here?"

"We are investigating a crime."

She waited, her eyes fixed on his face.

Annie felt as if she was watching a large cat toy with a cornered mouse. "Cruel." The word, scarcely audible, fell between her and Max.

He slid an arm around her shoulders. "He suspects her. He's trying to make her come out into the open. That's fair enough, Annie."

"Better than *The Shield*," Marian observed.

"Tell me what's going on." Elaine's voice rose.

Billy was brusque. "We responded to a 911 call at ten-fifteen this morning. Suspected homicide. The victim has been identified as Glen Jamison."

"Glen." Her voice shook. "Where was he found?"

"At the house. By Richard Jamison."

"They need me. The children . . ." She turned away.

"Hey, Chief." Lou's shout was robust. "I found something." He lifted the pole out of the water, stuck it in the mud a foot to his left. He gripped the landing net and eased the net down into the water. He made a scooping motion, lifted. Water sprayed from the net. Lou held the net aloft. A broken whiskey bottle dangled above the water. With a shake of his head, Lou used the net like a jai alai player and the bottle splashed twenty feet away. He grabbed the pole and resumed his slow exploration.

"Miss Jamison." Billy's voice was heavy.

Annie could see Elaine clearly, more clearly than she would have wished.

Elaine's face was stiff and pale, her eyes empty.

Billy took several steps, stood perhaps a foot from her. He stared down, his gaze intent and measuring. "You were observed this morning. What did you throw in the marsh?"

"I have nothing to say. I am going to the house now." She spoke wearily, as if she'd run a hard race and all her strength was gone. "I must see about the children. And about Glen." She took a deep, ragged breath.

Billy's voice was hard. "I can take you to the station for questioning."

"I don't know anything that will help you. Let me see about the children." Her control crumbled. She choked back a sob. "They've lost their father. I'll be there if you want me."

Billy watched in silence as she started, head down, for the verandah. He jerked his head toward Officer Harrison. "Stay with her. See what she says." He shouted to Lou, "Keep looking." He turned and strode toward the house.

Marian called out, "Do you have a person of interest?"

He ignored her call.

As he climbed the back steps and moved toward an open French window, Marian was sanguine. "I didn't think he'd commit this early, but it's pretty clear where he's going. Lawyer shot to death. Witness sees sister toss something, think firearm, into the muck. One plus one equals two."

Annie swung toward Marian. "I didn't see her throw anything."

Marian arched a dark brow. "You don't like being the finger, but that's the way killers get caught. Of course, Lou will have to have a shamrock on his shoulder to find anything out there." She gestured toward the marsh. "Although I'd be the last to pick Elaine Jamison to pull the trigger of anything deadlier than a perfume atomizer. Shows how much I know. Anyway, it's going to make a big-time story, even if I have to be careful how I play it." She glanced at her watch. "Speaking of, I got less than twenty minutes before deadline." She whirled and broke into a steady trot toward the road.

Max touched Annie's arm lightly. "Come on, Annie. I don't think there's anything we can do here."

"I've done enough, haven't I?" Her voice was shaky.

"You did what you had to do." He didn't go on to say that Elaine Jamison was digging her own grave by her lack of cooperation, but his eyes told her.

Annie swallowed hard. "I was here a few days ago and talked to Elaine. She was so open about Glen and the problems in the family. She would never have told me any of that if she'd intended to shoot him. She made it clear that she loved Glen. She said he wasn't at fault. She blamed everything on Cleo."

Max looked thoughtful. "Maybe it was Cleo's fault that Glen made his kids mad, but you said Elaine was furious that they were unhappy."

Oyster shells crackled beneath their shoes. They came out from beneath the shadow of a live oak and started across the rough lawn toward the car.

Annie made no answer. She couldn't disagree. Elaine had been angry with her brother over his treatment of Laura, Kit, and Tommy. Someone shot Glen Jamison in his study, which argued a killer near at hand. Elaine's distraught appearance this morning was suspicious. Moreover, the movement of her arm as she stood on the bank of the marsh indicated she had thrown something, and no murder weapon had been found in Glen's study.

Annie's steps slowed as they reached the front yard. She stopped and looked toward the steps to the wide verandah. "I have to go inside."

She walked swiftly toward the porch. Max didn't call after her. *Thank you, Max, thank you for understanding, thank you for knowing I have to be honest.* Steeling herself, she ran lightly up the steps.

The front door was unlocked, of course. So many were going in and out as part of the investigation. With a quick breath, Annie opened the screen door and stepped into the central hallway. A soft murmur of voices sounded from the drawing room.

Officer Harrison stood in the open doorway to the drawing room. She turned at the squeak of the hinges. She looked at Annie, unhooked the cell from her belt, flipped up the cover.

Annie moved as though she were confident of her reception. She lifted her voice, the better to be heard in the living room. "I have to speak to Elaine Jamison."

Hyla punched the cell. "Mrs. Darling wants to talk to Elaine Jamison."

Footsteps sounded. Elaine stood in the doorway. "Annie, we have great trouble."

"That's why I've come." Annie walked past the police officer, who listened, then pocketed the cell.

Apparently, Billy didn't mind Annie's presence as long as Hyla heard every word.

Annie glanced around the room. Obviously, Frank Saulter had finished taking the family members' statements because now they were all here. Kit Jamison huddled, knees to her chin, in a side chair. Laura and her brother, Tommy, shared a small sofa. Annie's gaze paused at Tommy. He'd combed his hair and changed into a larger shirt that fit him much better than the earlier tight polo. Richard Jamison stood by the window. His glance at Annie was quizzical.

Annie took a deep breath. Elaine deserved the truth. "I was in your backyard this morning. I told the police that I saw you come out of your cottage."

The silence in the living room was taut and stressed. Every face turned toward the doorway where Elaine and Annie stood.

Elaine raised a hand as if to ward off Annie's words.

Annie continued, her voice thin, her eyes meeting Elaine's stricken gaze. "You walked on the path toward the marsh. You were carrying a bunched-up blue cloth. I lost sight of you. I crossed the yard and looked around the cane. You were lowering your arm. I assumed that you had thrown something. However, I did not"—she emphasized the negative—"see you throw anything." If a gun wasn't found, they would have no physical evidence to link to Elaine. "You still held the cloth. You turned and ran behind your cottage and in a moment you drove out in your car."

Annie looked deep into pale blue eyes that held despair, not resentment.

Laura Jamison's voice shook. "Did you see anyone else?"

"The yardman." Annie continued to look at Elaine. "If Max and I can help you, call us." She waited for an instant, but Elaine's face registered nothing. Slowly, Annie turned away.

Voices rose. "What's this all about, Elaine?" "What's she talking about?" "Who is she?"

Annie walked away.

Elaine's voice sounded dull. "Annie Darling. I don't know why she came. What I did this morning doesn't matter. I didn't go up to the house. I didn't see Glen. I don't know what happened to him. I saw him last night. He was fine." Her voice broke, ended in a sob.

Annie pushed out the front door and hurried across the grass to find solace in Max's embrace.

Eight

Annie looked over the marina, smelled the salty scent of the water, and heard the clang of a buoy. She had stopped believing in pots of gold under four-leaf clovers by the time she was eight, but on this gorgeous, clear, brilliant morning she felt as if everything was going to come up roses. Even if Elaine Jamison had thrown away a gun yesterday in the marsh, she felt confident that Elaine was not a murderess. On the morning that someone shot her brother, maybe she'd thought a gun was nothing to have in her possession. Annie did not believe, could not believe, would not believe that Elaine lifted a gun, held the grip tight in her hands, squeezed the trigger, and ended the life of the brother she adored.

Annie plucked her cell from the pocket of her light and swirly georgette skirt with a bright pattern of tiny clamshells against a silvery background. She'd dressed with special care, her blouse a matching silver, a cool outfit for a warm day. She punched a button, held the phone up.

"Mavis, Annie again. May I please speak to Billy?" A black skimmer passed so near as it dove toward the water that she could see its brilliant black cap and red bill. "Billy? Annie." She got right to the point. "Did the search of the marsh yield anything?"

"Some information has been released to the media." His tone was matter-of-fact. What Annie would soon read in the *Gazette*, he was willing to share. "A search of the marsh was instituted. To date, investigators haven't found anything connected to the murder of Glen Jamison. Missing from the Jamison house is a semiautomatic 1911 Colt .45 registered to Glen Jamison. The gun was customarily kept in a gun safe in his study. The key was in the gun safe. The gun safe contained two handguns, a Smith & Wesson .357 Magnum and a Ruger Mark III semiautomatic .22 pistol. Neither had been fired recently and both were fully loaded. Glen occasionally went into Savannah to a gun club to shoot. About a week before the crime, he told his wife he had mislaid the key to the gun safe. He didn't mention the missing key again and she assumed he had found it. When and how the Colt .45 was removed from the gun safe and by whom is unknown. Ballistic tests indicate Jamison was killed by a forty-five-caliber bullet."

The brightness of the day dimmed as she clicked off the call. Billy clearly believed Elaine had thrown Glen's Colt into the marsh. Even if the gun were never found, Annie's statement would be damning. Annie walked slowly to Death on Demand and unlocked the front door. Agatha waited with her ears slightly flattened and her tail switching. The black cat's meow was distinctly annoyed.

"I only stopped at the marina for a minute." Annie clicked on lights, walked swiftly down the center aisle to the coffee bar.

Agatha nipped at one ankle.

"Okay, maybe five minutes." In a flash, Annie had opened a fresh can of salmon, filled the bowl, and refreshed Agatha's water.

Elaine threw away the murder weapon.

Annie brewed a pot of strong Colombian and wished she could will away the conclusion, but the conclusion seemed obvious and clearly Billy had made the connection. When Elaine's distraught appearance Tuesday morning was added to the possible disposal of the murder weapon, the likelihood of guilt was overwhelming. All Annie could offer in rebuttal was her memory of a sister's obvious devotion.

Annie poured coffee into one of her favorite mugs, *O Is for Omen* by Lawrence Treat. What she needed now, in addition to a jolt of super coffee, was a good omen for Elaine. She sat at a table and the first thing her eye saw was a Cat Truth poster. A magnificent Golden Shaded Persian with a malignant expression stared haughtily from pale golden eyes: *All we know are the facts, ma'am.*

Annie wanted to believe in Elaine's innocence, but deadly facts were deadly.

The tide was running out, exposing shallow pools with hard-ridged bottoms. The sun hung low in the west, splashing a burst of orange on low-lying dark clouds banked to the south.

Annie leaned back in the short-legged beach chair, sipped a limeade, and shaded her eyes from the still-vivid sunlight. "Not a cloud in the sky." She felt drained. All day at Death on Demand her thoughts had tumbled as she sought some means of helping Elaine. She'd been tempted to call Billy Cameron, but she had nothing to offer except her personal feeling of Elaine's innocence. After dinner, she'd agreed to go to the beach even though she felt as if she were letting Elaine down. But what could Annie do?

Max lay on a towel stretched out on the sand. His skin gleamed from coconut-oil sunscreen. Sand had dried to his yellow swim trunks. A soft, pale blue cotton bucket hat shaded his face. "We'll have some rainy days soon." This June had been uncommonly dry. "Then you'll sell a lot of books." His murmur was drowsy. "Hot today. Like the natives say, why do all these people come here when the sand burns your feet?" He didn't look, but the wave of his arm encompassed clots of tourists, many of them with peeling noses and sun-angry shoulders. They splashed in gentle surf, jogged, rode bikes, lunged for small black balls as they played Kadima, or lounged in beach chairs. "But it's a beautiful time to be on the beach."

"And everything is as it should be on a Wednesday evening in June." Her voice wobbled. On their beautiful sea island, life went on. Families played, lovers came together, old people lifted their faces to the warmth of the sun to remember when they were young and turned cartwheels on the sand.

Max tipped up the hat. His eyes sought hers. "You had to report what you saw."

"What if Billy arrests Elaine?" It was hard to force out the words. Speaking the threat aloud made Elaine's situation seem worse.

Max said quietly, "Billy makes decisions based on evidence. Right now he doesn't have enough evidence to charge Elaine."

Annie's reply was hot. "He needs to look at all the evidence. He brushed me off about Pat Merridew's murder and the photograph taken in the Jamison gazebo."

Max's dark blue eyes were thoughtful. He didn't answer directly. "When Elaine came out of the cottage, she was carrying a cloth wrapped around something, right?"

Annie saw Elaine's image clearly, haunted, despairing, driven, one arm pressed tight over the small bundle. "That's right."

His tone was neutral. "In Pat's photograph, the towel in the gazebo was wrapped around something."

"Oh, wait a minute . . ." But the words trailed away.

Max picked up some sand, let it trickle through his fingers. "You saw Elaine shortly after she had apparently thrown an object into the marsh. Glen's gun is missing and it was the same-caliber gun that killed him. One plus one, Annie. Elaine carried something wrapped in cloth and tossed something into the water. How hard is it to wonder if her cloth held the gun and if the towel in the photograph was wrapped around Glen's Colt?"

Annie wished she could blot out the words, but they buzzed in her mind, persistent as no-see-'ums. She understood Max's point. The Colt belonged to Glen.

Someone took it from his study. What then? The gun had to be hidden until it was needed. Elaine no longer lived in the house. It seemed reasonable to assume that if she stole the gun, she would have hidden it in a convenient spot but not in her cottage. The gazebo was only steps away.

"I guess that's how Billy figures it," Annie admitted. "If Pat Merridew was murdered because she took that photograph, she must have seen someone place that towel in the gazebo. More than that, Pat must have explored the contents of the towel. She knew who hid the gun. She invited that person for coffee to talk about what she had seen. Pat said enough over the phone that her guest came armed with the painkiller. I think the killer knew enough about Pat to slip into her house when she was away and take a handful of the pills."

"That would mean"—Max's voice was grim—"that Glen's murder was already planned. Pat died so that Glen could be shot."

"It didn't have to be Elaine." Annie's voice held a plea. But she looked away from Max's somber gaze. Only Elaine lived outside the house. "If it was someone in the house"—she didn't give up—"he or she probably wouldn't try to hide it in a bedroom."

Max was equable. "It's an argument."

But not one Annie felt she was likely to win with Billy.

Every path seemed to lead to Elaine.

An early-morning thunderstorm added another layer of humidity, though the rain was easing by the time she reached Death on Demand. Tourists wandered aimlessly around the store, avoiding the rain and enjoying the air-conditioning. Welcome to the Lowcountry in June. Happily, several carried hefty stacks to the counter. A big seller was Kathy Reichs's latest Temperance Brennan title.

Annie was glad for the influx of customers, but she was almost out of Danishes. Every table was taken.

A teenager, her nose coated with sticky white zinc oxide apparently in preparation for reading on the beach, approached her. The girl held a Cat Truth poster. "How much does this picture cost? I don't see a price tag. I'd love to have it, but I only have ten dollars with me."

Annie glanced at the photograph. An Egyptian Mau, round green eyes bright in a wedge-shaped face, fine silver-tan silky coat marked with random black spots, lay on his back, tummy exposed, feet in the air: *Lighten up. Serious is so yesterday.*

Inspiration struck. "All of the posters are available for exactly ten dollars and the money is contributed to the Animal Rescue Refuge." In a jiffy, she had placed the bill in a pottery bowl, added a printed card suggesting donations, and a happy teenager, her poster carefully sheathed in plastic wrap, hurried toward the front door.

"Tell everyone," Annie called after her. She was thrilled. Maybe she could get rid of some of the posters and help the animal refuge as well. "More than one way to skin a cat," she muttered. She felt out of sorts, but she knew her malaise wasn't caused by a rainy Thursday morning or the posters. Her malaise came from the growing conviction that Elaine Jamison was Billy Cameron's primary suspect and there was nothing Annie could do to change his mind.

If she could push away thoughts of Elaine, she would have a happy morning in her bookstore. Her gaze slid toward the Cat Truth posters. To tell the truth, she was becoming fond of the photographs and their captions. However, she didn't intend to confess her capitulation to Laurel. She might have to ante up ten bucks and hang one particular poster in her office. An American Shorthair Snowshoe with intent blue eyes and the telltale four white feet was perched on a brick wall, oblivious to pelting rain, fur plastered down, drenched to the skin. He peered at a svelte Siberian Forest Cat, elegant and unattainable behind a windowpane: *Hey, babe, come on out, the weather's fine and I'm a heckuva guy.*

She smiled and picked up the poster. Guys were guys, whether two-legged or four, and wasn't that wonderful. She shut the storeroom door, determined to push away all thoughts of Elaine Jamison. She settled at the computer, clicked a HarperCollins order form, entered a list of fall titles . . .

The phone rang.

"Death on—"

Marian Kenyon, her voice gruff, cut her off. "Cop shop just had a press conference on the Jamison kill."

Bubblegum wrappers littered the floor by Marian's sandal-shod feet. Her words were slurred by the wad in her left cheek. She looked like a bright, intelligent, industrious squirrel readying for winter. "I'm not a shrink. Maybe Billy's trying to pressure her. Whatever, Elaine's got to be the lead"—her fingers flew over the keyboard—"and true to form I got a call to show up for Q and A about twenty minutes ago and my deadline"—she scrunched her face in irritation—"is in nine minutes. Can't talk now. Read over my shoulder." She yelled across the room to Ferroll Crump, the city editor. "Gimme sixteen inches."

Ferret-faced Ferroll, a wizened refugee from the layoff surge that had swept through metropolitan dailies, grunted, "Yo." Divorced, in debt, fond of the ponies, he'd landed at the *Gazette* about a year ago. He wrote a weekly column, "A Damn Yankee in Bubbaland," which islanders vociferously applauded or condemned. Vince Flynn, the *Gazette*'s editor and publisher, told Annie that Letters to the Editor had upticked by 40 percent since the debut of Ferroll's column. Last week's diatribe began, *Thought somebody had dumped paste into my oatmeal but it turned out to be something called grits, which rhymes with spits . . .*

Five desks jammed the small newsroom. In addition to Ferroll and Marian, Big Bud Hoover manned the sports desk, Sally Sue Simpson handled society, and Tessa White was a summer J-school intern. Hoover glowered at a sports magazine. "No way McGwire goes in the Hall of Fame." Sally Sue cooed into a phone, "We'd love to feature your garden next week, especially the sedum in the terra-cotta jar . . ." The intern, eyes gleaming with excitement, eased up from her desk, edged near enough to join Annie and Max to watch Marian.

Energy and tension radiated from Marian. Her lead hit Annie like a karate chop:

Broward's Rock police chief, Billy Cameron, today announced that Elaine Jamison, sister of murder victim Glen Jamison, has been named a person of interest in the investigation into the shooting death that occurred at the Jamison residence Tuesday morning. Jamison, a member of a leading island family and well-known attorney, was fifty-two.

Chief Cameron announced that a Colt .45 registered to Glen Jamison is missing from a gun safe in Jamison's study. Cameron said Jamison died as a result of gunshot wounds from a .45 pistol. According to Chief Cameron, a few days before his death Jamison announced that the key to the gun safe was missing. When and how the gun was obtained and by whom is unknown at this time, Cameron said. A search for the murder weapon continues in a marsh behind the Jamison house. Miss Jamison's cottage is about twenty yards from the marsh. Chief Cameron said a witness observed Miss Jamison leaving her cottage shortly before ten A.M. Tuesday.

According to the police report, Glen Jamison was found dead in his study at the Jamison home at 204 Marsh Hawk Road at approximately 10:15 A.M. Tuesday. Chief Cameron said the body was discovered by Richard Jamison, cousin of the victim. Cameron said Glen Jamison was last seen alive by his daughter Kit at approximately 8:45 A.M.

Chief Cameron said Jamison's daughters, Laura and Kit, were present in the house when his body was discovered. Jamison's wife, Cleo, an attorney, had left the house to catch the 7:30 A.M. ferry to the mainland and was taking a deposition in Savannah when she was notified of her husband's death. Cameron said Jamison's son, Tommy, had spent the night with a friend and had not yet returned. Cameron said a yardman, Darwyn Jack, arrived for work in the backyard at eight A.M. Tuesday. Cameron said Jack did not see any unidentified persons in the backyard between the time he started to work and the arrival of authorities.

Glen Jamison, senior partner of Jamison, Jamison, and Brewster, customarily arrived at his office at nine A.M., firm secretary Edna Graham said. "He missed an appointment at nine-thirty. The client waited half an hour. I called his cell but didn't get any answer."

Richard Jamison, who discovered the body, said, "I came back from a jog. I poured a glass of Gatorade and started for the stairs. The study door was ajar. I was surprised to see the light on because Glen always left about nine to go to his office. I pushed open the door to switch off the light. I almost didn't see him because his body was partially hidden by his desk." Jamison declined to describe the appearance of the room.

Chief Cameron said the autopsy revealed that Jamison had been shot twice from a distance of approximately ten feet. One bullet struck the left side of his throat, right below the jaw. The second nicked the sternum and was deflected upward to lodge in his mouth. "Death would have been instantaneous from the wound in his throat," Cameron said.

Marian paused, chewed, made a face. She pulled the chunk of bubble gum from her cheek, retrieved a wrapper from the floor, and threw the wad into a wastebasket. "My mouth feels like cotton wool," she groused.

Annie tried not to picture the appearance of Glen Jamison's study. If the bullet in his throat severed his carotid artery, an explosion of blood would have stained the dead man and the area around him. She concentrated on thinking about cotton wool.

Marian hunkered back over the keyboard.

Jamison's family has a long history in the Lowcountry. His great-grandfather . . .

Marian typed fast, then her hands hovered above the keyboard as she reread the paragraph about the Jamison family. She made a last check of her notes, scanned the story from the top, then typed "30," clicked send. She glanced at the clock. "Made it with two minutes to spare. Whew. Got a throat dry as the Sahara. Come on, you two."

In the shabby *Gazette* break room, Marian sprawled like a tired surfer on a ratty sofa, its brown upholstery stained with spills and long-ago cigarette burns. She clutched a can of Coke and carefully dribbled into her mouth salted peanuts from a torn-open, one-ounce bag of Planters. She closed her eyes, paused, took a mouthful of Coke, drank and crunched. "Yeah." It was the heartfelt sigh of a climber safely at the top of the mountain.

Max leaned against the dingy, stippled-plaster wall. "Billy ladled out a lot of information."

"Mmmm." Marian took another mouthful. "God designed peanuts for Coke, trust me. Yeah. I'd say the chief's laying the groundwork for an arrest, making it clear to Elaine Jamison she'd better open up or go down."

Annie wriggled in an uncomfortable plastic bucket chair. She tried to sound positive, but it was a struggle. "It's a good story." She wished she didn't feel that every word pushed Elaine deeper into a hole.

Marian picked up on the unhappiness in Annie's tone. Her eyes slitted open. "Don't kill the messenger."

Max hastened to sound positive. "You obviously asked excellent questions, Marian."

Marian pushed to a more upright position on the sofa. "I know you guys like Elaine, but I got to tell you I don't pick up good vibes about her at the cop shop. If you want some deep background, but don't remember where you heard it, the skinny is that she's clammed up, demanded a lawyer, won't cooperate. That's not to say the innocent don't need legal advice, but the innocent who are trying to help cops solve a murder, especially of a nearest and dearest, don't yell for a lawyer when they haven't even been Mirandized." Marian's monkey-bright face suddenly split in a grin. "Hey, Annie, you got to save one of those cat pictures for me."

"My pleasure. In fact you can have"—she saw Max's reproachful glance—"whichever one you would like to have."

"Like they used to say before it got too trite, it doesn't get any better than the pix of that Bombay Tom, black as pitch, looking satisfied as a gambler with a royal straight, bright yellow eyes gleaming, and on the floor a broken fishbowl: *Don't look at me. I was at the vet's.* I'll bet"—Marian sounded callous—"Elaine wishes she had been at the vet's. Instead, she was johnny on the spot in her cottage. Or"—now her tone was silky—"up at the house."

Annie was sharp. "There's no reason to think she went up to the house. I saw her coming out of her cottage. Besides, nobody knows when Glen was shot. In your story, you wrote that he was last seen at eight forty-five by Kit and he wasn't found until a quarter after ten. Billy needs to find out where every member of the family was during that period." Her eyes narrowed. "How about Cleo Jamison?" She didn't know if the question was fair. As far as she knew, no one had suggested any kind of quarrel between Glen and his second wife. But a spouse was always sure to be looked at in the event of murder.

Marian yawned. "I checked that one out myself, not being a downy duck. Ben Parotti said she was on the seven-thirty ferry Tuesday morning. The ferry docked at eight-fifteen and her car rolled off going south. According to a secretary at the firm of Lampkin and Swift, she arrived at their offices at eight-fifty and was in a conference room with an L and S lawyer and his client and a court reporter when Edna Graham called."

"It would be nice if we knew exactly when Glen was killed." Max looked thoughtful. "Kit spoke to him at eight forty-five, Richard found his body at ten-fifteen. That's an hour and a half unaccounted for."

"Two shots." Annie looked puzzled. "Why didn't anyone hear them?"

"We don't know for sure that no one did." Max held out his hand and Marian reluctantly poured out a half-dozen peanuts. She jerked her head toward the vending machine. "More where these came from."

Max flipped the peanuts in his mouth, stepped to the machine, dropped in two quarters, and punched. He retrieved a bag of peanuts from the trough and tossed it to Marian.

She accepted the bounty as her due. "Unless somebody pops up and proves the shots occurred at the precise moment Elaine was entertaining the president of the League of Women Voters or, better yet, two fresh-faced Mormon missionaries, I'd say she's history."

Annie pushed up from the chair. "On that cheery note . . ."

They were in the break-room doorway when Max looked back at Marian. "You remember when I asked you about Elaine and you said you had an interesting tidbit about her?"

Marian's head jerked up. Her bright dark eyes gleamed. Without looking down, she ripped open the cellophane of the peanut bag with the skill of long practice. "Hey, hey, hey. You wanted to know about Elaine before we had a kill. What kind of inside dope do you have?" She pulled a soft-leaded pencil from the pocket of her jeans, along with a couple sheets of folded computer paper.

"Hey, hey, hey," Annie responded. "Maybe we can make a deal."

Max held up a warning hand. "Nothing's been released about—" He broke off, not mentioning Pat Merridew's name.

Annie had no such qualms. Billy Cameron either dismissed the possibility of murder in Pat's death or felt there would never be a way to prove murder. But she had every right to voice her own opinion.

Marian made notes as Annie recounted the background: Pat Merridew's late-night forays, her death from an overdose of an opiate, the fingerprint-free crystal mug, and the photograph in her BlackBerry of a towel wrapped around something. " . . . and the photo definitely was taken in the Jamison gazebo shortly after midnight on June thirteenth."

Face folded in disparagement, Marian ran a hand through her spiky, silver-frosted dark hair. "So what does any of that have to do with the price of rice in China?"

Max's gaze told Annie he felt she'd landed in a sticky patch all by her own effort. He shrugged. " 'Trust me not at all or all in all.' "

Annie didn't know whether to admire Max's erudition or whether he recalled her quoting from some of her cherished Miss Silver novels by Patricia Wentworth. Miss Silver often repeated the maxim from Alfred, Lord Tennyson.

Whichever, it was good advice.

Marian's eyes rounded as Annie described the bundle Elaine held Tuesday morning that probably contained the murder weapon and how Annie had told Billy and that led to the search of the marsh.

Marian stared at Annie. "So rewind to the gazebo and another bundle. Is it your idea that Glen's gun was in the towel and Pat Merridew saw who put it there, then tried a little genteel blackmail over coffee in crystal mugs, but wound up dead instead of counting ill-gotten gains? Have I got it right?"

Annie nodded.

Marian muttered aloud, "Okay, I think it all follows. The gun-safe key was missing. Probably we should pin down when that was known, see if it correlates with the towel in the gazebo. But it's kind of an ergo equation working backward. Tuesday morning Elaine had a bundle, which likely held the murder weapon, so the odds are that she's the one who put a bundle that might have contained a gun in the gazebo." She blinked at Annie. "At least you've got a date. When was the pix taken?"

"At twelve-oh-nine A.M., June thirteenth, that's just after midnight on Saturday, June twelfth."

Marian fingered more peanuts. "Sounds like a one-way ticket to jail for Elaine. No wonder she's a person of interest. I wonder what she was doing the night Pat died?"

"She was home. Alone." Annie felt discouraged.

Marian looked rueful. "Where's an alibi when a woman needs one? I guess she didn't spend that weekend in Savannah with her gentleman friend."

Annie asked, "Savannah?"

Marian's face had a waiflike quality. "Yeah. Savannah. That was my tidbit. Elaine Jamison and Burl Field are an item. I've seen her and Burl coming back on the early-morning ferry a couple of times. I have a niece who reads poetry at a coffeehouse and sometimes I stay over at her apartment on Saturday nights after her gig. In fact . . ." Her face squeezed in concentration. "Oh, wait a minute." Marian pulled an iPhone from her pocket. "I stayed with Cindy on, oh yes, I thought so, Saturday night June twelfth. I saw Elaine and Burl, yeah, it was the first ferry Sunday morning, June thirteenth. There's no ferry to the mainland after ten P.M. Saturday night, so Elaine didn't tuck a gun wrapped in a towel in the Jamison gazebo. Somebody else did the honors."

The morning clouds had fled and the day had heated up. In bright sunlight, Burl Field used a bandanna to wipe sweat from his red face. He braked the forklift and dropped to the ground. The forklift held a pallet of two-by-fours. "Yeah, Max, how can I help you?" A buzz saw whined in the cavernous interior of the lumber-yard warehouse.

Asking a man whether he spent the night with his lover could evoke a pugnacious response, but the conclusion seemed obvious. The last ferry to Broward's Rock left the mainland at ten P.M. The first ferry departed from the mainland at seven A.M. If Elaine Jamison and Burl Field had been on the early ferry from the mainland island on June 13, neither had been on Broward's Rock shortly after midnight on Saturday when the BlackBerry photo had been taken.

Max noted the lines of patience and good humor in Burl's heat-reddened face. He decided truth was the best offense. "Elaine Jamison's in big trouble, Burl.

You may be able to save her from criminal prosecution. Here's what I need to know . . ."

Annie parked in front of the Jamison house. As she hurried up the drive past several cars, skirting puddles from the morning storm, she glanced toward the garden. The time of day was different from her arrival here Tuesday morning. The humidity was heavier. The shrubs and trees still dripped from the morning storm. The wood of the gazebo gleamed wetly. But the scene was uncannily similar to Tuesday morning, except it was quiet without the shrill whine of a leaf blower. In the lagoon, Lou Pirelli moved slowly, the pole moving up and down, poking beneath roots, squishing into mud. Likely the fascination of the search had worn thin, very thin, for him.

Annie strode swiftly to Elaine's cottage, confident that she was on an errand that would lead to victory. She felt positive that the late-night photo in the gazebo had led inexorably to Pat's murder. Elaine spent the night on the mainland when the photo was taken. Therefore she was not the person Pat had invited to her house for Irish coffee. Annie never doubted that the deaths of Pat and Glen were connected. If Elaine was innocent of Pat's death, she was innocent of Glen's even if she had somehow come into possession of the murder weapon, which was still only a supposition. Billy Cameron might balk at Annie's conclusions even though everything she suggested was logical and reasonable. But there was no proof.

Annie knocked on the front door of the cottage.

The door was jerked open. Elaine Jamison's narrow, fine-boned face was wan, her expression haunted. She looked beyond Annie as if seeking something or someone, then slowly her gaze returned to Annie. She spoke as if from a long distance. "What do you want?" Her voice was dull and lifeless.

"To talk to you. To help you."

Elaine's lips trembled. "Help me? That's hard to believe. You followed me and told the police enough to make them suspicious of me."

"I was in the garden that morning. What else could I do? But I've told the police over and over that I know you didn't shoot Glen."

Something moved in Elaine's eyes. It might have been a flash of gratitude, but her face was still haunted.

"That's why I'm here." Annie spoke in a rush. "The police—" She broke off.

Elaine looked weary. "The police think I'm guilty." Her gaze was suddenly demanding. "Does everyone know the police are hounding me? They keep coming here. I told the kids not to come down here. I don't want them mixed up in this." She hesitated, then held the door open. "I have to talk to someone or I'll go mad."

In the living room, Elaine gestured to an easy chair for Annie. She herself settled into a corner of the sofa. She brushed back a strand of blond hair, tried to smile. "Would you like coffee? I have some made."

"No, thank you. Elaine, I think you found the murder weapon."

Elaine sat up straight and stared at Annie. "Are you going to hound me, too? Then go away. I'd rather be alone."

Annie persisted. "It's obvious you threw something into the marsh and everyone thinks it was the murder weapon. Where did you find the gun?"

"Where did I find the gun?" Elaine's voice shook. "At least you're original. Why don't you ask me why I shot Glen like the police do, over and over and over again?"

Annie was impatient. "I keep telling you. I don't think you shot Glen. But I do think you threw his Colt into the marsh. Did you find his body and take the gun? Look, if you did, go ahead and tell the police. I've got proof you didn't kill him."

Fear darted in Elaine's blue eyes. "What do you mean?"

Annie was confused. Instead of seizing upon Annie's belief in her innocence, Elaine seemed even more distraught. Annie spoke forcefully. "You were in Savannah the night Pat Merridew saw someone hide something in your gazebo. Marian Kenyon saw you and Burl Field on the first ferry from the mainland Sunday morning, June thirteenth."

Elaine pressed fingers against each temple. "Nothing makes sense." She massaged her temples, then her hands dropped. "What does Pat's death have to do with Glen?"

"Pat saw something she shouldn't have seen in your gazebo." Annie gestured toward the window. "After Pat was fired, she started coming here late at night . . ."

When Annie finished, Elaine's stare was incredulous. "Pat took a picture of a towel in the gazebo?"

Annie was decisive. "I think Glen's gun was hidden in the towel. Pat knew who hid the towel and she tried blackmail. I know it couldn't have been you. You were in Savannah with Burl."

"That doesn't sound likely to me." Elaine's voice was tired. She looked away from Annie, her gaze distant. "It doesn't make sense about Pat." It was as if she were processing the information about Pat's death against some inner knowledge, and the facts didn't jibe.

"The deaths must be connected." Once again Annie felt stymied. It was absurd to believe the murders weren't linked. She tried again. "Don't you see? Once the police know that you can't have committed the first crime, they'll realize you didn't shoot Glen. Now you can help them. Did you find the gun?"

Elaine looked defeated, weary, small against the puffy cushion. "I've told the police I don't know anything about Glen's murder. I don't know what happened." She lifted eyes brilliant with fear to gaze at Annie. "And that's what I'm telling you."

Max held his cell, waited for his call to be transferred.

"Chief Cameron." There was an undercurrent of impatience in Billy's voice.

Max felt he was on a short leash. "Hey, Billy. Annie and I saw Marian's story about Elaine Jamison being a person of interest. It turns out Marian saw Elaine Jamison and Burl Field on the early-morning ferry June thirteenth. That means Elaine was in Savannah the night Pat took that photo in the Jamison gazebo. Burl Field will swear to that."

"Thanks, Max. But"—Billy was brisk—"Elaine Jamison is a person of interest in the murder of Glen Jamison. Not," and he repeated with emphasis, "not in the possible homicide of Pat Merridew."

Max frowned. "Are you saying the murders are unconnected?"

"I'm saying we have one homicide and one unexplained death."

"Pat Merridew went to the Jamison backyard—"

"Got it from you. Got it from Annie. Several times." His tone was now gruff. "Sure, the BlackBerry photo's odd, but we will never be able to prove what was or wasn't in that towel. Look at it like this. *If* the Colt was in that towel, what was the point? I guess your theory is that the gun was hidden there until it was used to shoot Glen, which means premeditation. Maybe that's true, maybe not. We don't know who put the towel there or why. If it contained the gun, it's interesting to note that Elaine Jamison lives outside of the house. Very handy for her. That's not to say somebody in the house didn't put the towel there, but we are never going to know. As for rendering a verdict of innocent for Elaine Jamison on the basis of the BlackBerry photo, maybe the towel was hidden there the night before and Pat Merridew found it on the night of June twelfth. Maybe Pat Merridew came back every night to look and see who might be checking on the towel and that was when she saw Elaine Jamison. You can take it from me, and you can tell Annie, the timing of that photo doesn't matter and in no way does it knock out Elaine Jamison as a suspect in her brother's murder. If you want to spend time figuring what may or may not have happened, give a little thought to the murder weapon. The weapon hasn't been found. Annie saw Elaine Jamison shortly after she apparently threw something into the marsh. You want to take bets on whether she threw the murder weapon? If she had the Colt and threw it in the marsh, she was either trying to save herself, which makes her the principal suspect, or she disposed of the gun to save someone else. You know what that's called? Accessory after the fact."

The connection ended.

Max gave a soundless whistle. Annie was not going to be pleased at the course of Billy's investigation.

Nine

Max used a short stroke and the ball rolled up and over a slight ridge to curl beautifully into the hole of the indoor putting green. "Way to go." A successful putt was always a thing of beauty to him. Would Annie consider him derelict in his duty if he went over to the driving range? It was a perfect day to hit a bucket of balls and he wanted to practice his wood shots.

Max slid the putter into the bag. The phone rang. Annie. He smiled and punched his speakerphone. Maybe she'd join him. "Hey, Annie, let's go to the club and have lunch and—"

"I grabbed a sandwich after I went to see Elaine." Annie's voice was discouraged. "I told her I was sure she was innocent, but I felt like I was talking to a wall. She's like a cornered animal."

Max picked up a pen, drew a legal pad near, doodled an ostrich with its head in a hole. "She has good reason to be scared. I told Billy about Elaine and Burl in Savannah. As far as he's concerned, Elaine's whereabouts that night aren't relevant."

Her voice rose in protest. "He can't ignore what happened to Pat."

"Unfortunately"—Max spoke gently—"he can. Elaine is a suspect because of her own actions. She threw something in the marsh. If she got rid of the Colt, Billy believes she is either guilty or protecting someone. As he put it, an accessory after the fact."

Annie was subdued. "I want to help her. She won't cooperate."

Max drew a porcupine, quills flared. "She's an adult. She's made choices. Billy's a good cop. Let it go, Annie."

She was silent for so long he added five more porcupines to his row. "It's a gorgeous day. Let's play golf."

Annie's voice wobbled. "If I don't try to help her, I'll feel like I've turned my back on somebody in big trouble."

Max wrote in all caps: *BIG TROUBLE*. "She put herself in a deep hole. You didn't dig it, Annie."

"I can throw her a line, find a ladder, do something. If I thought she was guilty, I'd be glad to stay at the

store and be happy and not talk to people who are
upset and frightened. I would leave everything to Billy,
if I thought he was really looking. But he's made up his
mind. So I've got to see what I can find out. Maybe I'm
wrong. Maybe Elaine poisoned Pat and shot Glen. But
maybe she didn't. She doesn't want me to interfere, but
she doesn't have anyone on her side."

Max sketched a slender figure standing by a hole
with a lariat. Annie rarely met a lost cause she wouldn't
champion. "I understand."

"All right." Annie was abruptly vigorous, encouraged by her decision. "I'll talk to the rest of the family."

Max was sure Billy Cameron had already interviewed them, but perhaps one of them would say more
to Annie than to a police officer. Max drew a little halo
above a small cat with its fur on end, scrappy and determined. "Count me in. I'll nose around. We can't do
any harm and maybe we can find out something else
helpful to Elaine."

"Right. Here's what you can do . . ."

He jotted notes on the pad. "No stone unturned,
that's my motto." He clicked off the call and looked
at the list. It wasn't the way he'd planned to spend his
afternoon. He took a moment to fix a peanut-butter
sandwich in Barb's storeroom-cum-kitchen and carried
it to his desk with a glass of milk. He glanced at Annie's

picture with a whimsical smile. "So you've found an underdog you're determined to rescue." His tone was conversational. "Even if she doesn't want to be saved. Hey, that's why I love you." His smile dimmed. "But sometimes rescuers get bitten."

Annie punched the front doorbell of the Jamison house. She was surprised that Cleo Jamison opened the door. Cleo's beauty remained intact but it was muted, diminished by pallid skin, deep-sunken eyes, cheekbones made prominent by tightly compressed lips. The change in her appearance shocked Annie. The elegance was there, a crisp white cotton blouse, turquoise necklace against a tanned throat, beautifully tailored navy linen slacks, basket-weave navy leather loafers, but there was no trace of the confidence and, frankly, arrogance that Annie associated with Glen's young wife, now widow.

Cleo glanced at Annie's hands, then, with a flicker of puzzlement, said, "Yes?"

Annie realized Cleo had looked for a dish, the usual response from friends and well-wishers following a death. "Cleo, I'm Annie Darling." They had met casually several times at the country club. "I'm a friend of Elaine's and I'd appreciate it if I could visit with you for a few minutes."

"Is Elaine all right?" There was a ripple of apprehension in Cleo's husky voice.

Annie was encouraged by her concern. "I'm afraid not. She may be arrested. I'm trying to help her."

"Elaine arrested?" Cleo looked incredulous. "That's absurd. I'll have to call the police. That can't be true." She held open the door. "Please come in."

As Annie stepped into the hall, a young woman in a swim wrapper came down the stairs. A battered straw sun hat was perched atop glossy dark hair. She carried a beach bag and wore cherry-red flip-flops. Oversize sunglasses masked her eyes.

Cleo stiffened, her face bleak. "Surely you aren't going to the beach today."

"Surely I am." The reply was caustic.

"Laura, your father—"

"My father's dead. He's not even decently in a mortuary. Where do they take bodies of people who've been shot? Have you picked out a casket yet? Maybe Kit and Tommy and I should have something to say, but you're handling all the arrangements. The merry widow." She ignored Annie and yanked open the front door. "You kept telling Dad I needed to work harder. Well"—her voice shook—"I'm going to work this afternoon. I'd rather be a lifeguard watching out for sharks than be here. At least I'll be on the beach. Dad took us to the beach all the time when we were kids. I can remember him there. Without you." She bolted through the door and onto the porch.

Cleo's haggard face set in hard lines. She turned to Annie, spoke as if the ugly scene had never occurred. "I'll be glad to talk to you." She led the way down the broad central hall. Flower arrangements, large and small, lined either side of the hall and in some places were three deep. The scent of flowers was overpowering, cloying. The kitchen door at the end of the hall was ajar. There was a murmur of voices.

"We can go in here." Cleo opened the door to a small room at the end of the main hall. As they stepped inside, she murmured vaguely, "I'm trying to contact some of Glen's friends who live out of town." A game table was strewn with papers. A cell phone lay next to a mug of coffee. Cleo gestured at a wooden straight chair. "This is a catchall room, but I needed somewhere quiet."

When they were seated, Annie in a rickety Empire chair that likely was a castoff from an old dining-room table set, Cleo dropped onto a worn love seat with faded brocade upholstery. She gave Annie a searching glance. "Why would the police arrest Elaine?"

"It will be in this afternoon's *Gazette*. Elaine's been named a person of interest in the investigation." Annie knew her voice sounded grim, but her tidings were grim.

Quick comprehension flashed in Cleo's eyes. Cleo was a lawyer. Though she was in civil practice, she certainly grasped the import of Elaine being officially revealed as a person of interest in the investigation. Her response was immediate and emphatic. "Elaine wouldn't hurt Glen. That's impossible." She brushed back a tangle of dark hair. "Oh, I know they think she threw the missing gun in the lagoon. The police asked me if she knew how to shoot it. How would I know? Anyway, they haven't found anything. I don't believe Elaine shot Glen."

"I understand she was angry with Glen because of the children."

Cleo pressed her lips together. She folded her hands, stared down at them, seemed to draw upon some inner reserve. "I've always been lucky." She looked up at Annie with dumb misery in her gaze. "Ask anyone. That's what they'll tell you. The lucky lady. That's me. Beautiful, smart, quick, capable." It was as if she were describing a stranger from a remote distance. "And lucky." Her voice shook. "I made my own luck. That's what I wanted Glen to do. I wanted him to stand up and not let people take advantage of him. I thought they should take responsibility for their own lives. That's what I did. I worked. I supported myself. I earned scholarships. Nobody ever gave me anything. Glen's kids were leeches. Laura's twenty-four. She loses her job and whines because she can't find another cushy deal that pays her fifty thousand a year. The best she can do is wait tables or lifeguard. Whatever she earns, she should be living on it. Instead, she comes home and lives here for free and bleeds her dad for money. I tried to get Glen to see that Laura needed to stand on her own two feet. As for Kirk Brewster, Glen didn't owe him a place in the firm when times are tough. Glen said we had to cut back. That's why he wanted to drop Kirk. He didn't know Laura was going to go nuts when he gave notice to Kirk. That was a mess. As for Kit, I told Glen he put her through college and graduate school and here she was asking for more so she could go to Africa. Tommy was rude to me, day in and day out. He had his choice, be polite or go away to school. This morning . . . He was hateful. I told him to get out of the house, not come back until he could be civil. He slammed out the back door, barefoot, shirtless. I don't know where he's gone. I almost called Elaine but she hasn't been up to the house since—" Cleo broke off. "At least she's always treated me decently. Maybe she liked having the cottage. Anyway, it was better for her to have her own place. After all, I was Glen's wife. The house didn't need her still trying to run everything."

Cleo pushed up from the sofa, paced two strides one way, two strides back, making the room seem even smaller. Abruptly, she stopped and stared down at Annie. "I knew they'd be upset, but I never thought . . ."

Her words trailed away.

Annie asked quietly, "Never thought what?"

"That someone"—her voice was a whisper—"would kill Glen. If one of them shot Glen, it's my fault. My fault." A sob shook her voice. She stared at Annie, her face stricken with anguish. "The police said he was shot with a forty-five and his gun is missing. I don't see how a stranger could have the gun. Do you?"

Her eyes sought Annie, pleaded for an explanation.

"The gun may have been hidden in your gazebo." Annie described Pat Merridew's late-night jaunts and the photograph in her BlackBerry and Pat's death. ". . . one of the crystal mugs had no fingerprints."

Cleo sank onto the love seat. She leaned back, her expression skeptical. "You think Pat was killed because she saw someone hide Glen's gun? I don't believe that's possible. Why, she died four days before Glen was shot." Cleo's eyes narrowed. "When was the photograph taken?"

"At twelve-oh-nine A.M., June thirteenth."

Cleo rose, moved to the game table, picked up an iPhone, brushed the screen. She stared. "June twelfth was Saturday. It was on Friday that Glen couldn't find the key to the gun safe." She gazed at Annie, her eyes fearful with knowledge. "The key was missing Friday. You say something was hidden in the gazebo early Sunday morning." Her face looked haunted. She knew that the person who took the key had to be someone with access to the house, Glen's children, his sister, his cousin.

"If someone in the house took the gun, it would have to be hidden somewhere." Cleo spoke in a wondering tone. "Or if someone didn't live in the house, the gun had to be placed where it would be available." She returned to the love seat, sank onto it, obviously shaken. "I didn't actually think one of them could be guilty even though they're the only ones who gain by his death. Now everything Glen had will be theirs—the house, his estate."

Annie frowned. "You're his widow."

Cleo waved a dismissive hand. "I was his second wife. He had a family. We had a prenuptial agreement. Everything goes to them except for a hundred thousand to me and a portion of whatever he'd made since we married. The firm was in trouble and Glen's investments were down, but the estate still totals almost a million. And there's the house. It goes to them, but that's fine. I didn't marry him for his money. I don't need anyone's money. I'm a good lawyer."

"Did they know this?" Annie saw the faces in her mind. Laura Jamison was defensive about her stymied career and upset that Kirk Brewster was losing his partnership. Kit Jamison's sole focus was on her research and the grand opportunity that awaited her in Africa. Tommy Jamison's rudeness to his stepmother had resulted in Glen's decision to send him away to school. Tommy faced losing his senior year at the island high school and a starring role on the football team. Elaine Jamison wanted her nieces and nephew to be happy. All of them now would be able to do what they wished.

"They knew." Cleo was somber.

"Is there anyone else who profits from his death?" The Jamison siblings would inherit enough money to be able to do whatever they wished. Tommy would certainly be able to stay on the island for his senior year in high school. "What about Glen's cousin?"

Cleo looked startled. "Richard? No. He wouldn't have wanted anything to happen to Glen. Richard was about to persuade Glen to help him get loans to build resort condos in Costa Rica. He sure won't get any help from the kids. No, Laura and Kit and Tommy are the

ones who—" She broke off. "Oh." She looked thoughtful, considering. "One other may ultimately profit. I
guess will certainly profit. I hadn't thought about prof-
iting." The words came slowly. "I haven't been able to
think about anything besides Glen. Glen . . ." She took
a shaky breath. "They didn't let me see the study. I
didn't want to see it. They found someone to clean it."
There was horror in her voice. "Did you know there
are people who clean up terrible things like that? The
study's clean now, so they say. I've gone up to the door
and touched the knob, and each time I turn away.
Maybe if I went inside, I'd be able to get rid of the terrible picture in my mind. Sometimes it's worse if you
imagine something instead of seeing it as it really is. In
my mind, blood is everywhere and I want to scream,
but I can't. I've kept busy with letters and calls and
arrangements during the day and I take pills at night,
but the picture won't go away. I guess that's why I
didn't think about money. I should have told the police.
And he would know about Glen's gun." She stopped,
her face stricken. "I hate thinking this way, suspecting
people I know. Still, it's odd that Glen should die now.
If he had lived two more weeks, Kirk would have been
out of the firm."

"Kirk Brewster?" Annie was puzzled. "Is the fact
that he's still a partner affected by Glen's death?"

"Is Kirk affected?" Cleo's voice was thin. "Oh yes. He certainly is. To the tune of about two and a half million dollars."

Annie felt an instant of amazement. "That's a lot of money. How can that be?"

Cleo ran a hand through her shining dark hair. "Key man insurance. For Glen. I was against it from the first. I told Glen that the economy would get better but he worried about the firm's future if something happened to him. The firm was started by his great-grandfather. I thought the monthly payments were a waste. We would have been better off hiring a PR firm."

Annie wasn't deflected by Cleo's criticism of Glen's decision. What mattered was the timing. "What will happen since Kirk is still a member of the firm?"

"He and I are the two surviving partners. We are the beneficiaries."

"How much will the firm—you and Kirk—receive?"

"Five million dollars." She picked up the iPhone. "I'd better call the police." She paused before she dialed. "If you don't mind, you can show yourself out."

A man's voice droned beyond the partially open door. Max tapped on the lintel. "Miss Graham?" The legal secretary was listening intently to a cassette, her fingers flying over the keyboard.

She looked up in surprise. "Mr. Darling." She clicked off the cassette.

"I hope you can spare a moment. I'm here for Glen's sister."

"Please come in." She gestured toward a wooden chair to one side of her desk and reached for a pad. "What does Miss Jamison want me to do?"

Max wondered what would happen when Elaine Jamison discovered that he and Annie were prying into the personal lives of the Jamison family. He couldn't claim to have her approval. He owed Edna Graham the truth. "Elaine didn't send me. I'm here because the police have named her a person of interest in the investigation."

Edna's eyes widened in shock. Her face flushed with indignation. "Nonsense."

Max nodded energetically. "My wife and I agree. We're looking for information that would point the police in a different direction."

Edna clasped her hands. "If I can help, I certainly will."

"You may make a huge difference. No one had better insight into Mr. Jamison's day-to-day life. Was he involved in any legal matters that might have led to the murder?"

Edna Graham's strong-boned face was heavy and somber. "Mr. Jamison's practice did not include criminal matters." Her tone was a reproof.

Max hastened to reassure her. "Certainly not. But sometimes civil lawsuits cause hard feelings."

She shook her head decisively. "As I told the police, Mr. Jamison was always a gentleman. Even opposing counsel admired him." In a more everyday voice, she added, "Actually, he hadn't been very busy for the last few months. He'd done several wills and trusts and some bankruptcies, but nothing that had caused any controversy."

Max looked at her soberly. "I suppose the atmosphere was strained between him and Kirk Brewster." Would it have been kinder to have forced Kirk to clear out his desk and leave when the decision to drop him had been made? Max thought it must have been stomach-lurching ugly for the lawyer to return each day, informing clients, tidying up his cases and his desk, sending out résumés, knowing he soon had to leave the island and his chronically ill sister.

Edna stared down at her desktop. "Mr. Brewster kept out of Mr. Jamison's way. He will be leaving soon."

Max nodded. "Were you aware of some of the tensions between Mr. Jamison and members of his family?"

Edna's eyes shifted away from Max, but not before he saw a flash of something, possibly uneasiness, possibly uncertainty. "The police officer asked if Mr.

Jamison had quarreled with anyone. I didn't know if it would be called a quarrel. Last week Mr. Jamison's cousin came here to see him. He left the door ajar when he went into the office and I couldn't help overhearing. Mr. Jamison told his cousin that he was sorry but he wasn't in a financial position to help him. They talked for a while. It all sounded pleasant enough, but when his cousin came out, his face wasn't . . . nice." She added quickly, "Maybe he didn't feel good. Everything sounded very pleasant."

Max's smile was reassuring. "That's probably exactly the case."

She looked sad. "I can't believe Mr. Jamison won't be coming into the office in a little while." Tears welled in her eyes. She reached for a Kleenex. "I'm sorry." She wiped her eyes. "You are very kind to try and help Miss Jamison."

Max rose. "All of us need to help the police if we can."

As he left, she turned to her computer, but she sat motionless, head lowered.

Max left the door ajar as he had found it. He glanced up and down the hallway. He turned to his left. Next to an open door was a wooden plaque with Kirk Brewster's name, gilt letters against redwood. The door was wide open.

Max lifted his hand to knock, then paused. He had an odd sense of déjà vu. Tuesday morning in the living room of the Jamison house he'd watched as Tommy Jamison swung toward the hallway and blundered away. Now he looked into Kirk Brewster's office and gazed at a young man staring out the office window. There was the same suggestion of youth and strength, the same bush of curly blond hair, the same muscular shoulders, the same powerful legs. Tommy had worn a too-tight polo and khaki shorts. The man at the window wore a close-fitting mesh polo and cutoff jeans.

Abruptly, the stocky figure turned. A man in his late twenties stared at Max with an unsmiling, guarded face. "Who are you?"

"Max Darling." Max took a step inside the office. "Kirk Brewster?"

The young lawyer's eyes were light blue. His hair was sandy like Tommy Jamison's, but his face was older, the features stronger, a beaked nose and thin lips. No one would mistake him for Tommy Jamison from a front view. "You got a warrant?" His light eyes were defiant, but there was an air of desperation about him as he rocked back on his heels.

"I'm not a policeman." Max saw a flicker of relief.

Kirk shoved a hand through the thick tangle of blond hair. "You don't have an appointment. I'm not seeing people anyway. I'm not lawyering now. I'm packing up my stuff." He gestured at the cardboard boxes lined up in the center of the office. Framed prints and plaques leaned against a wall. "Whoever you are, whatever you want, I'm not interested." He turned away, walked back to the window.

Max again recalled Tommy Jamison as he strode out of the living room Tuesday morning. The casual clothing and stocky build accounted for the similarities even though the teenager and the man seen face-to-face could never be confused in person. Tommy Jamison had been upset, frightened, grieving. Kirk Brewster was upset, frightened, and a very worried man, of that Max felt certain. "Even though you had good reason to be unhappy with Glen Jamison, I'm sure you want his murderer found."

Kirk jerked around. "I don't know anything about his murder."

"How angry were you when he fired you?"

Kirk's face twisted in a scowl. "You ever been told to take your stuff and hit the road? Yeah. When I got fired, I got mad. Why shouldn't I?" He was defiant. "Glen was a patsy for that overbearing bitch he married. I hated her more than him. But I never thought about shooting him. Or anybody else. Not even her."

"Were you here Tuesday morning between a quarter to nine and ten-fifteen?"

"Talk about hitting the road, it's your turn. You aren't a cop. Get out." He turned and moved back to the window. His rigid stance shouted anxiety.

Max left him standing at the window in the office with its bare walls and half-filled boxes. He walked down the hallway. What was Kirk looking for or waiting for? Whatever the lawyer imagined or feared, he was waiting for something to happen.

Max opened the outside door. The pretty young receptionist's cheerful admonition to have a good day added a surreal element. She was untroubled, in sharp contrast to Edna Graham's mournful face and Kirk Brewster's apprehension.

Max was halfway down the front steps when a police cruiser pulled to the curb.

Max reached the sidewalk and waited.

Billy Cameron and Officer Benson moved swiftly. Billy looked big, capable, and serious. Coley Benson's eyes gleamed with excitement, but he was clearly making an effort to appear matter-of-fact.

Billy stopped at the foot of the steps, his big, square face grim. He jerked a thumb toward the front door of the well-kept brick building. "Did Annie sic you on Kirk Brewster?"

Max understood now. Kirk Brewster was waiting for the police. Max held up his right hand as if taking an oath. "Not guilty." That was true. He'd come to the law office to check with Edna Graham. "I haven't talked to Annie about Kirk." Billy didn't need to know the gist of his conversation with Annie and the next task on Max's list. "Why?"

Irritation flickered in Billy's blue eyes. "I got a call from her. She'd talked to Cleo Jamison. She's probably quizzing the rest of the family now. Whatever. I've already interviewed them. She can't do any harm. But now I find you here and I haven't talked to Kirk Brewster. So far as I know"—his voice was sharp—"nobody's asked either one of you to interfere in a criminal investigation."

Max dropped his hand. "Definitely we don't intend to interfere. We're just talking to people informally. Speaking of"—he tried a winning smile—"you might want to ask Glen's secretary about Richard Jamison's visit here with Glen last week. And, yeah, since I was here, I went down the hall and tried to talk to Kirk Brewster. He wasn't up for a chat. I'd say he's a worried man."

Billy's expression was grim. "Did you ask him anything substantive?"

Max knew Billy wasn't fooling around. It was time for him to be precise. "I asked Kirk if he was mad when Glen fired him and I asked him where he was Tuesday morning. I got a yes on the first, no answer on the second."

Billy looked relieved. "That's all right. And"—he cleared his throat—"we appreciate the efforts of good citizens. But"—he started up the steps, paused beside Max—"don't screw up any evidence."

Annie pushed through the swinging door to the kitchen. A tall, slender woman with a kerchief over graying hair worked at the sink, up to her elbows in suds. Tommy Jamison stood on a kitchen ladder, reaching for china plates high on a shelf. Freshly washed plates glistened in a plastic drainer on the counter to the left of the sink.

Cleo said Tommy had stormed out of the house earlier, barefoot and shirtless. He was still barefoot, but he wore a baggy, wrinkled green polo as well as brown cotton Bermuda shorts.

Kit Jamison was on the telephone. " . . . appreciate your call. We will welcome everyone here after the memorial service. Yes, it will be Monday. Dad would have been pleased to know you can come." She hung up the landline. Her ascetic face drooped in sadness. She brushed back a thin strand of blond hair and pressed trembling lips tightly together.

Tommy thudded to the floor, holding a stack of saucers. He carried them to the sink, giving Annie a sharp glare in passing.

The woman murmured, "Thanks, Tommy." She lifted a yellow-rubber-gloved hand to slip the stack into her dishpan.

Annie looked toward Kit, then up at Tommy. "I need to talk to you both. Will you step out on the porch with me?"

Kit hesitated, then shrugged. "Come on, Tommy."

The brawny teenager followed his sister onto the porch, leaned against a pillar, big, muscular, and sullen. Kit folded bony arms and faced Annie, her face questioning. Her gaze was cold. "What do you want?"

"I want to help Elaine."

Kit gave an angry half laugh. "I'd say you're a little late. You didn't do her any favors Tuesday morning."

"I happened to be in the backyard Tuesday morning about ten. Your dad was shot at some time between eight forty-five and ten-fifteen." Annie's voice was sharp. "I had to tell the police what I saw."

"Why were you spying on Elaine?" Kit's narrow face jutted in disapproval.

"Yeah." Tommy took a step nearer. His face was heavier, but equally hostile.

Annie watched the brother and sister carefully as she told her story of Pat Merridew, the photograph in the BlackBerry, and the crystal mug with no fingerprints.

"Wow." Tommy, for the moment, looked neither sullen nor angry. He shoved back a thick tangle of blond curls, stared at Annie. "Hey, that's weird. Who'd put Dad's gun in the gazebo? If it was his gun."

Kit, too, appeared astonished. A sudden eagerness lit her face. "That means somebody from outside shot Dad."

Tommy swung toward his sister. "Well, duh. Did you think one of us did it?"

"Tommy, don't be a fool." Kit glared at him.

"Anyway, that's why I was here Tuesday morning." Before Kit could frown again, Annie rushed ahead. "Elaine wasn't on the island the night Pat took that picture. I told the police that, too." Of course, Billy had an easy answer for why Elaine's absence that night meant nothing. "But Elaine still won't describe what she did Tuesday morning. Please try to persuade her to talk to the police. Otherwise, I'm afraid they'll arrest her."

"Arrest Elaine?" Tommy looked shocked. His big hands hung loose at his sides. "That's crazy."

"I agree. But she won't tell the police how she got the gun, if she did. If not, what did she throw in the marsh and why won't she tell them? And where did she go? Please persuade her to cooperate. Or she may go to jail."

"Oh God." Tommy turned and thudded down the steps and hit the uneven ground, running fast down the central path.

Kit looked out into the garden at the glimpse of cottage beyond a sweep of azaleas. "Elaine said for us not to come down. But maybe she needs to know what's going on. I'll talk to her, too. I don't care what the police think, Elaine would never, never hurt anyone." She frowned with a swift, bitter intensity. "Look, on the road that runs by the cottage. There's another car. People are awful. Driving by, coming up Elaine's road like we were animals in a zoo. They're the animals."

Annie recognized Max's dark green Jeep. It made a U-turn and was soon out of sight, dust rising behind the back bumper. He wasn't a curiosity seeker. Max was setting out on the search she had asked him to make. "Kit, I'm sure there are things the police don't know." She spoke calmly, hoping to encourage Kit. "Can you tell me about Tuesday morning? Did you see your father at breakfast?"

Kit's thin shoulders hunched. "Just for a minute. I wasn't very hungry. I ate a bowl of cornflakes."

"Was he just as usual?"

Her mouth twisted. "I guess so. This summer he acted like we were all strangers. He never wanted to talk about things. She had him jumping through hoops. She didn't want Dad to have anything to do with us."

Annie had no doubt that she was referring to Cleo. "I understand he was worried about money."

"Because of her." Kit's voice bristled with anger. "She resented us. Dad always encouraged us. Or he used to. Tuesday morning, I tried to talk to him again about my trip. I came downstairs and he was sitting at his desk and he looked really tired. But I was running out of time. I have to get my tickets by next week. He told me he wasn't in a position to help. I told him—" She broke off, choked back a sob. "I told him I hated him and now he's dead."

Annie spoke gently. "That doesn't matter now. People who have died understand who loved them. What's important is that you did love him."

"I went up to my room and I was pacing back and forth."

"Did you have your door open?"

Kit nodded. "And the windows."

"Did you hear any noise?"

"That leaf blower. It was driving me crazy. I shut the windows because the leaf blower made so much noise. I was trying to work on my laptop."

"When you shut the windows, did you see anyone in the garden?"

"No."

"What other rooms overlook the garden?"

"Our rooms are right in a row, Tommy, Laura, and me."

"Had your father quarreled with anyone recently?"

Her narrow face was instantly wary. Was she thinking of her older sister or perhaps her brother or even Pat Merridew? She spoke in careful, measured words. "Nothing big. That I knew about." Suddenly her gaze narrowed. She stared out into the garden.

Annie looked, too. Richard Jamison came around the stand of cane. He walked with his head down, hands in the pockets of khaki shorts. His dark brown hair was cut short. He walked like a man deep in thought, head bent, steps slow.

Kit's voice shook. "I told the police about him." She pointed toward Richard, her face accusatory. "That big officer, the captain, he listened like it didn't amount to anything. But I know it was wrong. I saw him looking at her just a few days ago. He wanted her. She looked at him and it was like I was in a bedroom with them. Then she turned away. But I know what I saw. That evening after dinner, he went out on the terrace. I went after him. I asked him if Dad knew he had the hots for Cleo. He laughed and said he always admired good-looking chicks but he didn't make it a practice to seduce married women. He started to move away and I said it looked like she was hot for him, too. He stopped and shook his head, said that wasn't true. He said I didn't need to worry, he was going to leave next week."

Richard reached the path to the house. He looked up, saw Kit and Annie, came to a stop.

Kit drew in a sharp breath. "I thought he was wonderful. He's been everywhere around the world, the kind of life I'd like to have. Dad called him 'little buddy.' Dad said Richard had always been his favorite cousin. How could he care about her?" The harsh pronoun exuded venom. "She's awful. She always has been."

Kit whirled away, slammed into the house.

Annie walked down the steps toward Richard.

Max pulled up to a four-way stop sign. A larger road intersected the dirt road that led to Elaine's cottage. A gray shanty, lopsided from storms and years of weathering, was on his right. Sitting on the sloping porch, resting in a red rocker, was a tiny little woman in a voluminous purplish dress. To his left, a neat and tidy oyster-shell parking lot welcomed shoppers to a two-pump gas station and small cinder-block convenience store.

Max pulled up to a pump. On the mainland, payment was required in advance. On the island, you could pump first and pay later. He removed the gas cap, filled up with regular.

A bell jangled as he opened the door. At the counter, he looked out through the plate-glass window as he handed a twenty to a middle-aged woman with a thin mouth. "Guess you can see everyone coming and going."

She glanced outside without interest. "Yeah. If I cared." Her tone indicated she found little of interest in her view, in her job, and likely in her life. She handed him a dollar and seventeen cents in change.

"Were you working Tuesday morning?"

Her gaze sharpened. "Why do you care?"

"Just a bet with a friend." His tone was easy. "A yellow Corolla came past about ten o'clock. I think it turned right, but my friend's sure the car turned left. Do you happen to remember?"

She picked up a pack of spearmint gum, ripped the top, pulled out a stick. "I didn't pay no never mind."

Outside, Max glanced across the road at the small frame house. In a moment, he turned the car into a rutted driveway. He swung out of the Jeep and walked toward the porch.

The old woman looked up from the Bible in her lap. Raisin-dark eyes in a wrinkled brown face studied him. " 'Good people bring good things out of their hearts, but evil people bring evil things out of their hearts.' " Her voice was as deep and calm as water in a sheltered lagoon.

Max knew Scripture when he heard it. "Yes, ma'am."

She tilted her head to one side, those bright eyes never leaving his face. "Are you in search of truth?"

"Yes, ma'am. I'm trying to help a woman who has been unjustly accused." In Max's view, designation as a person of interest qualified Elaine Jamison as falsely accused.

The deep voice intoned: " 'But let justice roll down like waters and righteousness like an ever-flowing stream.' "

Max smiled. "Justice might get a big boost if you were rocking on your porch Tuesday morning."

"Sit, boy."

He didn't take umbrage at the designation. He would guess she was ninety, perhaps older. He settled on the rocker beside her. "I'm Max Darling."

"Lula Harmon." She rocked and the runners squeaked on the wood flooring. "I been sitting here most days. My boy don't let me work anymore. He says, 'Mama, you rest and read your Bible, that's the best work you can do for me and for God.' So if I can serve the Lord from my rocking chair, I will. 'Learn to do good: seek justice, reprove the ruthless; defend the orphan, plead for the widow.'"

A bumblebee, striking in its black-and-yellow stripes, hovered near honeysuckle on a trellis at the end of the porch. The summer afternoon murmured with the chirp of birds, the hum of insects, the rustle of live-oak leaves. Max looked into intelligent eyes, bright and sharp, despite age. He had a sense of wonder. Had Lula been sitting on this porch on this sunny day waiting for his question? He shook away the thought as fanciful, yet he could not keep the eager hope from his voice. "On Tuesday morning about ten o'clock a yellow car came this way and stopped at the intersection. Which way did that car turn?"

Annie contrasted Richard Jamison's vigor with her memory of his older, thinner cousin. But Richard's hair was brown and his skin tanned. He looked ruddy, outdoorsy, masculine, and attractive. Light green eyes looked at her curiously. "Hello."

He listened politely as she spoke, then shook his head. "I see no reason why I should talk about Tuesday morning with you."

Annie felt a flicker of anger. "Don't you care what happens to Elaine?"

His eyes narrowed. "If Elaine needs help, she can hire a lawyer. And now I've got things to do."

As he started to brush past her, Annie said sharply, "Cleo's a widow now. Are you still leaving the island?"

He stared at her, his eyes glinting with anger. "I guess Kit's been spinning stories. I don't owe you any explanation. But if it makes you feel better, lady, I never for a minute forgot that Cleo was Glen's wife." The muscles in his jaw bunched. "Believe it or not, I cared about Glen. I don't know who shot him. Or why. I hope the cops figure it out. Fast."

At the stop sign, Max turned left. A right turn led eventually to the island's small downtown and the ferry landing. Side roads offered other possible routes. But turning left, the road—Sea Oats Lane—plunged into untamed brush. Foliage crowded to the very edge of the dirt road. Trees and ferns encroached on the sandy soil. Branches interlocked as the lane narrowed. He drove the Jeep deeper and deeper into a dim and shadowy tunnel of greenery. The lane ended in a turnaround. Faded red letters on a worn wooden sign announced: KITTREDGE FOREST PRESERVE.

A quick thought made Max jam the brakes. He stopped about five yards from the widened area that was mostly clear except for broken palmetto fronds and a portion of a broken live oak split by lightning.

He turned off the motor. A faint path near the side curved into woods and was lost from sight. Ferns, vines, and creepers flourished. In an instant, no-see-'ums swirled through the open window. Birds chittered and insects hummed, a symphony of summer sound. Max stared at the trail. This was the Lowcountry unhomogenized, unfiltered, as raw and wild as it had been when hardy rice growers cleared the land. Death was common then, from fevers, malaria, smallpox.

Max opened the door, studied the ground before he stepped onto a broken palmetto frond. He waved at the cloud of insects. There was nothing he could do about the wheel marks of his Jeep, which likely had obliterated previous tracks. But he had stopped well short of the turnaround. It would take a careful piece of maneuvering to turn the Jeep for his return, but he would manage somehow. He was determined to leave the turnaround as he had found it.

He gazed slowly, carefully, back and forth across the semicircular patch of ground. He spotted tire tracks, fresh and deep in the sandy soil. He would have bet a bundle that the tracks matched the tires on Elaine Jamison's Corolla.

He lifted his eyes to the narrow entry to the woods. Whatever Elaine had done when she reached journey's end here on Tuesday morning, she had not come this way to commune with nature. She had been visibly distraught when she had hurried out of her cottage. Apparently, she had thrown something into the marsh, turned away clutching a blue cloth. Then she'd driven away. Mrs. Harmon had seen her car turn onto the nature preserve road at shortly after ten, so this must have been her destination.

Max stared at the inhospitable woods, thick and dark and deep, home to rattlesnakes and water moccasins, wild boars, cougars, and alligators. The preserve encompassed acres of wild country.

Billy Cameron suspected that Elaine had thrown the murder weapon into the marsh. Annie saw Elaine lowering her arm. In her other hand, she held a cloth. She'd turned away from the marsh, carrying the cloth, and in only moments, her car had come careening from behind the cottage. She had driven here. If her objective had been to discard the cloth, she'd chosen a wild area where hundreds of searchers could look and look again and never find anything hidden beneath a log or thrust into a hollow of a tree or shoved deep into a thick tangle of underbrush.

Elaine's actions might further convince Billy of her guilt. But Max had discovered too much to stop now.

Swatting at the insects, evading a buzzing yellow jacket, he climbed into the Jeep, shut the windows to avoid the assault of the insects, and turned on the motor. In the stifling air, sweat slid down his face. As he punched his cell, the air-conditioning began to cool the car's interior. "Hey, Billy, I may have found something of interest to you. You remember how Annie saw Elaine Jamison leave in her car on Tuesday morning? I followed the same road. At the first four-way stop, I asked a few questions. I think I've found where she went."

Ten

Annie stood on the boardwalk at Blackbeard Beach. The tide was out. Sunbathers stretched on towels. Sun-reclusive vacationers lounged in blue canvas chairs beneath red umbrellas. Joggers clipped along hard-packed gray sand exposed by the outgoing tide. Surfers paddled out to catch the first wave. Dolphins flashed in the sun, silver gray and lovely. Annie spotted tendrils of dark hair poking from beneath a battered straw hat at the third lifeguard stand.

She skirted two brawny teenagers tossing a football. She came around the back of the stand. "Laura."

The straw hat tilted as Laura looked down. Sunglasses masked her eyes. Her face appeared rigid, cheekbones jutting, lips unsmiling. There was a suggestion of banked anger and possibly fear. "Yes?"

"I'm Annie Darling. I—"

"You were at the house Tuesday. You made the police suspicious of Elaine. And today"—her tone was accusatory—"you came to see Cleo."

Annie felt a ripple of anger, but she kept her voice pleasant. "I'm trying to help Elaine."

Laura's mouth curved down in disdain. "You sure helped her Tuesday. The cops are still mucking around in the marsh." She lifted her head, looked out beyond the surf.

"Do you want the person who killed your father arrested?"

The dark lenses jerked back toward Annie. "Of course I do. It's horrible. I can't believe something like this could happen. It doesn't make any sense. Why would anyone kill Dad?"

"For money?" Annie's voice rose in a question. She wished she could see Laura's eyes.

Laura's mouth twisted in disgust. "Has Cleo been filling you up with lies? She hates us. She always has. She probably told you that Kit needs money to go to Africa and Tommy didn't want to go away to school and I'm broke and a parasite. She's the one who wants money. She's greedy."

"She was in Savannah when your father was shot."

"I don't care. She's still greedy." She spoke harshly.

"Maybe so." Annie dropped the words like pebbles in a pond, knowing ripples would spread. "But she doesn't inherit any of his estate. However, you and your sister and brother will be able to do what you want to do. And Kirk Brewster will be a very rich man."

The lifeguard's thin shoulders tightened. She gripped the arms of the high wooden seat. "Kirk? He won't be a partner much longer. There's no money for him."

"The firm paid for a key man life-insurance policy on your father. The proceeds—five million dollars—will go to the surviving partners, Cleo Jamison and Kirk Brewster." Annie paused. "Did you know about the policy?"

"No." She scarcely breathed the answer.

"When did you last see Kirk?"

"Not since Cleo talked Dad into firing him. I know it's her fault. Dad told me he had to let Kirk go because the firm isn't making enough money. I called Kirk but he said he wouldn't come to the house, that he'll call me when he's found a job. I haven't heard from him." Laura's lips quivered. "Kirk didn't hurt Dad. I know he didn't." Her words were jerky and she struggled for breath.

Annie shaded her eyes, stared upward. "Where were you Tuesday morning?"

She hesitated. Finally, she said slowly, "I always sit on the upper verandah in the mornings."

Annie had a clear sense that she would never have admitted her presence there, but feared someone else in the family would know the pattern of her mornings.

Laura swallowed. "My shift here doesn't start until one o'clock. Cleo thinks I'm lazy. She never sits around. She was too busy figuring out ways to spend money Dad didn't have." She radiated resentment. "I was out there from right after breakfast until Richard knocked on my door. I wasn't"—she spoke with heavy sarcasm—"shooting my father."

"Did you see anyone in the backyard?" The upper verandah overlooked the garden and the cottage, though shrubbery and trees would have blocked a complete view. Nonetheless, anyone approaching the terrace would have been visible at some point.

There was sudden stillness in Laura's posture. She swallowed, then said quickly, "Of course not. No one but the yardman." But there was a telltale quiver of her dark red lips.

Annie looked up at unrevealing dark lenses. Laura had answered quickly, forcefully. Annie felt sure she was lying.

"Thank you." Annie took a step away, looked back. "If Elaine's arrested, perhaps your memory might improve."

"I didn't see anyone." Laura was emphatic.

Annie walked across the sand. At the boardwalk, she looked back.

Laura huddled in the broad wooden chair. Even from this distance, Annie could see how tightly her hands gripped the arms of the lifeguard seat. Did she stare out to sea, watching for swimmers in trouble or was she picturing a summer-drowsy garden on the morning her father died?

Dark eyes intent, the black-and-tan bloodhound sniffed at the gauze pad. Lou Pirelli waited patiently. He knelt near the dog, holding the pad in a plastic-gloved hand. "Should be a good smell of the Jamison dame. Swabbed the seat of her car. Had her permission. Have to say she doesn't have a clue what we're up to. That picked up enough scent for Durante to find which way she went—if she went this way."

"Durante?" Max looked at the floppy-eared, long-nosed dog.

Lou grinned. "My grandma has all of Jimmy Durante's old radio programs." He whistled a bar from "Inka Dinka Doo." "Nobody has a better schnoz than this dog."

The dog lifted his head, gazed at Lou as he stood.

The officer paused. "The chief said you can come along, but stay behind me and don't touch anything. If we find anything, I got to make sure the evidence isn't contaminated."

Lou spoke firmly. "Track."

The dense-furred dog swung his head, long ears dangling, and headed for the opening in the woods. Lou picked up a backpack from the ground, shrugged into it, and followed.

Max stayed a few feet behind in the dim tunnel.

The dog broke into a lope.

"Steady," Lou called.

The bloodhound slowed enough for the sweating men to keep up and jolted to a stop when Lou's foot caught in a vine and he flailed into the brush. When Lou was back on his feet, wincing from thorn scratches on his right arm, he heaved a long-suffering sigh. "I thought wading around in the marsh was bad enough. I couldn't wait to hand those waders to Hyla. This is worse." His glance back at Max was dour. "Thanks, old buddy. Nothing I'd rather do"— he swatted ineffectually at swirls of insects—"than go head to head with mosquitoes big enough to play in the line."

Durante pulled on the leash, snuffling, making low sounds in his throat.

As the dog set out again, the trail grew less distinct. Vines and tendrils hung from tree limbs, wavered in the dusky gloom. Masses of insects swirled until the air looked speckled. The men walked another quarter mile, then the dog swerved from the path into an area of trampled ferns.

Lou was quick. "Heel."

The dog stopped, planted his big paws, waited.

"End of the line," Lou announced. "She came this far, went off the path here." He studied the crushed grasses. "Looks like she went about five feet." He peered at the thicket.

Max's tone was thoughtful. "If we've guessed right, she came all this way to get rid of a cloth. For some reason, maybe she was afraid it wouldn't sink, she didn't throw the cloth into the marsh. Instead, she came here and went off the path . . ." Max scanned the tangle of shrubbery and ferns and palmettos.

Lou nodded. "Let's see if Durante can get us a little closer." He gestured off the path. "Track, boy."

The dog padded two feet off the path, stopped.

"She wouldn't take a chance on throwing it. It might snag on a limb." Lou stepped carefully. He pulled some canvas gloves from a pocket. He knelt beside Durante and began to pull aside leaves and ferns. He worked slowly, methodically. "Oh, hey." His voice rippled with excitement. "Max, unzip the top of my backpack, get out the Nikon. I'll hold the stalks apart and you can get some shots."

Max found the digital camera, leaned over Lou's shoulder.

Lou's voice was crisp. "That brown smear looks like blood."

In the beach parking lot, Annie paused in the shade of a magnolia. She touched a creamy-white blossom for luck and enjoyed the sweet scent. She almost turned to go back to the beach, then shook her head. Laura Jamison had no intention of revealing who or what she had seen from the upper verandah the morning of her father's murder. Annie had a quick memory of Tuesday morning, the whine of the leaf blower, the distress so evident in Elaine Jamison's face as she hurried out of the cottage.

Did Laura see Elaine walking toward the house during the critical time period when Glen was shot? Or did Laura see Kirk? Did she hear the shots? Two shots had been fired. No one admitted hearing them. It seemed likely the gun had been fired when the young yardman was at work, blowing needles out of the flower beds.

The yardman . . . Laura had not been the only person with a clear view of the Jamison backyard. Annie hesitated, then punched a number.

"Hey, Marian."

"You got something?" The reporter's husky voice quivered with eagerness.

Annie pictured Marian grabbing a notebook and pen, balancing the phone between cheek and shoulder. Marian rarely quidded without a pro quo. "You didn't hear it from me, but Glen's law firm had taken out key man insurance. The beneficiaries: Cleo Jamison and Kirk Brewster. We know where Cleo was Tuesday morning. It might be interesting to know where Brewster was." If Kirk Brewster had nothing to fear, Marian's inquiries wouldn't cause harm and might, in fact, be helpful to him.

"Oooooh."

Annie doubted an alligator sighting a succulent blue-winged teal would have sounded any happier.

"Got it. Tha—"

Before Marian could disconnect, Annie said swiftly, "In return. What's the name of the yardman at the Jamisons'?" She had no doubt Marian had a concise list of everyone in the vicinity of the crime Tuesday morning.

Marian didn't hesitate. "Darwyn Jack. He's quite the boy. Fights off the dames. But not very hard. I've seen him at Beau's Bodacious."

Annie raised an eyebrow. The beer joint was fairly new on the island, where nightspots had a tendency to open, flourish, fail. Some neighbors complained of noise beyond the three A.M. closing time.

Marian's laughter was hearty. "Sometimes I'm like that old Garth Brooks song 'Friends in Low Places.' I like to sling back a cold one and the barflies at Beau's keep me up-to-date on island gossip that may come in handy. Some of us go after work on Fridays. I've seen Darwyn there."

"Do you have a phone number?"

"Not personally." She sounded amused. "He bunks with his grandmother Bella Mae Jack. Good woman. Hold on, I'll look up her number. I think they live on Killdeer Lane. Here you go."

Annie scratched the number on the back of an envelope from her purse.

"So why the interest in the handsome Darwyn?"

"He was in the backyard. I want to know if he saw anyone."

"Other than Elaine? I talked to him and that's all I got. He got there about eight that morning, said he didn't pay much attention to people going in and out, why should he?"

Annie wasn't surprised. Disappointed, but not surprised. Still, she wanted to talk to him. Had he noticed Laura on the porch, or, perhaps, not on the porch?

"Thanks, Marian."

"Give me a yodel if you find out anything." The connection ended.

Annie pulled her cell phone from her pocket. She dialed Bella Mae Jack's number.

"Is Darwyn there?"

"Darwyn's at work. He'll be home about five-thirty."

"This is Annie Darling. We need help with some tree trimming. I was hoping to get it done fairly soon. Can you tell me where he's working this afternoon? I'll drop by and talk to him." And not about trees.

Annie scratched an address on the envelope. She knew the area, a fairly new development of turreted and gabled homes in the gated plantation. She drove from the public beach and turned left on Sand Dollar Lane. The guard at the entry gate waved her through. He didn't need to see her decal. She came through every day from the north end of the island and their old refurbished antebellum home en route to the marina and Death on Demand.

She turned on Laughing Gull Road, turned again on Mockingbird Lane, and pulled up in front of a two-story Tudor with an actual sweep of lawn that must have cost a fortune to create in the sandy ground. Grass flared from beneath a riding mower. The shirt-less driver's back glistened with sweat. His thick hair glowed tawny in the sunlight.

Annie parked and walked to the drive, awaiting the mower's approach. She lifted a hand, gestured.

The mower reached the end of the row and came to a stop. He turned off the motor and swung lightly to the ground. He made no move toward her, standing with his hands loose at his sides.

Annie hurried toward him. Marian said Darwyn had arrived to work around eight A.M. He would have been visible to Laura on the upper verandah. Had he looked up, noticed her? Perhaps Laura's uneasiness had another source. Had she been on the verandah as she claimed?

The skin of his face was smooth and perfect. He watched her approach with appraising brown eyes. His full lips curved in an impudent half smile.

Annie stopped a foot or so away. "I'm Annie Darling, a friend of Elaine Jamison's. You were working there Tuesday when I came by."

He wiped sweat from his face. "I remember. The day the old guy got killed."

Annie had a quick memory of thick-lipped Marlon Brando in his debut movie, which was a favorite on the old-movie channel during Academy Awards week. The young man who watched her with sleepy eyes had the same unlined face and animal magnetism.

"I'm hoping you can help Miss Jamison."

Darwyn gave her a puzzled glance. "She got a problem?"

"The police have named her as a person of interest in her brother's death. That means—"

"Yeah. I know what that means." He was disdainful. "What's that got to do with me?" He didn't move physically, but it was as though he had stepped back. He was wary.

Annie gestured toward a rose garden. "You were working in the Jamison garden Tuesday morning."

He folded his arms. "Yeah. So?" His tone was combative.

Annie felt the moment was moving from inquiry to confrontation. She made her tone admiring. "You can be very important."

"Look, like I told the cops, I was working. I wasn't looking out for people. I saw the yellow car go like a bat out of hell. It went tearing down the drive, kind of like X Sports. Man, I thought she was going to flip over when she went around the curve."

"Did you see her throw something in the marsh?"

For a minute he looked puzzled. "You mean before the car roared out? No. I guess I was in the pines. Anyway, I saw you and then the car."

"How about Laura Jamison? Did you see her?"

"In the garden? Not that I noticed." He looked bored. "She was up on the verandah. Sitting there cool as you please while I sweated. But that's how it always is."

"How long was she there?"

He folded his arms, gave her a look of disgust. "I was working. I was in and around the pines and up and down the garden. I don't have time to watch people who don't do anything. And"—his sacrasm was heavy—"speaking of work"—his glance was dismissive—"I got to get back to mowing."

"Darwyn, wait, tell me about the leaf blower." More than likely, he would not have been likely to notice much while handling the bulky loud machine.

"The leaf blower." Something moved in his dark eyes. "What's such a big deal about the blower?" His voice was soft, his gaze intent.

"What time were you using it?"

He looked blank.

She took a step nearer. "I'm trying to get a picture of where you were in the garden. When did you use the blower?"

"Oh. I get you. I probably had my back to the house when I was blowing leaves. I started about nine-fifteen, finished up a little after ten."

Annie looked into his brown eyes that held a glint of disdain. "Have you told the police about the leaf blower?"

His expression was cool. "Lady, they know I was using a blower."

"Did you tell them the time?"

"I guess."

Annie felt a flicker of irritation. Darwyn obviously didn't care what the police knew, if anything.

"Did you work near the house?"

He gave her a hard stare. "You asking if I looked that way?" He thought about the question. Finally, his full lips parted in a slight smile, a very slight smile. "Maybe."

Annie felt an intimation of danger. She spoke sharply. "If you saw anything that could help the police, it's your duty to tell them."

Now his amusement was clear. "I don't like cops. Let them figure out stuff. If I saw something, it would be bad news for somebody, wouldn't it?"

"Darwyn—"

He cut her off with a laugh. "No problem. Like I told the cops, I didn't see anybody." He turned away and walked to the mower, swung up into the seat, and the motor roared.

Billy Cameron ignored swirling insects, including a yellow jacket that hung between him and the small area of crushed grasses. "Don't let the cloth get snagged on a bramble."

Billy's wife, Mavis, was a crime-scene tech as well as a police-station dispatcher. She knelt on a piece of cardboard. The bloodhound lay on the path a few feet behind her, big head resting on his paws, dark eyes watchful.

Max and Lou stood a few feet to the other side of Billy. Max held back a frond of a palmetto shrub for a better view.

In repose, Mavis often appeared remote and wary. Despite her happiness after she met Billy, she carried the baggage of an earlier marriage to an abusive husband. Her face always lighted when she looked at Billy and her gentle mouth eased into a soft smile. Now she was intent, focused on her job, well aware that evidence must be gathered properly. Each gloved hand held a handle as she nudged the flat-jawed pincers gently between bent stalks of underbrush and clamped the tool head to a piece of blue cloth. She tugged slowly, steadily. Suddenly she stopped. "I'm afraid the cloth is caught on something."

Lou turned toward a cane thicket. Using strength honed by years of baseball and weight lifting, he snapped off a five-foot piece of cane. "Here, Chief."

Billy grabbed the cane and poked behind the cloth. "There's a patch of stickers." He tossed the cane back to Lou, pulled some plastic gloves from a pocket, and knelt beside Mavis. He reached carefully below the wad of cloth and tugged. The cloth quivered. "Try now."

Mavis pulled. As she stood, the wadded-up cloth fell free.

Billy joined her in the middle of the path. He studied her trophy and gave a satisfied smile. He used his camcorder. "Man's blue polo shirt found hidden"—he glanced at his watch—"on Thursday, June twenty-fourth, at—" He glanced at Lou.

"Three twenty-seven P.M."

"—three twenty-seven P.M. by search dog Durante and handler Officer Lou Pirelli a quarter mile into the Kittredge Forest Preserve, approximately three feet to the east of the path." Billy turned back the collar. "Tommy Hilfiger. Men's size large. Sky-blue color. The shirt had been rolled into a ball and secreted among a cane stand. On the front of the shirt is a reddish smear approximately six inches in length. The heavier concentration is on the upper end of the smear. The brownish stain may be blood. Laboratory tests will be run. The shirt was taken into evidence at"—he glanced at his watch—"four-seventeen P.M. by Crime Tech Mavis Cameron." He clicked off the camcorder.

Annie poked her head into Max's office, Confidential Commissions.

Barb beamed. "How about a slice of banana cream pie?" Max's ebullient secretary's hair, piled in its usual beehive, looked closer to strawberry than blond this afternoon. Barb said a woman's hair was her own to fashion and always made a statement. Gold, she was a diva; red, she was a siren; strawberry, and she was betwixt and between.

Annie was tempted, but she'd left Ingrid on her own at Death on Demand for far too long. "Have you heard from Max?"

"He texted a while ago. He's following a dog and probably won't be back in the office this afternoon. He told me to close up shop when the pie came out. I just took it out of the oven. Hey, let me cut you a piece to take with you."

Annie walked next door to Death on Demand. Dog? Whatever. Max was obviously caught up in something interesting. She'd give him a ring after she checked on the store. She smiled as she stepped inside. Actually she carried two pieces of pie, each in a Styrofoam container. Barb was always prepared. One container held a slice for Ingrid.

Ingrid was dealing with a long line at the front counter. Annie quickly slid in beside her. She tucked the small boxes and her purse onto a shelf, smiled brightly at a young woman whose nose rivaled Rudolph's. "May I help you?"

The customer pushed forward a stack of paperbacks, three by Laura Childs, two by Elizabeth George, and four by Harlan Coben.

Annie eyed her with interest. She either had wide-ranging tastes or was a work in progress.

Ingrid slid five hardcovers into a bag for her customer.

Annie automatically noted the titles: *Shutter Island* by Dennis Lehane, *Dead in the Family* by Charlaine Harris, *Look Again* by Lisa Scottoline, *In Big Trouble* by Laura Lippman, *The Chocolate Cupid Killings* by JoAnna Carl.

Ingrid turned a thumb toward the back of the store, murmured, "Elaine Jamison's waiting for you at the coffee bar. She's upset. Uh-oh, here she comes."

Annie glanced down the central aisle.

Elaine Jamison's narrow, aristocratic face was strained. She was moving fast, coming toward the cash desk like a woman in a very big hurry. She stared at Annie, her eyes hard and cold.

Uh-oh, indeed.

"I have to talk to you." Elaine's voice was thin.

Annie made a gesture toward the long line. "I'll be with you in a minute."

Elaine came even with the main counter. "I'll wait outside." She slammed out the front door.

Annie dreaded talking with her. She was grateful for the customers and a moment's reprieve. As always, she noted the authors as she rang up the titles: Ed Gorman,

Parnell Hall, Bill Crider, Robert Crais, then a spate of women authors—Donna Andrews, Rhys Bowen, Julie Hyzy, Laura Joh Rowland, Joanne Fluke, Lisa See. The last of her customers plopped a dozen M. C. Beaton titles on the counter. "I can't get enough of Agatha Raisin."

Annie managed a smile. "You're in good company. She's one of our bestselling authors."

As the front door sighed shut behind the Agatha Raisin fan, Annie bent to retrieve the Styrofoam containers. She handed them to Ingrid. "Barb's banana cream pie. One for you and please put mine in the fridge."

Annie stepped out into late-afternoon warmth, but she felt as cold as a calving iceberg when she stopped beside Elaine. They stood at the railing by the marina. A horn sounded as an excursion boat neared its slip.

Elaine's eyes were red-rimmed, her face pale. She looked wan and insubstantial in a pale blue linen dress and latticed white leather sandals. "You talked to everyone in the family. You had no right to do that. They think you're helping me. I don't want your help." Her voice shook. "You mean well, but you are making things harder for me." She broke off, clasped her hands tightly. "Nothing you can do will make a difference." Her voice was scarcely audible. She sounded like a woman nearing the limit of her endurance. "Leave me alone, leave the family alone."

"Elaine." Annie spoke loudly, hoping to break through Elaine's shell of fear. "You need to help yourself. You can't go on ignoring the police."

"I don't have anything to say to them. I've told you and told you."

"They're going to arrest you." Annie stared into anguished eyes. "I don't think you shot him, but that's what they believe."

"I didn't." It was a cry of heartbreak.

"Then help the police find the murderer. I discovered a great many facts today." Annie ticked them off, one by one. "Kirk Brewster is two and a half million dollars richer since your brother died this week while Kirk is still a partner." She described the key man insurance.

Elaine's eyes widened in shock.

"Kit insists Richard is interested in Cleo. Laura was on the back upper verandah Tuesday morning. She claims she didn't see anyone. I think she's lying."

Elaine stood frozen, staring at Annie.

"Maybe Laura saw Kirk Brewster. And that's not all. Darwyn Jack may have seen something in the garden, too. He was in the best position to have spotted someone near the French window to your brother's study. Darwyn said he told the police that he didn't see anyone, but he was taunting me with the idea that maybe he did see someone after all. The police can check out all of these things. Max is looking around, too. You need to tell the police what you know."

Elaine flung out a hand in despair. "You don't understand. It's too late. Stop hounding me. Leave me alone." She turned to go, looked back, her face twisted in misery. "Stay away from us." She ran then, her shoes slapping on the boardwalk.

Annie watched until Elaine disappeared around a pittosporum hedge. She had hoped the woman might listen to reason. That hope was gone. Her suggestion that Laura or Darwyn or perhaps both of them might have seen someone in the garden had clearly upset Elaine even more. Elaine had no intention of telling Billy what she knew and it was becoming ever clearer that she knew something, some fact that she was determined to hide.

Annie pressed her lips together. Elaine had made her choice. She didn't want Annie's help. But Annie knew she had discovered facts that Billy should have. The more he knew, the more likely that some piece of information ultimately would reveal the truth. She pulled her cell from her pocket and rang the police station. Instead of Mavis, Annie recognized Hyla

Harrison's cool, reserved voice. "Hyla, Annie Darling. May I speak with Billy?"

Hyla gave no indication she had any acquaintance with Annie.

Annie didn't take Hyla's formality as an affront. The police officer had very definite ideas about the proper behavior of a public servant.

"Chief Cameron is not available. May I connect you with his voice mail?"

Several clicks later, Annie spoke. "Billy, Annie." She made her report crisp and brief. "Tuesday morning Laura Jamison was sitting on the upper verandah. I think she saw someone in the garden, possibly Kirk Brewster. Darwyn Jack hinted that he saw someone, then backtracked, insisted he hadn't seen anyone. Kit Jamison's convinced Richard was hot for Cleo and vice versa. Richard denies it." Her face wrinkled. "He sounded sincere." She hoped this last didn't brand her as naive. Certainly anyone who committed murder would present themselves in the best possible light. "Anyway, maybe some of this will be helpful. You'll be glad to know I am returning to full-time bookselling. I'm sure Elaine Jamison is innocent, but she's made it absolutely clear she doesn't want any help."

Annie dropped the cell in her pocket. It was time to make good on her pledge to be a full-time bookseller. She shivered as she stepped back inside Death on Demand. The chill did not come from the air-conditioning, usually so welcome after the sun-drenched boardwalk. She carried with her Elaine's despair and unhappiness and unequivocal rejection.

Ingrid lifted a book from the romantic suspense shelves as she spoke to a middle-aged man with sandy hair. "That's tough that she stepped on a horseshoe crab. She'll feel better soon. Some Mary Stewart books will definitely please her. Here's one of my favorites, *Madam, Will You Talk?*"

Annie slipped past Ingrid and the kindly husband. The bookstore was fairly quiet as early evening approached. She would check her e-mails and go home. As ever, her heart gave a happy leap. Home meant Max. They would share what they'd discovered today, make sure Billy knew everything. Maybe they'd helped. Maybe not. In any event, Elaine's opposition seemed insurmountable. They had done all they could—or should—do.

Annie was almost to her office when she glimpsed a Cat Truth poster: a cinnamon-apricot Oriental Shorthair, a striking Siamese with no pointing, green eyes huge in a big-eared triangular face, back arched in a crouch, poised to spring, mouth agape in a hiss: *I'm warning you, back off.*

Annie cut generous wedges of key lime pie. She carried dessert plates to the kitchen table.

Dorothy L, their fluffy white cat who adored Max, lay on the counter by the phone, watching them with hope in her green eyes.

Annie put down the plates, reached out to stroke the cat.

Max lifted the silver carafe. "More coffee?"

"Lots more." She slid into her place. "And"—her tone was considering—"I think I'll add some cinnamon and cream and a dash of chocolate syrup." She popped up and retrieved a jar of clotted cream and the Hershey's syrup from the refrigerator.

Max evinced shock. "Are you really going to pair the best pie a man can make with coffee that would stagger a horse-size sweet tooth? You definitely have eclectic taste."

She bent as she passed to kiss the back of his neck, then settled at the table with a smile. "What a nice way to say you deplore my dessert creativity." She plopped a tablespoon of the yellowish cream into her coffee cup, added a spurt of syrup, looked thoughtfully at the cup, repeated the procedures. She stirred, sipped. "Heavenly."

Max looked at her for a moment, murmured, "Be right back." He returned from the living room carrying a Cat Truth poster. A curly-whiskered American Wirehair, dark tabby markings accented by white, turned its broad face, the tip of the tongue protruding, to study a lifted paw: *That's a taste for the ages. Where have I been?*

"Tiptoeing through mashed squirrel, no doubt," Annie said equably. "Don't knock it till you—"

The phone rang.

Dorothy L bolted from the countertop with a look of outrage.

Annie hurried to answer. She checked the caller ID. "It's Billy." She punched the speakerphone.

Max was beside her. He held up his hand, mouthed, "Let me talk to him."

Annie shrugged. Max had a point. Possibly Billy was more than a little weary of her helpful calls.

"Hey, Billy. Thanks for calling." Max reached down for Dorothy L, restored her to the counter. "Any news on the shirt?"

"Blood type matches Glen Jamison's. We don't know yet who the shirt belongs to." He cleared his throat. "Hey, Max, that was good work to call us from the preserve so we could make the search. The chain of evidence wasn't compromised. And you can tell Annie I'll check out her suggestions."

Annie spoke up brightly. "I'm here, Billy."

"Hey, Annie. Thanks for the tip about Laura. What happened in the backyard is critical. The telephone lineman had a clear view of the Jamison front porch from eight o'clock until the cruisers arrived around ten-nineteen. He didn't see anyone go inside. Or come out."

Annie understood the import of Billy's calm pronouncement. If no one entered the Jamison house from the front, the murderer either came from inside or across the backyard. "And Darwyn?"

"He sang a different tune when Lou talked to him." Billy sounded wry. "He claims he didn't see anybody, anywhere, no way."

"Darwyn said he didn't like the police." She paused, tried to bring back the uneasiness she felt when speaking with the Jamisons' yardman. "It was like he was laughing at me, at the police. But there was something about the look on his face that scared me. I think he saw something that he thinks might be connected to the murder."

"He's a smart-ass. That doesn't mean he knows anything. He'd get a kick out of stringing us along. I'll try again tomorrow, but I doubt I'll get anything from him. I'll warn him, make it clear he doesn't want to kick sand in a killer's face."

Eleven

Agatha's swift black paw clipped a small, hollow plastic bounce ball that contained a bell. A tiny jingle sounded as the pink ball caromed down the center aisle. Agatha bounded after her prey.

From behind the cash desk, Ingrid observed drily, "Such a dear little instinct to kill. Happily, this morning Agatha's whopping a plastic ball and not your ankle."

Annie's glance was reproachful. "Agatha never means to hurt me."

A muffled thump sounded and Annie's head swung toward the coffee bar.

Ingrid grinned. "The good news is that it's nothing breakable. The bad news is—depending upon your perspective—Agatha's probably dumped Laurel's latest offerings." At Annie's anguished look, she said reasonably, "It isn't in my job description to tell my boss's mother-in-law to take her posters and"—Ingrid paused for effect—"carry them elsewhere on a sunny summer morning."

Annie was already on her way down the central aisle. She skidded to a stop by the coffee bar. Posters slewed out of a portfolio onto the heart-pine floor.

Agatha stood on the counter, staring down with an interested expression.

Annie couldn't help but laugh. A photograph of her elegant, silky-furred black cat with her attitude of inquiry would have served as a great Cat Truth poster: *See what I did! Am I great or what?*

Annie looked around the coffee bar. Several blank spots on the walls indicated posters that had been sold, but there wasn't room for all of the new batch. However, she would hang them somewhere. As she gathered them up, she scanned each poster, admiring the subjects, then paused to look at a silvery Chartreux in an attitude of attack, ears flattened, golden eyes glittering. Behind her, only the tip of a tail exposed, another Chartreux huddled beneath a shawl: *Don't even think you can get him, he's my brother.*

Annie stacked the posters, slipped them into the portfolio, and faced another truth: Elaine Jamison was protecting herself or someone she loved. Accessory after the fact. Accessory to whom?

Annie leaned the portfolio against the wall by the fireplace. Elaine would want to keep safe her nieces and nephew, but she surely would not protect her brother's murderer. No, the greater likelihood was that some piece of evidence in the study pointed toward one of the family and Elaine was trying to shield an innocent person from the police. Perhaps one of the children had come to her with the Colt, upset and panicked, but claimed to be innocent. Elaine might very well decide the best solution would be to get rid of the gun. Surely that was the case. But no matter if Elaine was hiding information for what she felt to be a good reason, she was, in fact, hiding information, and that made her an accessory after the fact.

Elaine would protect Laura, Kit, and Tommy Jamison.

Annie's information about Pat Merridew and the photo in the gazebo must have been a great shock to Elaine. If Annie was right and the towel held the gun, Glen's murder had been planned well in advance. That would explain Elaine's reluctance to believe the towel photographed by Pat had any connection to Glen's murder.

In any event, Annie had done all she could do. She needed to order some petits fours for Kathryn Wall's signing next week. Lemonade would be tasty, too.

The front doorbell sang.

Annie continued on her way to the storeroom. Ingrid didn't need help at the cash desk. The day was warm and sunny. Customers would drop in after a day at the beach or on the water. As she reached for the knob to the storeroom door, loud and purposeful steps thudded in the central aisle. Annie didn't believe in portents, but there was something ominous in the sound. She turned.

Officer Harrison strode toward Annie. The officer's somber face and her crisp, almost military progress, shouted that this was an official visit.

A half-dozen police cars and two unmarked Ford sedans lined the Jamison driveway. Officer Harrison parked expertly. "Here we are."

Annie climbed out of the car, looked inquiringly at the angular, serious-faced officer.

"The chief wants everybody to wait on the terrace." Officer Harrison gestured toward the group standing on the flagstones behind the Jamison house.

Annie followed her across the uneven ground, but stumbled to a stop when she saw Darwyn Jack's body sprawled facedown at the foot of the gazebo steps. She folded her arms tight across her chest.

Uniformed officers moved unhurriedly, each with a specific task. Investigation at a crime scene followed protocol. First the M.E. must arrive and certify that the presumed victim was dead. Only then could the body be touched and identified and the investigation begun. Who was the victim? When did the crime occur? Were there witnesses? What was the manner of death? Was there a weapon? What physical evidence was available at the scene? The body would remain unmoved until the surroundings had been carefully screened and evidence, if found, cataloged.

Hyla looked back, made an impatient gesture.

Numbly Annie moved forward, still gazing at that scene of desolate finality. Yesterday Darwyn Jack had been superbly alive with the animal magnetism of a young athlete. Now a flaccid shell remained.

Yellow crime-scene tape fluttered from stakes driven in a rectangle that included the gazebo. A man in a Beaufort County Sheriff's Office uniform spoke into a camcorder as he walked the perimeter of the marked-off area. Officer Coley Benson stood near the steps to the gazebo. His eyes surveyed the ground, then dropped to a pad as he made notes. Annie noticed several other unfamiliar faces and knew Billy had called for assistance from the mainland.

Billy Cameron, former chief Frank Saulter, and the medical examiner stood near the crime-scene van. The side doors were open. Mavis Cameron was bent over an open carrying case. Billy's gaze was intent as he listened to the M.E. Sunlight glinting on his shaggy gray hair, Doc Burford made a chopping motion with his right hand. Frank turned one hand at an oblique angle. Billy Cameron nodded.

Marian Kenyon stood next to the fluttering yellow tape. She looked intent and determined, pad in one hand, pen in the other. The reporter craned to hear the low voices of the investigating officers.

Hyla Harrison said, kindly enough, to Annie, "It's better on the terrace."

The body would not be visible behind the row of palmetto palms.

Hyla led Annie to a group standing beneath the spreading limbs of a century-old live oak. Silvery-gray tangles of Spanish moss moved in a gentle breeze. In the marsh, yellow-green cordgrass gleamed in the sunlight.

Officer Harrison was polite. She spoke to Annie and the group at large. "Chief Cameron will be with you shortly." She stepped back a few feet.

Gathered were the members of the Jamison family. If Elaine Jamison had appeared pale and shaken before, today her face was waxy. Kit Jamison watched the movement of the police, her eyes huge and staring. She looked bony and ill at ease in a shapeless cotton shift. Every so often she pushed wire-rim glasses higher on her nose. She wore no makeup and her face was extraordinarily pale. Laura's eyes were again hidden behind sunglasses. She had apparently dressed hurriedly, her glossy black hair scarcely combed, a yellow tee a mismatch with pink shorts. Blond hair tousled, Tommy was shirtless and barefoot, hands jammed into the pockets of khaki shorts. A few feet away, their backs to the siblings, Cleo waited with Richard. The bones in Cleo's face jutted. She was crisp in a blue blouse and beige linen slacks. Richard's short brown hair and T-shirt were damp with sweat, as were his Nike running shorts. He gazed toward the gazebo, his face drawn in a tight, worried frown.

"The cop's coming." Tommy Jamison's young voice was shaky. His blue eyes skittered toward Elaine.

Oyster shells crunched as Billy Cameron and former chief Frank Saulter strode toward them. Frank's cold brown eyes were alert and questioning. Frank looked tough and impervious. He held a notebook and pen.

Billy scanned the waiting faces. "Does anyone have information pertaining to the murder of Darwyn Jack?"

A crow cawed. Magnolia leaves crackled in the breeze. A distant *tick tick tick* announced the presence of a clapper rail slipping unseen through marsh grasses.

No one spoke.

"From the progression of rigor mortis, death is estimated to have occurred between ten P.M. and two A.M. with the likelihood that he was dead by midnight." Billy's words were as grim as the tolling of a funeral bell. "Did anyone here speak with Darwyn Jack last night?"

His question was also met by silence.

Billy swung toward Elaine, his gaze probing. "You called 911 at a quarter to ten this morning."

Elaine braced herself against the bench railing with both hands. "I was going to work in the flower bed behind my cottage, but I couldn't find my gardening gloves. I thought I might have left them in the greenhouse." She gestured to a small structure between the cottage and the marsh. "That's why I came out my front door. As I went down the steps, I glanced toward the gazebo and saw someone lying on the ground. It didn't look right. The person was so still. I dropped my trowel and basket and ran as fast as I could. As soon as I got near, I knew he was dead. The back of his head . . ." She wavered on her feet.

Cleo eyed Elaine speculatively, then spoke to Billy. "How was he killed?"

"The cause of death was blunt trauma to the back of the skull. From the way he fell, it appears he may have been seated on the top step when a weapon with a sharply planed surface struck him with enormous force."

Tommy moved uneasily on his bare feet. "Somebody hit him?"

"Somebody hit him." Billy's voice was heavy. "Did anyone hear a disturbance last night?" He waited. He looked at Cleo. "Mrs. Jamison?"

Cleo brushed back a strand of dark hair, looked wearily at Billy. "Obviously"—her voice was crisp, a ripple of irritation evident—"if anyone—other than a murderer—knew something about the attack on Darwyn, they'd speak up. I want to know what you are doing in this investigation. Glen was killed Tuesday, and so far as we've been informed"—her gesture included all of the family—"you haven't made any progress in solving the crime. Now Darwyn's dead. He worked in the yard. He was here Tuesday morning. Did he know something about Glen's death? Did you talk to him?"

Billy's response was measured. "We interviewed everyone in proximity of your husband's death. Mr. Jack told us he neither saw nor heard anything."

"He must have lied." Cleo's tone was sharp. The breeze stirred her dark hair. Her face was pale. She, too, wore no makeup. There was a grim hardness in her gaze.

"That is a reasonable assumption. Now"—Billy was crisp—"I want to know if any of you spoke with Mr. Jack between Tuesday morning and last night. I'll start with you, Mrs. Jamison."

Cleo massaged one temple. "I think it was yesterday. I believe it was. I called and told him I wanted the front yard raked and cleaned this morning. The memorial service will be Monday. People will come to the house afterward." She pressed one hand against her eyes for a brief instant. "That was all. He said he'd take care of it. That was the last time I ever spoke to him."

Billy went from person to person.

None of the Jamison children acknowledged contact with Darwyn.

Elaine shook her head. "I don't know anything about him except he did the yard work. He was new this summer. I didn't hire him. Cleo did."

Billy turned back to Cleo.

"Someone told me about him." Her tone was off-hand. "I don't remember who it was." She looked toward Elaine. "Yesterday I stepped out to pick some roses. It was about noon. I was surprised to see Darwyn's truck." She glanced at Billy. "He worked here Tuesday mornings. I guess that's why I stood there and watched. I thought he'd left some tools behind or perhaps he wanted to check out the ladders for trimming." Cleo turned back toward Elaine. "He got out of the truck but he didn't come this way. He knocked on the front door of the cottage." Her tone was tentative.

Elaine lifted a hand to her throat. "I answered the door. I don't know what he wanted. He acted very odd. His manner was threatening."

Billy walked closer, looked down, his heavy face challenging. "You didn't mention this earlier."

Elaine's lips trembled. "I asked what he wanted. He looked at me with a kind of smirk. I can't really describe it, but he didn't act normally. I didn't like his attitude. I asked him again, very sharply, what he wanted. He said that he wondered if I'd be interested in knowing what he saw Tuesday morning. I told him I didn't know what he was talking about and again he gave this half smile. Then he said"—it was as if she was trying to recall each and every word precisely—" 'I was working in the yard.' I told him I knew that. I wondered if he was trying to say he knew something about the person who shot Glen. I said if he knew anything that would help the police, he should tell them immediately. He rocked back on his heels and laughed. It was not a nice laugh. He said, 'I'll be in touch,' and he turned away. That was exactly what happened."

In the silence that followed, Annie looked from face to face. Richard's frown was dark. Cleo looked cold and thoughtful. Kit's face creased in a worried frown. Laura's lips quivered. Tommy stared at Elaine, his expression beseeching.

Elaine's head jerked toward Billy. "It isn't what you think. I don't know why he came to me."

Billy scarcely gave her time to finish the sentence. "Did you meet Darwyn Jack in the gazebo last night?"

"Absolutely not." She seemed relieved to be questioned directly. "I did not meet him. I did not kill him. I don't know who did."

Billy glanced toward the portion of the gazebo that was visible beyond the azaleas. "Darwyn Jack met someone last night in the gazebo. His truck"—he jerked a thumb toward the dusty road that ran behind the cottage—"is parked out of sight around a curve. It seems reasonable to assume that Darwyn Jack observed someone enter or leave the study window during the time period in which the murder occurred. He very likely made a demand for money to keep his mouth shut."

Annie wondered if Darwyn's death would bolster her argument that Pat Merridew had been a murder victim. That Glen Jamison's murderer would not succumb to blackmail was evident—to Annie—from Pat's death. In fact, would Darwyn be alive today if Glen and Pat's murders had been publicly linked? That was a possibility, but Darwyn Jack had likely been too young, too sure of himself, too alive to envision danger.

Billy turned back toward Elaine, his expression stolid, his eyes scouring her face.

She lifted her hands as if in self-defense. "No." Her voice was high. "He did not ask me for money. I did not meet him in the gazebo. I had nothing to do with his death. I swear it. I didn't shoot Glen. I loved Glen." Her voice broke.

Billy turned to Annie. "Tell me exactly what Darwyn said to you."

Annie tried to give an accurate picture. "He may have been making things up. That's the impression I had. He acted as if he might have seen something or someone and then he said, 'I don't like cops. Let them figure out stuff. If I saw something it would be bad news for somebody, wouldn't it?' He laughed and said he didn't see anything. Maybe he didn't. Maybe he went around to everybody and pretended he knew something."

Billy asked each family member in turn, "Did Darwyn Jack approach you and suggest he saw someone in the garden Tuesday morning?"

Cleo's head shake was definite. "Absolutely not."

Richard looked grim. "I'd have knocked him flat."

Laura looked nervous. "I never talked to him. I didn't like him. We went to school together. People said he was mean. I didn't like the way he looked at girls in the hall."

Kit twined a strand of light hair around a finger. "He never spoke to me." She glanced toward her sister. "I know what she means about the way he looked at women."

Tommy shrugged. "That dude never came near me."

Elaine's voice was shrill. "I'm telling the truth. I don't know what he knew or didn't know. I told him to go to the police."

"That was good advice. He might be alive if he'd followed it." Billy turned to Cleo Jamison. "Mrs. Jamison, I wonder if you can help me with another matter. You are Glen Jamison's widow. Are the house and grounds, including the cottage and outbuildings, now your property?"

Cleo briefly closed her eyes. Her lips moved. " . . . widow . . ." She pressed her lips together, stared at the ground for an instant, then lifted her face, spoke wearily. "The house and grounds . . . Actually, I've not seen Glen's will. I had no reason to see it. We signed a prenuptial agreement. I have no claim on anything prior to our marriage. The house very likely now belongs to Kit and Laura and Tommy. I'm sure he made some provision for Elaine. Whatever Glen earned since then, I share with his children." Her face twisted. "I received a settlement at the time of our marriage. What is the point of your question?"

"I would like the permission of the home owner to conduct a search of the house and grounds, including the cottage and its garage, without a warrant. I can easily obtain a warrant, but if I can have signed approval from all of you, we can proceed now. Does anyone object?"

Cleo shrugged. "I'll be happy to sign, but I am quite certain the house has been left to Glen's children."

Billy's eyes moved to Glen's children.

Kit turned her hands over. "Sure. Why not?"

Laura nodded, then shivered. "I want this to end. Look anywhere you want to look."

Tommy's shoulders hunched. "Yeah. Whatever."

Billy's blue eyes reached Elaine.

"Of course you should search." Her voice was thin but steady.

Frank Saulter swiftly wrote a statement. He held it out to Billy. "This provides that the Broward's Rock Police Department had the permission of the presumptive heirs of Glen Jamison to undertake a search of the property in regard to the murder of Darwyn Jack."

Billy gave the sheet first to Cleo. She signed.

The sheet was passed to each of the Jamisons except for Richard. When everyone had duly signed, Elaine handed the sheet to Billy.

Billy nodded in satisfaction. He turned and walked away from the terrace.

There was silence.

Cleo glanced at Officer Harrison. "Are we required to remain on the terrace?"

Hyla looked bland. "If you have no objection, Chief Cameron would appreciate each of you remaining until the search is completed."

Cleo shrugged. She looked at Elaine. "There's no reason for us to stand." She gestured at several wrought-iron tables and accompanying chairs. "We might as well be comfortable. I'll make some coffee." She turned to Richard. "If you'd lend a hand?"

He nodded and followed her into the house.

Kit, Laura, Tommy, and Elaine sat together. Kit watched Cleo and Richard walk into the house. Her face was hard and suspicious.

Annie walked to a path that curved among the azaleas. She had a clear view of the gazebo. Billy Cameron spoke to a cluster of law officers, some on his staff, some from the mainland. He gestured toward the gazebo, up at several trees, and at the cottage, greenhouse, and garages.

Annie stood with her arms folded. She supposed the search was window dressing. The marsh glittered in the morning sunlight, the broad expanse of water an open invitation to a murderer seeking to discard a weapon. Tuesday Elaine Jamison had successfully thrown something into the marsh. A continuing search had yielded nothing of interest. It seemed very likely that Glen Jamison's Colt was even now submerged in the murky water and was likely to remain there undisturbed.

Annie watched EMSA techs ease Darwyn Jack's body into a black crime-scene, envelope-style body bag. The techs stood on each side, gripped the vinyl handles, lifted the bag to a gurney, and wheeled toward a waiting ambulance.

Two uniformed officers strode past the cottage and lifted the door to a white frame garage.

Steps sounded on the flagstones behind Annie. She turned.

Lack of makeup accentuated the sharpness of Cleo Jamison's features. She looked exhausted. "Would you care to join Richard and me for coffee?"

"Thank you." Annie appreciated Cleo's invitation. She followed to a table at the far end of the terrace. Annie wondered if the space between Cleo's table and that of Glen's family was a deliberate effort to avoid contact.

Annie added two teaspoons of sugar and a splash of cream.

Cleo stirred sugar into her cup, then looked at Annie. "I know you've tried to help Elaine." She paused, glanced at Richard. "Elaine seems determined to put herself in as deep a hole as possible. It's awkward. I can't believe she would shoot Glen or"—she shot a bewildered look into the garden—"kill a yardman, but I have to assume she's declining to talk to the police because she is afraid whatever she says would incriminate her. That's very . . . troubling."

Richard shoved a hand through his thick brown hair. "She should be doing everything possible to help find out who killed Glen." His voice was angry.

"I think she's protecting someone." Annie took a sip of the sweet, creamy drink and found it comforting.

Cleo's gaze moved to the table at the far end of the terrace where the others sat. "I don't have any sympathy for her, if that's the case." Her voice was cold. "Glen's dead. And now—" She gestured toward the gazebo. "You talked to Darwyn yesterday afternoon.

He was killed last night." She eyed Annie with a demanding gaze. "What did he know?"

Annie looked toward the gazebo. "I think he saw someone. I think he knew that he had important information and decided to see what he could get out of it."

Cleo's eyes narrowed. "Did he say what part of the yard he was in? If we knew where he was working, it would give us an idea of what he could have seen."

"He was using the leaf blower near the flower beds. He probably had his back—" Annie sat bolt upright. The leaf blower . . .

Suddenly the dark moments of Tuesday morning seemed crystal clear. She came to her feet. "I need to talk to Chief Cameron."

Richard paused with his coffee cup midway to his mouth. "Why?"

"I think Glen was shot while Darwyn was using the blower. Darwyn said he ran the blower from a quarter after nine to a few minutes after ten o'clock. That's why no one heard the shots. The noise was covered by the leaf blower. Otherwise someone would have heard the shots and possibly raised an alarm before the killer could get away. Excuse me. I need to tell Billy about the time." Narrowing the time when the murder had occurred might not matter. But it might be important.

Annie started for the path.

Officer Harrison barred the way. "The search is in progress. Please return to the terrace."

"Hyla." Annie saw the quick stiffening. "Officer Harrison, I have information that may be helpful. I'll go carefully. I won't get in the way." She looked toward the cottage. "I'll stay on the drive."

Hyla unhooked her cell, clicked. "Chief, Annie Darling wants to speak with you." She nodded. "Yes, sir." She gave Annie a quick nod.

Annie walked briskly, glad to leave behind the strained group on the terrace, the family so clearly divided, Glen's children and sister at one table, his widow and cousin at another.

Billy Cameron stood outside the open door to the garage. He stood with his head jutted forward, his concentration evident. He held a video cam and spoke into it. ". . . white leather golf bag found three feet inside garage door next to west wall. Deputy Keith McKay removes clubs one at a time."

In the garage, Mavis Cameron watched intently as a sheriff's deputy lifted a golf club from the worn leather bag propped against a side wall. The tall, angular detective wore plastic gloves. He bent over, revealing a bald spot on the top of his head, and placed the club, a six iron, on the oil-stained floor of the garage next to a row of clubs. He came upright and turned back to the bag.

Annie stopped beside Billy. He looked serious, imposing, and expectant.

A few feet away, Marian Kenyon gave her a brief once-over, then focused again on the deputy as he reached into the golf bag.

Billy noted Annie in his peripheral vision. "Yes?" His gaze never wavered from the garage.

"Yesterday I asked Darwyn about the leaf blower."

Billy nodded, indicating he was listening even though he continued to watch the deputy.

"Darwyn said the blower ran from about nine-fifteen to a few minutes after ten." She spoke to Billy, but she, too, turned her eyes toward the search. "I think Glen was shot on Tuesday because Darwyn worked at the Jamison house on Tuesdays. The killer wanted the leaf blower to hide the sound of the shots."

"That's what I'd figured. It seems likely the killer picked Tuesday because Darwyn was there. Thanks for narrowing the time. He was vague about the leaf blower when I talked to him. But otherwise, the shots—"

The deputy abruptly straightened. He held a five iron aloft, firmly grasped between plastic-gloved thumb and index finger. "Hey, it looks like there's blood and tissue on the club face."

Billy strode forward. He held the video cam to photograph the club as he described the scene.

Marian Kenyon gave a soft whoop. "In at the kill." She tucked the pad under one arm, poked the pencil behind her right ear, grabbed the Leica that hung around her neck, and began to shoot, muttering, "Yeah, yeah, yeah, turn a little this way. Oh, good, that's a great shot. I can see the heads: 'Murder Weapon Found' or maybe 'Deadly Chip Shot,' or better yet 'Final Swing.'"

Mavis Cameron stepped nearer and grasped the iron in pincers.

Billy finished recording and spoke to the deputy, his words inaudible. He nodded. They turned together and started up the drive toward the house. They passed Annie and Marian, walking fast. The tall thin deputy made Billy appear even heavier and stronger than he usually looked.

As soon as they were past, Marian headed for the house, too. Annie took a deep breath and followed. Her mind pulsed with thoughts: Darwyn struck from behind, Frank Saulter's oblique chop with his hand, a five iron, a white golf bag in the garage of the cottage.

At the terrace, Billy walked directly to the table where Elaine sat with her nieces and nephew. "Are you a golfer, Ms. Jamison?"

Elaine looked past Billy as the deputy approached with the five iron. Elaine's face looked frozen. She lifted a hand. Blue stones in a bracelet glittered in the sunshine. "Where did you get that club?"

Tommy's face squeezed in puzzlement. Kit watched her aunt with an uncertain expression. Laura bent for a better view of Mavis.

"Are you a golfer, Ms. Jamison?" His tone was steely.

Her hand dropped. "I play golf." Her voice was thin. "That looks like my five iron." Her voice shook. "Why do you have that club?" She came to her feet.

Billy jerked his head and the deputy came nearer. He was near enough to the terrace that the smear of dark matter on the club face was readily visible, but not so near that anyone could reach the five iron.

Billy's eyes never left Elaine's face. "The club was found in the white leather golf bag in the garage adjoining the cottage. Does that golf bag belong to you?"

Elaine slowly nodded.

Billy took a step nearer. "When did you last see the club?"

"I played golf last week. I haven't touched the club since then." Her voice had an edge of horror.

"Can you explain the discoloration on the face of the club?"

She stared, her eyes wide and strained. "No."

Billy watched her carefully. "The club will be submitted to the forensics laboratory for testing."

Marian Kenyon piped up. "Does the stuff on the club face appear to be human tissue and blood?"

Elaine cried out, "I haven't seen my five iron since last week."

Cleo pushed back her chair. She crossed the width of the terrace, stopped a few feet from Elaine. "I am not your attorney, but you might find it wiser to choose to remain silent."

Elaine looked at her in despair. "Cleo, I swear to you. I don't know anything about what happened to Glen or to Darwyn. If that club killed Darwyn, someone took it from my bag and used it."

There was silence on the terrace.

Billy was matter-of-fact. "Is your garage kept locked, Ms. Jamison?"

"No. I never lock it."

Cleo almost spoke, shrugged.

Elaine said jerkily, "I'm innocent. I shouldn't have to be quiet."

Billy eyed her curiously. "You have had very little to say about your actions on Tuesday morning. What did you throw in the marsh?"

Elaine seemed to shrink. Her eyes dropped. She folded her arms across her front.

"Speaking of Tuesday morning, Ms. Jamison, there is another matter you might wish to explain."

He unclipped his cell, lifted it, punched. "It's time, Officer."

Clearly, his crisp order was setting into motion a previously designed plan of action. Billy walked to the edge of the terrace, looked toward the line of official cars parked along the Jamison drive.

Behind him, chairs scraped on the flagstones. One by one, the Jamisons stood. Kit, Laura, and Tommy moved close to Elaine. Cleo and Richard remained a few feet away.

Lou Pirelli stepped out of a parked police car. His coal-black hair gleamed in the sunlight. A black-and-tan bloodhound clambered out to join him. They walked toward the crime-lab van, Lou holding the leash. The hatchback door was open. Beyond the van, detectives continued to investigate the crime scene near the gazebo, but everyone on the terrace watched the uniformed officer and the dog in his leather harness. Man and dog stopped at the rear of the open van.

Mavis Cameron held a large, clear plastic container. She hopped lightly to the ground. She lifted the hinged lid. A plastic-gloved hand lifted out blue cloth. She dangled the cloth before the bloodhound.

Lou spoke loudly. "Track."

Mavis returned the cloth to its container.

The dog snuffled, then turned and meandered back and forth. He stopped near a volleyball net, smelled intently, then headed for the terrace, Lou moving fast to keep up. The dog went straight to Tommy Jamison, lifted his head, and bayed.

Tommy backed away. "What's wrong with him?" He pointed at the bloodhound.

The dog kept pace.

Lou pulled on the harness. "Stay."

The bloodhound stopped, his dark eyes staring at Tommy.

"What's the dog for?" The teenager's voice was high. "What's going on?"

Billy lifted his voice. "Crime tech."

At the crime van, Mavis Cameron nodded. She strode swiftly toward her husband. At the edge of the terrace, she placed the container on the ground, used both gloved hands to hold up a man's blue polo shirt. In the soft sunlight, the brownish smear across the front was distinct.

Billy walked back toward Elaine. "Tuesday morning you were observed walking toward the marsh carrying a bunched-up cloth." He looked toward Annie. "What color was the cloth?"

Annie stared at the stained shirt. "Blue."

"Did the shade of blue you saw Tuesday morning match the shade of this polo shirt?"

"Yes." Annie looked toward Elaine, wished that she had not. Elaine's face reflected a welter of emotions: fear, despair, frantic thought, disbelief, panic.

Billy folded his arms. His voice was uninflected and perhaps even more menacing for its very lack of drama. "Ms. Jamison, we know what you did with this shirt. You drove away Tuesday morning in a great hurry. You turned left on Sea Oats Lane."

Elaine stared at him, her eyes widening in shock.

"On Sea Oats Lane"—the police chief sounded authoritative, a man with facts at his fingertips—"you proceeded to Kittredge Forest Preserve. You parked in the turnaround. Tire tracks there match the tread on your 2009 Corolla."

Elaine clasped her hands tightly together.

"You proceeded on foot into the preserve. You walked precisely eight-tenths of a mile. You left the trail to secrete the exhibit"—he pointed at the blue polo shirt held by Mavis—"beneath a resurrection fern. The shirt was photographed in situ, removed by an officer, and submitted to the crime lab for testing." Billy pointed at the stain. "Ms. Jamison, why did you hurry away from the site of your brother's murder and hide a bloodstained shirt in the forest preserve?"

Elaine looked sick and frightened.

"Surely you remember what you did that morning and why. Perhaps I can assist you in recalling." He was matter-of-fact. "The shirt is stained with the blood of your dead brother. Is that why you disposed of it?"

"Stop it." Tommy's cry was hoarse and desperate. "Dad's blood . . ." Tears filled his eyes.

Billy swung toward Tommy. "It's your shirt, isn't it, son?"

"Yeah." He was struggling to breathe. "My shirt . . ."

Cleo Jamison stalked toward the teenager. "Did you shoot Glen? Oh God, did you kill him?"

Tommy took a step back. "I didn't. I didn't. I—"

"Leave him alone." Elaine plunged to Tommy's side, grabbed his arm. "I'm sorry, Tommy. I just grabbed anything. I didn't know it was your shirt. I didn't know what it was, I was so upset. God, I'm sorry." She clung tightly to her nephew's arm as she faced Billy. "Listen to me, I can explain. I came up to the house to talk to Glen. I went to the door of the study that opens off the terrace. I pulled the handle and stepped inside. I wasn't looking around the room. I was thinking about what I was going to say. I wanted Glen—oh well, it doesn't matter now. But that's why I didn't realize what had happened. I went in and my foot hit something. I looked down. I saw Glen's gun. I'd kicked it. I couldn't imagine what it was doing on the floor. I thought it was odd but I knew the key to the gun safe had been lost. I took a few steps and bent down and picked up the gun. It wasn't until I straightened up that I saw shoes. Glen's shoes. And his legs. I walked around the desk. He was lying on the floor and there was blood. So much blood, blood everywhere. I dropped down and touched his arm. I guess that's when I got blood on my hand. I got up and I was going to call for help and then I looked down and I saw the blood on my hand and I had the gun in my other hand. I was afraid. I wanted to call the police, but I thought they'd think . . . I was terrified. I ran into the hall and through the kitchen and that's when I grabbed Tommy's shirt from the dirty clothes basket in the laundry room. I wiped my hand off and rolled up the gun in the shirt and went outside."

The teenager, his eyes huge and frightened, stared at his aunt. "Elaine—"

She tightened her grip on her nephew's arm. "I'm sorry, Tommy. I didn't know the shirt belonged to you. But now everything's all right." She looked defiantly at Billy. "I know it was stupid. I should have owned up. But that's what happened." She pushed back a strand of blond hair, stared with a pinched and desperate face. "I didn't shoot Glen. I didn't see anyone on my way to the house or on my return. But I didn't know what to do. I went in the cottage. I ran to the phone. But I was afraid."

"You didn't call." The police chief's tone was considering.

Her thin face rigid, she answered in a small voice. "I knew I'd messed up any fingerprints on the gun. In fact, I wiped it off with the shirt and then I wrapped it up and carried it to the marsh and threw it away."

"Ms. Jamison, I am taking you to the police station for further questioning. You have the right to speak to an attorney. Anything you say may . . ."

Twelve

As the police car carrying Elaine Jamison disappeared around a curve, Cleo gripped Richard's arm. "I can't believe Elaine would hurt Glen." She looked upset, verging on tears.

Richard's face was taut. "No family ever expects murder. But it seems pretty clear that Glen was shot by someone he knew."

Her plain face outraged, Kit Jamison glared at him. "Not by Elaine." Without another word, she turned and ran for the house. She slammed inside.

Laura looked bewildered and scared. Tommy appeared utterly miserable. He turned toward Laura, then stopped and shook his head.

In a moment, Kit was back on the verandah, a purse clutched in one hand, car keys in the other. She called to her sister and brother, "Come on, we're going to the police station."

The sisters and brother moved toward the driveway.

Annie hurried after them. As Kit opened the door to a faded VW Beetle, Annie said quickly, "Elaine needs a top lawyer. Call Handler Jones in Savannah."

"Handler Jones." Kit repeated the name as she turned the ignition. Laura slid in the front passenger seat. Tommy climbed into the backseat, looking big and burly in the confines of the small car.

By the time Annie turned to look toward the terrace, the back door was closing. Cleo and Richard had returned to the house.

She pulled out her cell phone as she walked to her car. "Max . . ."

Dishes clattered and voices rumbled, almost drowning out "That Old Black Magic." As always in the summer, Parotti's was booming with business. The hubbub made conversation private.

Annie poked a succulent, hot french fry into ketchup she'd laced with fresh black pepper. ". . . but, Max"—her voice was forlorn, the french fry cooling in her grasp—"I think Elaine made it up as she went along, about the polo shirt and what she did."

Max squeezed lemon on grilled flounder. "Why?"

"She talked too fast. It was like she was thinking as she went, trying to come up with a rationale for the shirt and the gun."

Max forked a piece of flounder. "Are you saying she shot Glen?"

Annie welcomed the cool freshness of iced tea. She looked thoughtful and possibly a bit uncertain. "That's what it looks like, but I don't think so."

Max was skeptical. "If she didn't shoot him and if she didn't go to the house, how did she get the gun? Or the shirt?"

Annie ate the french fry, absently noting that it was lukewarm. "I don't know. I wish I could help her. I've never seen anyone look more alone when Billy took her to the squad car."

Max's face softened. "You helped her. As soon as you called, I got in touch with Handler Jones. The kids had already talked to him. He'll be over tomorrow." The Savannah criminal lawyer with boyish good looks and Southern charm was well known for his courtroom successes.

Annie's face squeezed in unhappiness. "Do you suppose they'll keep her in jail?"

"Handler didn't think so." Max's smile was wry. "Another advantage of living on a sea island. Billy knows she can't get away without taking the ferry and he'll have alerted Ben."

Annie looked across the restaurant. Ben Parotti owned the island's only ferry as well as its most successful eating establishment and various other properties. He was smart, energetic, and a very good friend. He saw Annie's glance and in a moment was at the booth, carrying an iced-tea pitcher. He refilled their glasses, peered at Annie. "Heard you were rounded up by Hyla this morning, taken to the Jamisons'." He rocked back on his heels. "Kind of strange, Glen Jamison shot on Tuesday, Darwyn Jack murdered in Glen's backyard last night."

Annie wasn't surprised at Ben's knowledge. He knew everyone, heard everything.

Ben gave the pitcher a shake and ice rattled against the plastic interior. "Got an order from the *Gazette*." It was an answer to her unasked question. "Talked to Ferroll." His leprechaun face folded in a frown. "I told him anybody who thinks grits tastes like paste don't have the good sense God gave an inchworm. Anyway, Ferroll said all hell was bustin' out and it sure looked like Elaine Jamison was up a creek without a boat, much less a paddle." His frown grew darker. "Ms. Jamison is a real nice lady." In Ben's world there were real nice ladies and all other women.

"A nice lady wouldn't have no truck with someone like Darwyn. He worked here for a while. I told him to take a hike. I was sorry because his grandma is a real nice lady, but Darwyn, he had a mean streak. I caught him out in the alley on a break, treatin' one of the girls like she was no 'count. That was that as far as I was concerned."

Annie wasn't surprised. She'd felt uneasy when she talked to Darwyn.

Max cut a piece of flounder. "The best guess is that he saw Glen's killer Tuesday morning and asked for money."

"Maybe." Ben's tone was ruminative. "But maybe he was mixed up in something. You know I own Jasmine Gardens."

Annie hadn't known, but Ben's real-estate holdings on the island were extensive. Jasmine Gardens offered cabins with a marsh view that could be rented by the week, month, or year.

"I keep an eye on things. I was over there a week ago, talked to my manager, Marva Kay Murphy. As I pulled in to park, a beat-up pickup came out too fast. I saw the driver. Darwyn Jack. I asked Marva Kay about him. She didn't have anybody by the name of Jack as a renter. I described him and she said oh, sure, that was a guy named David Harley, Cabin Nine.

He paid by the month. Cash. I didn't like that for nothing. Marva Kay said she didn't usually take cash, but rentals have been down the last couple of years and she thought it wouldn't do any harm. Maybe not if she'd rented to a guy really named David Harley, but I knew Darwyn Jack and I wouldn't trust him around the corner. I told Marva Kay when he came to rent for the next month to tell him the cabin was no longer available."

Max looked puzzled. "I don't see how anything Darwyn saw Tuesday morning could have a connection to his renting a cabin. Maybe he had a girlfriend."

Ben raised a grizzled eyebrow. "I don't mean to sound snooty but I don't see where Darwyn could afford my cabins. Anyway, I called and told the cops, but that Hyla Harrison didn't sound interested either." He sounded faintly aggrieved, a leprechaun with mud splashed on his green frock coat.

Annie retrieved another french fry. "Ben, you're great to want to help. We'll see what we can find out. I'll tell you what—why don't you ask Marva Kay to keep that cabin locked. I'll drop by and take a look."

Ben looked at her in approval. "I'm thinking you'll find something there. It don't make sense that Darwyn rented the cabin. I'll tell Marva Kay to let you in." He started to turn, then stopped and added obscurely,

"Ms. Jamison was a peach to help Miss Jolene when she had the flu last winter."

As he walked away, Max grinned. "Is this your Be-Kind-to-Ben ploy?"

Annie pensively ate another french fry, then picked up her sandwich, crisply fried flounder with Thousand Island dressing. "Okay, so it's a long shot. But if someone wanted to get rid of Darwyn, how clever would it be to set up a meeting at the Jamison gazebo? Everybody on the island knew Glen Jamison had been murdered. Who would ever believe a second murder there wouldn't be connected to the first?" She took a bite, mumbled indistinctly: "Right, right. There's the golf club to account for. Maybe the murderer brought a weapon but nosed around for something linked to the scene." She took another bite. "Is our garage locked?"

Max put down his fork, folded his arms on the table. "That, Mrs. Darling, is unworthy of you."

Annie laughed. "Nobody locks up on an island. Anyway, I know it's unlikely but," and now she was serious, "Darwyn at Jasmine Gardens is out of the ordinary. That makes it worth exploring."

Max took a bite of the house salad. Today's version was homegrown tomatoes, iceberg lettuce, and a sprinkling of pepitas. "So you want to keep on looking even though you think Elaine lied this morning?"

Annie slowly nodded. "Billy's investigation is over, isn't it?"

Max met her gaze. "He has motive, opportunity, and physical evidence."

Annie sighed. "All Elaine has is us."

Max reached across the table, touched her cheek. "Everybody thinks Jude is the saint of desperate causes. They don't know about you."

"Maybe Saint Jude will help us help Elaine." She took a last bite of flounder. "So, where do we start?"

Max snagged a paper napkin from the dispenser in the middle of the table. "What don't we know?"

Annie scrambled in her purse for a pen, handed it to him.

"Okay." She tried to sound like a woman with a plan. "Here's what we do know. One—"

Max marked a numeral, waited.

"—Darwyn probably saw someone either going into Glen's study or coming out. Two—a telephone lineman was working across the street from the house and would have seen anyone entering the house from the front. Three—Darwyn used the leaf blower from nine-fifteen to a few minutes after ten. Four—Laura was on the upper verandah and saw something that she is desperate not to reveal. To me, that spells Kirk Brewster."

Max used another napkin, sketched the Jamison house and the garden. He placed an X in the front yard with an arrow to a telephone pole. "The telephone lineman's bird's-eye view makes it simple. If nobody came in the front door, then the murderer was either someone in the house, Kit, Laura, or possibly Richard, if he lied about his jog. But Darwyn's murder suggests the killer came through the backyard. Otherwise, how would Darwyn have known anything dangerous to the killer?"

Annie spoke slowly. "If the murderer came from the backyard, that clears Kit and Laura. Neither had any reason to go outside."

Max looked thoughtful. "If the murderer came from the backyard, the possibilities are Richard and Elaine and maybe Kirk Brewster or whoever Laura saw."

Annie had no doubt Billy had already reached this conclusion. "Richard found the body. He could easily have shot Glen, then raised the alarm. But he was trying to get money from Glen. He needed Glen alive."

Max shook his head. "According to Edna Graham, Glen turned Richard down. She said when Richard came out of Glen's office, his face wasn't"—Max's tone put the word in quote marks—" 'nice.' "

Annie's eyes narrowed. "Maybe we're getting close. Richard wanted money. Glen said no. Maybe Richard wanted both Glen's money and his wife. Kit thought Richard was attracted to Cleo. I wonder"—her tone was thoughtful—"if Richard knew about the key man insurance."

He raised an eyebrow. "He'll never admit he knew, if he did. But the important point is that Kirk Brewster absolutely knew about the insurance. Two and a half million is a pretty nice incentive for a man who was going to be broke and looking for a job and unwilling to leave the island because of his sister's health. I'm sure Billy has checked out Kirk's whereabouts Tuesday morning, but I'll see what I can find out."

Annie was stubborn. "Maybe Richard Jamison had good reason to believe he could cash in if Cleo came in for her share."

Max leaned back against the booth. "Do I pick up on a little hostility toward Richard? Or are you willing to toss him under the bus to save Elaine?"

Annie's tone was scathing. "What kind of man comes to his cousin's house and hangs around like a squatter trying to get money out of him?"

Max laughed. "Not a fine specimen of the Puritan ethic, according to the Annie Laurance Darling Doctrine?"

It was a long-standing divide between them. Max grew up rich, enjoyed dabbling, and never felt he had to prove anything by hewing to a career. He would have been happy traveling and collecting art, supporting good causes, and eschewing personal achievement. Annie grew up counting pennies, always worked hard, and did her best at whatever task she attempted. They achieved peace by making accommodations: Max dutifully created Confidential Commissions and found he enjoyed solving problems for people; Annie discovered devotion to work could be balanced with impromptu walks on a winter beach, late-morning breakfasts, and, of course, some afternoon delight.

Annie was stern. "If a man lacks character in one respect—"

Max held up both hands in negation. "It doesn't mean he'd shoot his cousin."

She placed her elbows on the table. "He came looking for money. And"—her tone was portentous—"maybe when he got here, he wanted more than money. Maybe he wanted Cleo."

Max was impatient. "We're making everything up here. We don't have any reason to believe Cleo was cheating on her husband."

"But maybe she was."

"Maybe. A love affair between Cleo and Richard would give him a motive in addition to money. I'll do some checking on the two of them. But we know for sure that Kirk Brewster had only a couple more weeks before he lost any chance to profit from the key man insurance. I'll see what I can find out about Kirk, too. And you?"

Annie looked across the room at Ben Parotti. "I like Ben's instinct. I'll drop by Jasmine Gardens."

Max gave a wistful glance at his indoor putting green but went directly to his computer. He settled behind his massive mahogany desk and turned on his computer. He opened his file on the Jamison family and reread the biographical material on Richard Jamison. After a little digging, he had three names. Thanks to the ubiquity of cell phones and modern humans' apparent inability to be out of touch, he soon spoke to the skipper of *Pretty Girl*. "Captain, I'm putting together a movie in Beaufort County"—the county had been home to the filming of several feature films— "and I'm looking for a recommendation for Richard Jamison. I believe he sailed with you for a couple of years."

The crusty voice rumbled, "Good hand. Got a quick head in emergencies. Kept his nose clean. Broke up a cocaine ring once. Don't want that kind of crap on my ship. Hire him anytime."

"Did he tip you to the smuggling?"

"Damn right. Helped me set it up with the feds. Caught 'em. Almost a half-million dollars' worth of cocaine."

"He sounds like a good hire. Now, I have kind of a funny question"—Max made his voice easy, amused, sharing a joke—"but we have an actress who likes good-looking men. Do you suppose he'd be willing to be nice to the lady?"

A roar of earthy laughter. "Richard's your man. Hardly ever met a woman that didn't have the hots for him. He likes the ladies, so long as he can love 'em and leave 'em."

"No problem there." Max was equally hearty.

As he replaced the receiver, he studied a smiling picture of Richard from his Facebook page, tanned and fit, muscular in a pale green guayabera shirt and khaki shorts and docksiders. He stood at the stern of a cabin cruiser, a breeze stirring sun-streaked brown hair. His lopsided smile was exuberant. He was a man who liked sun and sex, and he was always looking for the route to easy street. But he'd drawn the line at drugs. Max wrote on his legal pad, underlined *drugs* three times.

He made two more calls.

The first was to Sam Whistler, who was still bartending at the Ship Ahoy in Boca Raton. "Sam, I understand Richard Jamison worked there last year. I'm looking for a manager for the Fast Catch here on the island. What can you tell me about Richard?"

". . . good joe . . . easy to talk to . . . handles crowds . . . careful about money. You can trust him . . . Women? I don't know what his secret is. They love the man. But he makes sure they understand the rules before he plays. He's one smart dude."

The final call was to a childhood friend now teaching Spanish at Clemson. "Richard? So he's back on the island. I doubt that lasts long. He's a wanderer. He never met an open road he didn't want to take or a beautiful woman he didn't want to make love to." A faint sigh. "Richard's not a nine-to-five guy."

Max ended the call, pulled the legal pad nearer. He drew a road, a pair of sexy female legs, a condo marked by a huge X, and a rectangular package that would hold a kilo of cocaine.

It was time to talk to Richard Jamison.

Palmetto palms stood like Southern sentries on either side of a short oyster-shell road. The Jasmine Gardens cabins weren't visible from the main road. A small white sign hung from a steel stanchion near an office-cum-cabin. The inscription read:

JASMINE GARDENS

MANAGER

INQUIRE WITHIN

Annie parked. She smelled the banana sweetness of pittosporum. Five steps led to a small front porch. The cabin was built about five feet above the ground, always a wise precaution on a sea island. Annie admired its blue shutters and white siding. The style reminded her a little of Bermuda. Ben Parotti had evidently been feeling romantic when he approved the design.

A skinny redhead, her hair pulled back beneath a yellow do-rag, gave Annie a bright smile. "We have a vacancy," as if Annie were a lucky winner of a sweepstakes. "Each of our cabins is built behind a private screen of bamboo and bayberry. Each cabin has its own parking space on one side. The cabins are fully furnished, once-weekly maid service—"

"Maid service." Annie felt a surge of panic. "Has Cabin Nine been cleaned?"

"Oh." The manager sighed. "You must be Annie Darling. I thought you looked kind of familiar. I took my mom to your bookstore once. I'm Marva Kay.

Ben called and said you'd be by to see that cabin. He said not to touch it. I told Linda Lee to skip nine this week." She turned and reached inside the door. "Here's the key."

"How long had Darwyn been renting the cabin?"

She squinted at Annie. "He signed the register David Harley. He paid cash, plus a two-hundred-dollar deposit, so I didn't ask for an ID." She frowned. "I wonder who'll get the deposit back."

"I'd hold on to it. What's most important, please don't have the cabin cleaned until Ben gives the go-ahead."

"Sure enough." Marva Kay looked rueful. "I got plenty of others to rent."

"Did you see much of Darwyn?"

She gave a little laugh. "I don't see much of anybody. See, every cabin is completely private. It's like they're supposed to be love nests. Or something like that. We used to get a lot of couples from Savannah but not so many now."

"Did you ever see anyone with Darwyn?"

She looked wise. "His girlfriend? Nope. But one afternoon I got a call from the lady in ten and she was panicked. Seems like a raccoon was trying to get in the back door. I told her just to leave him alone and he'd go away but she insisted I come and do something. I got Buster, my hound. I knew that raccoon would scoot

faster than a floozy who sees a patrol car. We took
the path, and like I said, it's plenty private behind the
bamboo, but I heard, well, you can take it from me,
they weren't playing tiddledywinks in nine. I walked
a little faster. No business of mine. Then I heard the
sliding door shut and I figured that was good. I like
the heavy breathing to be inside. Some kids might be
wandering around. So, I never saw anybody but him.
For sure, he didn't rent the cabin to work on his abs.
Not that they needed any work."

Back in the car, Annie drove cautiously on the
narrow, twisting lane. As Marva Kay had said, each
cabin was its own world. She pulled into the parking
slot next to nine. She walked to the front steps. The
old-fashioned metal key was distinctive, a shiny silver
color with a heart-shaped bow.

The door swung in. Dust motes danced in the
splash of sunlight. The air was still and hot. The air-
conditioning was off. The living room's island decor
was cheerful, wicker chairs with red-and-yellow cushions, a ceiling fan, a rattan sofa, tiled floor. One wall
featured a mural with a great blue heron standing in a
marsh.

There was no evidence of recent occupation. No
newspapers. No magazines. No glasses. Annie glanced
into the small kitchen. It, too, appeared unused. She
didn't touch the refrigerator or cabinets.

In the single bedroom, she felt as though she were chasing phantoms. The double bed was made, the spread tightly tucked beneath the pillows. The bolsters common to hotel rooms were absent. Unless she was very much mistaken, the room had been cleaned since it last served as a rendezvous for lovers. There was no hint as to the identity of the woman who had met Darwyn here, nothing in the closet or in the drawers of a wicker chest, no scrap of papers in the wastebaskets, nothing that had rolled beneath the bed or the sofa.

She locked the cabin behind her, returned the key, and walked to her car. She'd had great hopes of finding some clue about Darwyn's girlfriend. Of course, there was no guarantee she knew anything at all about what he had seen in the Jamison backyard Tuesday morning.

Still, it would be nice to have the opportunity to ask her.

Barb poked her head into Max's office. "Richard Jamison is here." Her expressive face registered a warning.

Max rose from behind the refectory table that served as his desk and walked toward the door.

Richard Jamison stopped a few feet inside, folded his arms. His gaze was cold. "You called me out of the blue, started asking questions. I don't know you.

I don't have to talk to you." He was island casual in a loose orange polo and baggy shorts and huaraches, but his face was brooding and unpleasant.

Max looked at him coolly. "But you came."

Richard's face hardened. "Because of Cleo. I'm warning you. If you spread rumors about Cleo and me, I'll sue you for defamation of character."

Max was forceful, though he kept his voice even. "I don't spread rumors. I'm asking about you and your cousin's widow because his daughter Kit told my wife that she thought you were having an affair with her stepmother."

"No." Richard's answer was violent. "There's no truth to that. You want the truth? I'll tell you the truth even though you don't have any right to ask me a damn thing. I loved my cousin. I looked up to him. Glen was great to me when I was a little kid. And yeah, Cleo's an amazing woman. Sure, I'm attracted to her. But I don't screw a man's wife when I'm living in his house. I'd decided to leave. I was going next week and then somebody shot Glen. It wasn't me. I'll talk to Kit." He turned to go.

Max's tone was sharp. "Are you still leaving town?"

Slowly Richard faced him. "I'm staying for a while."

"I suppose you'll help Cleo sort out her financial future."

"Her finances are none of my business."

"She'll be able to help you swing the loans for those condos in Costa Rica."

Some of the tension eased out of Richard's body. "You got that wrong, just like you got it wrong about me and Cleo. All Cleo gets is prenup money and that wouldn't make a dent in what I need."

"What about the proceeds from the key man insurance?"

Richard looked puzzled. "I don't know what you are talking about."

Max spoke softly. "Somehow I thought you might know. The firm took out insurance payable on Glen's death. Cleo might be able to find what you need out of the two and a half million she'll receive."

Richard appeared stunned. "Two and a half million?"

Max saw Annie's theory—Richard deciding to kill Glen both for his wife and the money she would receive—dissolve like a sand castle with the tide running in.

Richard swung around and left without another word.

Max wondered: Was Richard a shocked and bewildered man, or was he a very fine actor?

Thirteen

Annie pulled in to the curb in front of the Broward's Rock police station. She scanned the street for Kit's VW. As she climbed the front steps, she checked the parking lot to the north. No little black car. She opened the front door and stepped into the narrow space in front of the counter.

Mavis Cameron's angular face looked tired, but she managed a smile. "Billy's not here, Annie. He went to the mainland."

Annie didn't take that calm statement as a good sign for Elaine Jamison. Very likely, Billy had gone to Chastain for a conference with Circuit Solicitor Brice Posey, who was not and never had been a favorite of Max and Annie's. However, Annie felt certain Mavis would not volunteer any information in regard to the status of Elaine Jamison, either as a suspect or as a prisoner. "Actually, I'm looking for Laura Jamison. She and her sister and brother came here to see about their aunt."

Mavis pushed back a strand of auburn hair. "They left a little while ago."

Annie nodded her thanks. As she turned to go, Mavis added, "I'll tell Billy you dropped by."

Outside, Annie pulled her cell from her purse and called Elaine's cottage. No answer. She called the Jamison house. "Is Laura there?" It might be better not to identify herself unless asked to do so. She listened. "No thanks, I won't leave a message."

In the car, she made a U-turn. In a way, she wasn't surprised to learn that Laura had gone to the beach. Was she taking solace from the sweep of the water to the horizon or was she simply trying to escape the worry and fear at home?

Annie found a parking space without a vestige of shade at Blackbeard Beach. She hurried to the boardwalk. She wished she could be there for pleasure, enjoying the scent of coconut oil and sea salt. Waves crested in lines of silver foam atop the green water. Just like yesterday, dolphins arched above the waves, graceful as ballerinas. Annie picked her way around umbrellas and among sun worshippers stretched on towels. At the third lifeguard stand, she again looked up at a thin face masked by sunglasses.

"Laura."

Laura looked down. "Kit was going to call you. Thanks for helping us. We contacted that lawyer. He's coming over tomorrow. They let Elaine come home. They're going to talk to her when Handler Jones is here."

So Billy had permitted Elaine to leave the station. Annie knew her name popped up on Elaine's caller ID when Elaine used her cell. If she was in the cottage when Annie called, she'd chosen not to answer. However, Laura had no way of knowing that Elaine didn't want to talk to Annie, and Laura clearly felt indebted to Annie for the connection to Handler Jones.

Annie strove to appear relaxed, as if in no way she and Laura were at odds. "That's wonderful news. He will certainly be helpful. As I said when I talked to Elaine"—if Laura assumed this conversation was recent, that was her privilege—"it's important to come up with the most complete information possible. Now that Elaine has cleared up the confusion about the gun, we're counting on you for absolutely critical information."

"Me?" Laura sat rigid.

Annie nodded energetically. "You were on the upper verandah. You saw Darwyn."

"Oh." Laura relaxed. "Yeah. I wasn't paying a lot of attention. He was blowing pine straw. Then I lost sight of him. He must have come up close to the terrace."

With the toe of one shoe, Annie drew a line in the sand. "Okay. That's the edge of the terrace." She walked a few feet and dragged her heel to make a line perpendicular to the first. "Here are the pine trees." Annie turned and walked several feet toward the water. She stamped her feet twice. "Let's say this is the cottage." She returned to the first line. "If you looked down, you could see the pine trees and flower beds and Darwyn. If you looked straight, you saw the cottage."

"Not exactly. There's a willow in front of the cottage."

Annie was impatient. "But you would see anyone coming from the cottage to the house once you were past the willow."

"Yes." Laura sounded reluctant. This line of questioning was clearly making her nervous and wary.

"When did Elaine come up to the house?" Annie had seen Elaine leave her cottage and hurry toward the marsh around ten. It would help narrow the time frame for Glen's murder if Laura knew when Elaine had walked to the house.

Laura looked relieved. "I didn't see Elaine."

Annie was puzzled. "Yesterday you said you were on the verandah the whole time. You should have seen her."

Laura shifted uneasily in the high seat. "Oh. I guess I wasn't there the whole time. I went inside for a few minutes. That must have been when Elaine came."

Annie had the clear sense that Laura was scrambling for an explanation. She glanced at the imprints in the sand. Darwyn had been in the pines or in the flower beds near the terrace. Definitely Laura should have seen Elaine either coming or going unless she had been absent from the porch for longer than just a few minutes. Was Laura protecting herself? It was possible that she had slipped downstairs to the study and that was why she hadn't seen Elaine. There was no reason for her not to admit having seen Elaine. Yet Annie sensed a lie somewhere in Laura's choppy responses.

She tried to work out the times. "How about Richard?"

Laura looked relieved. "I saw him. He was sweating. He'd been jogging. He came up to the terrace and went inside and then in only a few minutes the police came."

Annie imagined herself on the upper verandah. If Laura glimpsed someone leaving the house after having shot Glen, she would have seen that person walking—or running—toward the cottage and the lane that ran behind it. "Between the time you went out to the porch and before Richard arrived, did you see anyone heading toward the cottage?"

"I didn't see anyone." Her voice was strident.

Yesterday Annie had suspected that Laura was lying. Today she had no doubt that the girl was hiding something. Was she hiding the reason for her absence from the verandah or the identity of someone walking away from the house?

"Did you see Kirk Brewster?"

Laura's fingers curled on the strap of the binoculars in her lap. She drew a swift breath. "No."

Annie looked up and knew her face was grim. "You saw someone. I think it was Kirk. If you don't speak out, your aunt is going to be arrested."

Edna Graham hesitated. When she spoke, her voice was thoughtful but firm. "Mr. Darling, I'm positive Mr. Brewster didn't have anything to do with Mr. Jamison's death. But I've heard," and now she sounded worried, "that the police have arrested Elaine."

"That isn't correct." Max tried to sound reassuring. "The police simply wish to question her. Along that line, that's why I want to visit with Mr. Brewster." He kept his voice pleasant and hoped she concluded that he posed no threat to the young lawyer. "We're trying to collect as much information as possible to assist the police. I know Kirk has already been questioned and I'm sure he was helpful. I'm hoping he might offer some insights into the family dynamics."

"Oh. Well, of course. He's off-island this afternoon. He took his sister into Savannah to go to the doctor but"—as a good secretary, she had every partner's location at her fingertips—"you might find him at the youth center in a little while. He didn't intend to come back into the office. His nephew Sam has a baseball game at four o'clock."

Annie sat at the coffee bar. She sipped a cappuccino with a double dash of caramel. "Thanks, Henny. You're a sweetheart to pitch in while I'm running around the island not accomplishing very much." She felt discouraged and knew she sounded discouraged.

Henny's voice was firm. "You're doing your best. If it weren't for you, the police wouldn't know that Pat Merridew was murdered."

Annie felt even more discouraged. "We may know that someone poisoned Pat because she saw Glen's gun hidden in the gazebo, but Billy doesn't think there will ever be any way to prove that her death was deliberate."

"She won't be labeled a suicide." Henny's eyes flashed. "That matters to me and that matters to her sister. I finished packing up everything in Pat's house. Those travel brochures for the Alaska cruise never did show up." Henny Brawley poured herself a fragrant tropical tea. She came around to look over Annie's shoulder at a sketch pad of the Jamison front and back yards with arrows and Xs. "Your drawing looks like one of those old John Dickson Carr books. Maybe we should read *The Three Coffins* and see if we get some inspiration."

Annie was emphatic. "There's always an answer to a locked-room puzzle if you know where to look. But this time, I don't see any way out of a box." She pointed at the sketch. "There's the telephone lineman. He had a clear view of the front door to the Jamison house. According to Billy Cameron, the lineman said nobody came in or out until the police cars arrived, sirens blaring. So we can't have an unknown who popped in the front door, went down the hall, and shot Glen. Then . . ." Her index finger tapped the squiggle that represented the terrace and the backyard. "There's Laura on the upper verandah. She claims the only person she saw was Darwyn. She said she didn't see Elaine. Now she says she wasn't on the verandah the entire time. That wasn't what she said yesterday when she claimed she sat there the entire time from breakfast until Richard knocked on her bedroom door. If she was on the verandah and if she's telling the truth, then the only people who could have shot Glen are Kit or Laura from inside the house or Richard and Elaine from the backyard. I think Laura saw someone. Just like Darwyn did. Who would she protect? Kirk Brewster. Who has a gold-plated motive? Kirk Brewster. Did she see Kirk?"

Henny studied the drawing. "The possibilities come down to Kit and Laura, who were in the house; Richard, who claimed he found Glen dead; Elaine; or maybe Kirk. It looks bad for Elaine. She's the one who threw away the murder weapon and hid a bloodstained shirt."

Annie slipped down from the seat, wandered restlessly toward the fireplace. More Cat Truth posters were now mounted on the wall on either side of the fireplace and at the ends of bookshelves. No doubt Laurel had dropped by simply to lend a hand and, of course, improve the bookstore's decor in passing.

Whatever.

Annie's gaze slid across the photographs. Which was the most gorgeous? She admired new posters with the wide-open gold, almond-shaped eyes of a fawn-coated Somali (*Always say yes to adventure*), and an elegantly marked European Brown Tabby pressing a paw on the remnants of a mouse (*Don't knock it till you try it*). Among the original posters, she admired again the cinnamon-apricot Siamese with no pointing, green eyes huge in a big-eared, triangular face, back arched in a crouch, poised to spring, mouth agape in a hiss: *I'm warning you, back off.*

Just like Laura.

Annie shook her head in puzzlement. Why hadn't Laura admitted seeing Elaine? Elaine claimed she'd grabbed up the gun in a panic, gotten blood on her hand, dashed through the house, and grabbed Tommy's shirt from the laundry basket.

Tommy's shirt. The bloodhound smelled the shirt and came straight to Tommy.

Annie remembered Tommy in the living room after arriving home from his friend's house the morning of his father's murder. A too-tight, green-and-orange-striped polo had emphasized Tommy's stocky build. Was it possible . . . Slowly she reached for the phone, punched a familiar number.

"Yo, Annie."

"Marian"—Annie clung to a hope that the inde-fatigable reporter could help her—"can you give me a good physical description of Kirk Brewster?"

"Sure. What's in it for me?"

"If I find out anything big, you'll be the first to know." Annie's fingers were crossed. She would share with Marian at some point, but right now what mat-tered was discovering the truth.

"Blood oath?" Before Annie could erupt, Marian relented. "Okay, okay. I'll trust you. Okay. He's about five nine . . ."

Annie clicked off the phone and stared at another poster. A Highland Fold with an aura of age appeared comfortably settled on a red cushion. Perhaps it was clever photography, but there was a hint of a satisfied smile on the aging cat's large, rounded face: *All cats are gray in the dark.*

Ben Franklin's famous comment on the pleasures of older women after the candles were snuffed was far afield from crime, but Annie repeated the legend aloud. "All cats are gray in the dark." A picture formed in her mind. She yanked her cell phone from her pocket, punched a familiar number.

"Strike two . . ." The tall, skinny home-plate umpire balled his right hand into a fist and punched.

The wooden bleachers held about fifteen admiring onlookers. Kids played in the shade beneath the seat. An American flag fluttered from a staff at the top of the modest grandstand.

A wiry pitcher wound up and threw a high fastball.

The towheaded batter connected, and the ball dribbled into the outfield.

"Run, Sam. Way to go." Kirk Brewster yelled and whistled.

Dust flew as the little boy slid into first. The first baseman swiped with the ball, lost his grip, and the ball bounced into the outfield to be retrieved by the shortstop.

Max clapped loudly.

The lawyer gave Max a sour look. "You don't have to join Sam's cheering squad."

"He's a good hitter. I like baseball." Max's tone was mild. Without a change in tone, he asked, "Were you in the Jamison backyard Tuesday morning?"

Kirk gave a strangled hoot of laughter, but he didn't look amused. "Greased that question in, didn't you? Ever cross-examine a witness?"

"Not since practice court." Max was proud of his law degree and had been admitted to the bar in New York, but he was always quick to make it clear that he didn't practice law.

Kirk shoved a hand through his thick, tawny hair. "Let's get this straight. I wasn't there. I don't know anything about Glen's murder. I understand the cops are looking at me fish-eyed because of the insurance. I didn't kill Glen for the money."

"Although"—Max was still conversational—"it's convenient for you that he died before you wouldn't have been eligible for the payout."

"Yeah." Kirk sounded troubled.

"I assume you will accept the portion due you?"

Kirk's face hardened. "You're damn right I will, if for no other reason than to keep the bitch from walking away with five million." He glanced toward Max. "I was pretty upset that I was being pushed out, but I didn't blame Glen. Cleo yanked his string and he danced. It was as simple as that."

"So there's no reason why Laura Jamison might think she saw you in the backyard Tuesday morning?"

Kirk looked disturbed. "Is that what Laura said? But I didn't come."

Max tried not to look excited. "I guess she got it wrong."

Kirk shook his head, his expression bemused. "Man, I finally had a piece of luck. Laura kept begging me to talk to her dad one more time. I knew Cleo was going into Savannah for a dep, so I promised

Laura I'd drop by Tuesday morning. At the last minute I chickened out. I drove halfway there, then turned around and came back downtown. I went to the pier and walked up and down. Finally I decided to go to the office. I knew it wouldn't do any good to talk to Glen. He wasn't going to cross Cleo. That's why I didn't show up. Man, was that lucky. I'd be in the dock if I'd been on the spot when somebody shot Glen." He frowned. "Laura's called me a couple of times. I haven't answered. She doesn't know about the insurance. I didn't want to tell her. I feel kind of bad taking it, but I'd feel worse to leave it all to Cleo. I need to talk to Laura." Suddenly he gave a whoop as Sam darted from first, stole second.

As Max joined in the cheers, his cell phone rang. He took it from his pocket, glanced at the caller ID, answered. "Hey, Annie." He listened, then gazed at Kirk. "Yeah. I saw him from the back the other day. Yeah. You sure could make that mistake . . . Sure, hold on." He looked at Kirk. "What were you wearing Tuesday morning?"

Kirk looked blank. "Wearing?"

"Your shirt."

Kirk looked puzzled, but answered readily. "A short-sleeve madras plaid." His expression was touched with sadness. "I didn't want to look like a bum at Glen's house. I wish how I dressed was all that mattered on Tuesday."

The Crawford house on Heron Point was a ranch style, probably built in the late fifties. Annie always shook her head at homes that rested flush on the ground. A force-three hurricane would put all but a small portion of the island's center under four feet of water from the storm surge.

A scrawny teenager, maybe five feet six and weighing a hundred and ten, dribbled a basketball up the drive, dodged an imaginary opponent, turned, and threw. The basketball bounced on the rim, teetered, plopped to the drive. He caught it on the bounce.

Annie shut the car door and walked swiftly across the yard. "Buddy?"

The boy turned and looked at her politely. "Ma'am?" He appeared helpful and well mannered, apparently accepting without thought or question that a woman he didn't know knew him.

"Did Tommy Jamison bring your shirt back?"

Buddy looked shocked and uncertain. The direct question implied knowledge. Buddy's thumb rubbed hard against the seam on the basketball. "Tommy's shirt?"

"The one he borrowed Tuesday morning after he came back."

Buddy looked bewildered. "How'd you know?"

Annie's gaze was pleasant. "He was seen in the backyard at his house and now we are simply getting the times straight. When did Tommy leave your house?"

Buddy shuffled his feet.

Annie was firm. "We know what happened and it will be better for Tommy if you can confirm what time he left here and when he returned. He was wearing a blue shirt when he left, but when he came back to your house, he didn't have on a shirt." She saw indecision and, finally, resignation. She watched him grope through his thoughts. He'd promised Tommy he'd keep quiet, but somehow Tommy had been found out.

"Yeah. Well. Tommy didn't want me to tell anyone. See, his shirt—"

Annie interrupted. "The blue polo."

Buddy nodded. "Yeah. He got blood on his shirt." Buddy looked at her in entreaty, big brown eyes filled with concern.

Annie knew she was taking advantage of a teenager's credulity. She'd set out to prove Elaine Jamison innocent of murder. Everything about Elaine—her gentleness, her obvious devotion to her brother, her desperate unhappiness since his murder—had combined to convince Annie that she needed help. But perhaps Annie was beginning to understand Elaine's plea to be left alone to do what she felt she must do. Elaine loved her brother but she loved Tommy, too. It took an effort for Annie to speak. She knew her voice was thin. "It's better to straighten things out." She wasn't at all sure that clarifying the truth about his shirt was better for Tommy Jamison.

"Yeah, well, I didn't mind loaning him a shirt. He came back and he was all upset. Poor guy. He was shaking and crying. He found his dad dead and somebody had shot him. Tommy accidentally kicked the gun and then he picked it up."

Annie heard the echo of Elaine's explanation.

Buddy looked earnest. "He wasn't thinking. He was scared. He was afraid to call the police because he and his dad, well, they'd had a fight, and that morning Tommy had gone home to have it out with him about school and everything. He said if his dad didn't come around, he was going to run away and then his family could wonder what had happened to him. He got up to the study door and it was open and he pushed inside, ready to yell at his dad. He said that's maybe why he was moving so fast he didn't see the gun, but when he kicked it, he stopped and picked it up. Then he got really freaked. He had blood on his hand and he wiped it on his shirt. He ran out of the house and pulled the shirt off. He ran down to the cottage and his aunt took the gun and his shirt. She told him to go back to my house. Anyway, he got on his bike and came back here. He didn't know what to do. I told him maybe it would be better when he got home to act like he didn't know anything. I gave him one of my shirts to wear."

Annie looked sympathetic. "I guess he was really scared to call the police since he'd told you he was going to go home and have it out with his dad once and for all."

Buddy turned the basketball in his hands. "Well, he wouldn't have sounded so mad at his dad if he'd known somebody was going to shoot him."

Mavis Cameron smiled at Annie. "Billy said to come on in." She clicked to open the locked door to the interior of the police station.

Annie stepped into the corridor. She forced herself forward, stopped at the door with Billy's name on frosted glass. When she revealed what she knew, Tommy Jamison might become the prime suspect. If she didn't tell Billy, Elaine Jamison would be arrested. She took a deep breath, turned the knob.

Billy looked up from his desk. Lines of fatigue pulled at his sturdy, broad face. He managed a faint smile as he stood and gestured toward a straight chair in front of his desk.

She moved forward and sank onto the chair.

Billy eyed her sharply. "You look about as grim as I feel."

Annie took a deep breath and began without preamble. "Tommy Jamison . . ."

Billy listened intently, making notes. When she finished, he looked thoughtful. "I get the picture. His aunt lied to protect Tommy. That doesn't surprise me. She never seemed right for a killer. For one thing, so far as we've been able to find out, she's never shot a gun in her life. To hit her brother twice in the throat was more than blind dumb luck. And why the throat? To watch blood spew? The instinct is to go for the chest or, if you're a really good shot, the head."

He leaned back in his chair, stared out the window toward the harbor. "I'll talk to the kid. He'll probably open up when he finds out his friend let it all hang out. But even if he spills his guts, if it's the same talk about kicking the gun and getting blood on his shirt, that won't clear Elaine."

Annie edged forward on the hard chair. "When Laura realizes she didn't see Kirk and that you know Tommy was there, she can tell you exactly what she saw."

Billy's expression remained dour. "Here's what we've got. Laura was on the porch. Darwyn Jack was down in the yard. Laura saw somebody and now we know it was Tommy. She didn't see anyone else until Richard Jamison came in from his jog. He found Glen and immediately raised the alarm. Laura said she didn't see Elaine. If she'd seen anyone besides Tommy, she would have told us long before now. That leaves us with Kit and Laura in the house and Tommy crossing the backyard. Why would Kit or Laura come outside? No sense to it. And Tommy crossing the yard lets out the cousin, too. Darwyn told us Richard ran through the yard and out the road by the cottage around eight-thirty. Kit saw her father alive after that. By the time Richard came back from his jog, Tommy had already hurried to his aunt's cottage and given her the gun and the shirt stained with his dad's blood. You saw Elaine at the marsh before Richard returned."

Annie tried to sort out the timing in her mind. Kit and Laura in the house. Tommy in the backyard. Her lips felt stiff. "The murderer has to be Tommy." Blood on the blue polo . . .

Billy slammed a hand on his desk. "I've been a cop for a long time." He looked angry and frustrated. "I never thought Elaine was the killer. Now we have

Tommy in her place. But you know what, the murder of Darwyn Jack knocks everything screwy."

Annie was puzzled. "He must have seen Tommy."

Billy nodded shortly. "Right. The easy answer is that Tommy killed him because Darwyn tried blackmail, though I don't know how much money he could get out of a high school kid." He waved a hand. "I know, Tommy inherits, but I doubt he can get his hands on big money." His mouth twisted in a wry smile. "Even semibig money. So now, and I'm saying it like the circuit solicitor will see it, the easy answer will be that Darwyn tried to blackmail Tommy and Tommy killed him. The easy answer before that, and the circuit solicitor was hot for me to arrest Elaine, is that she killed Darwyn. But I don't believe either one of them cracked his skull. Darwyn's murder was planned down to the last detail and that includes Elaine's golf club. He was lured to the gazebo—the prosecution will argue he was there for a payoff—and what happened? Darwyn came to the gazebo. He sat on the top step. The killer then moved behind him and picked up Elaine Jamison's five iron and gave an almighty swing." Billy leaned forward and his words came in a staccato rush. "That doesn't play with me. Let's take Elaine Jamison. Tuesday, when her brother was killed, it's obvious she threw the murder weapon in the marsh. Smart move, right? We still haven't found the gun. We can't drain the marsh. My guess is we'll never find that Colt. Someday we may have a force-three hurricane and nature can play some tricks and a rusted pistol might be found wedged in a live-oak tree. Stranger things have happened. For now, we don't have the weapon. Fast-forward to Thursday night. The murderer used Elaine Jamison's five iron, which we later find in her golf bag. The club face wasn't even wiped off after it struck him. We had plenty of tissue to test. The lab results are back and her club was the murder weapon." He looked disgusted. "Does that make sense? She had the smarts to throw the Colt into the marsh and she was under pressure because she knew any minute Glen's body would be found. So I'm supposed to believe that Thursday night she takes her own five iron with her fingerprints all over the shaft, tucks the club away in the gazebo where it will be handy, meets Darwyn, cracks his skull, then marches back to her garage and puts the dirty club in her bag? Baloney. I didn't believe it then. I don't be-lieve it now. Besides that, you know what we found hidden up in a crook of a tree near the gazebo? Her gardening gloves. Now, why would she wear gardening gloves and not wipe off the fingerprints from the club? She had all night to throw that club in the marsh and put the gloves away in her gardening basket. We might have checked her bag and discovered the five iron was missing and been able to prove the wound was consistent with having been made by a five iron, but that doesn't compare to finding her club and proving it was the murder weapon."

"None of it makes sense." Annie thought of murder deep in the night, Darwyn lying facedown at the base of the gazebo steps. Elaine would have been a fool to keep the club. And there was no point in hiding the gloves up in a tree.

Billy was gruff. "You bet it's screwy. She's cool and smart and quick Tuesday morning when the pressure's on, but she panics and shoves the stick in her bag when it's the middle of the night and no one else is around, plus scrambles up in a tree to tuck her gloves in a crotch. There's a lot to be said for MO. People act the way they're going to act. You can't have smart-as-a-whip and dumb-as-a-post in the same person. That's what I told Brice."

Brice Willard Posey, the circuit solicitor, rarely heeded advice.

Billy shook his head. "Brice never met a fact he'd pay attention to. He was hell-bent to arrest Elaine. I staved him off, at least until after tomorrow. She and her lawyer will show up here at nine. Now the solicitor will switch horses and ride Tommy. He'll say I was right on the button and the club in the bag was a trap for her. He'll say Tommy Jamison used the club and hid the gardening gloves and left his aunt holding the bag. The solicitor will love it: deranged teenager from old island family guns down father, knocks off a blackmailer, and frames his aunt. Do you know why that scenario stinks?"

"Not the same MO?"

He shook his head. "The MO's the same. The key to the gun safe disappeared before the murder. That shows planning, just like Darwyn's murder shows planning. This time it has to do with character. Tommy Jamison's got a reputation for a bad temper. A couple of fights after football games, sometimes some rough stuff in the locker room. Apparently, he loses his cool, then pretty quick snaps out of his rage and is an all-around good guy. If he'd shot his dad, then had been stricken with remorse, that would be one thing, but Glen's death was planned down to the last detail. For example, Darwyn only worked there on Tuesday mornings. That's when the leaf blower would hide the sound of the shots. Lots of planning, so same MO. That doesn't sound like Tommy Jamison. Besides, when he found his dad dead, if he was dead, who did Tommy run to? His aunt. She came through for him big-time. Unless he's like Rhoda in *The Bad Seed*, he'd frame anybody but his aunt.

Who tried to save him? Who took his shirt and hid it and lied for him when we found it? His aunt."

Annie remembered that moment when the bloodhound loped up to Tommy and began to bay and when the shirt was identified as his, how Tommy had begun to speak but Elaine cut him off. His instinct had been to tell the truth and save his aunt.

Billy glanced toward a gray folder that sat by itself near his in-box. He reached out, tapped the cover. "And there's Pat Merridew. We'll never prove she was murdered, but too much has happened in the Jamison gazebo to act like that picture in her BlackBerry didn't mean anything." He gave Annie a wry glance. "You kept telling me, right?"

Annie felt as if she'd planted a flag atop a mountain.

Billy gave her a thumbs-up. "Counting her as another murder victim makes it clear that the crimes were carefully planned. Admittedly, we have three deaths from different means—poison, shots, and a blunt instrument—but if the deaths are linked, somebody's thinking on all cylinders. There's no way Tommy Jamison can figure for the Merridew death. Was Pat Merridew going to invite a teenager over for Irish coffee? I don't think so. That puts it back on Elaine, but Laura didn't see her cross the backyard plus Elaine was off-island when the BlackBerry pic was made."

Billy shoved his hand through his thick short hair. "It's an almighty mess. I don't believe the murderer is Elaine or Tommy. Yet somebody close to Glen Jamison shot him. Only someone with access to the house could have obtained the Colt. But when we look, we eliminate suspects one by one. The wife was in Savannah. The cousin left when Glen was alive and came back after"—Billy emphasized the word—"the kid got blood on his shirt. Laura didn't see Elaine in the backyard during the critical period. That leaves Laura herself, her sister Kit, or Tommy. Kit and Laura had no reason to go outside, so Darwyn didn't see them. That brings us back to Tommy, but the idea rubs me wrong." He looked weary. "The circuit solicitor wants somebody's hide nailed to the wall. The only good thing is Posey won't harass me tomorrow because he doesn't work on Saturdays. Monday morning he'll summon me. He'll say it's time I moved, made the arrest, slapped Tommy Jamison in jail. The hell of it is, we've got enough evidence. Do you think Posey cares if I know in my gut that somewhere something's wrong?"

Cricket frogs cheek-cheeked, bull frogs whorummed, barking frogs yapped, and Southern toads shrieked. Cicadas whirred and crickets clicked. Annie stood on her and Max's back verandah, looking through the dusk toward the darkness of the pond, but she found no peace in the summer serenade. "I was smart, wasn't I? I figured out about the shirt and now Tommy Jamison's going to be arrested."

Max slipped an arm around her shoulders. "Sometimes"—his voice was gentle—"what we see is what is there."

Annie felt as if her thoughts had raced around and around ever since she talked with Billy. No matter how she figured, there didn't seem to be any way to save Tommy.

"Kids kill." Max was somber.

Annie knew he was right and yet Billy thought the equation was wrong. So did she. She turned to Max, lifted her chin. "We can't give up. Tomorrow, let's try one more time. Darwyn was one sexy guy. We know he had a girlfriend." She pictured the cabin at Jasmine Gardens. "He would have talked to her about the morning he was working at a house and a man was killed. I mean, that was too exciting to ignore. Maybe I can find her."

Max gave her shoulders a squeeze. "I'll tilt at a windmill, too. Richard Jamison claims he wasn't having an affair with Cleo. If he was, what are the odds he'd know about the key man insurance? It's a small island. If they were meeting on the sly, there should be some trace."

Dimly Annie heard the ring of the telephone in the kitchen. She almost ignored the sound, then turned and hurried inside. She raised an eyebrow at the caller ID, answered in a neutral voice.

"Annie Darling?" Cleo Jamison's voice was low and hurried, but Annie had no difficulty recognizing the rich contralto.

"Yes."

"I hope you don't mind my calling you at home." Cleo sounded uncertain. "I want to know what's going on. I have a right to know what's happening. Glen was my husband." There was a hint of anger in the pronoun. "The police have been here. The chief wanted to talk to Tommy about his shirt. I advised him to decline to answer questions until he was represented by counsel. I understand he and Elaine will be interviewed tomorrow. Chief Cameron left and now the family's shut me out. You'd think they would appreciate my effort to help. Maybe I shouldn't help them. If one of them killed Glen, I want them arrested. But I have trouble believing Elaine or Tommy would shoot Glen. Since Laura was sitting there, I didn't want to say anything, but it looks to me like Kirk is the one the police should be investigating. Cameron said the information about Tommy's shirt came from you. What exactly did you tell him?"

Annie hesitated. Obviously, Billy had given only the bare minimum of information. Was it his intent to let the family worry and wonder until the interview tomorrow?

Cleo attacked. "I have a right to know. Glen was my husband."

Annie pictured Cleo clutching her cell phone, perhaps secreted in the small study, keeping her voice low in a house where she was the outsider.

She did have a right to know.

Annie spoke soberly. " . . . and so it turned out that Laura saw Tommy."

"Oh my God." Cleo's voice was faint. "Poor Glen. Oh, poor Glen." There was a long pause. Finally, shakily, she said, "I only wanted Tommy to be nice to me. I'll never forgive myself if Glen died because I made Tommy mad. But we'll see what happens tomorrow. I'll be there. I hope the police chief is wrong." A long pause. "But he may be right." The last words were scarcely audible. "If you learn anything else, call me."

Fourteen

B ella Mae Jack was composed. "If I knew something to help the police, I would have told them."
A frown furrowed her pale face. "I always worried that
Darwyn would get himself in trouble. The police think
he wanted money to keep quiet about what he saw the
morning Mr. Jamison was killed. I wish I could say that
Darwyn wouldn't do such a thing. I was always afraid
Darwyn could turn bad." Her voice was weary, tired
with heartache and loss and disappointment. "Darwyn
wanted more than he had any right to have and there
was a hard spot in his heart. He loved me. I loved him.
I wish that had been enough."

Annie felt the hot burn of tears. Her hand trembled
as she lifted the coffee mug. Darwyn's grandmother
had insisted that they sit at the old-fashioned white

table in the kitchen and have a piece of sherry cake and a cup of coffee. The old woman, her shoulders stiff beneath her crisp dress, was a gallant figure, accepting that life was full of trouble and woe.

Bella Mae Jack reached across the table and patted Annie's hand. "You are a good girl. And nice to come for Darwyn."

Annie put down the coffee mug. "Mrs. Jack, did Darwyn have some close friends I could speak to, maybe a girlfriend? Perhaps he might have told someone what he saw that morning."

Bella Mae's long face was somber. "Darwyn kept to himself. He never had anyone over. As for girls"—she averted her gaze—"I'm afraid he didn't treat girls the way he should. He'd be with one for a while and then another, but he never cared about them. The last one kept calling but he wouldn't talk to her. I heard she moved to the mainland last May." She looked faintly surprised. "I don't know that he was seeing anyone the last month or so. He was home most nights."

Annie scrambled for some hint, some reflection of Darwyn's last days. "I don't suppose"—she hated asking, forced herself—"that there was anything in his pockets"—the police would have cataloged and returned his personal effects to her—"that might lead to someone he saw recently?"

Bella Mae took a breath. "I don't think so. But you're welcome to see." She pushed up from the table, led the way down a short hall, opened the first door to her left, stood aside for Annie to enter.

"I put the things on his desk." She gestured toward a light pinewood desk against the opposite wall.

Annie noted the single bed against one wall with a dark green spread. Two rock posters hung above the bed. A boom box sat against one wall, next to a rotating gun rack that held two rifles and a shotgun. Mounted antlers on one wall made the room look small.

Bella Mae stayed in the doorway. "I laid everything out."

Annie stepped past her. At the back of the desktop sat a wine bottle with a candle stub in the neck, a canteen, a duck whistle, a pair of field binoculars, several boxes of ammunition, a soft canvas camouflage hat, a hat-clip light, a pinewood rack with three pistols, a Braves baseball cap, a deck of well-thumbed playing cards, a set of red-feathered darts.

She had no difficulty discerning the contents of Darwyn's pockets on the night he died. The items were ranged in an orderly row: car keys, brown leather wallet, assorted coins, pocketknife, crumpled receipt from a Gas 'N Go, pack of condoms, small plastic container of mints, one metal key to Cabin Nine of

Jasmine Gardens, laminated card with the Braves baseball schedule, a half-dozen lottery tickets, cell phone.

Max pulled up in front of the Gypsy Caravan, a seedy
motel next door to an equally unprepossessing beer
joint with a tin roof and red barn siding. He glanced at
his list. Nine names were now scratched through and
they were the better motels on the island. Broward's
Rock had fishing cabins, apartment houses, and rental
condos, but fewer than a dozen old-fashioned motels.
He'd spoken to managers and yard workers and a few
occupants. No one had recognized a photo of Richard
Jamison or Cleo Jamison. He squinted against the
bright sun. This was not a milieu for Cleo Jamison.
On the other hand, she could be confident that no one
she knew would likely be found here. Max sighed and
opened the car door. Annie admired thoroughness,
tenacity, and unswerving commitment. He would
finish what he had set out to do, but unless he was
mightily surprised, Richard Jamison had not arranged
any on-island liaisons with his cousin's wife. Now, as
for off-island . . .

Max strolled toward a ratty office with smeared
windows and a sagging screen door. As Annie had
pointed out, Richard appeared to have taken up squatter's rights at the Jamison house, but Cleo practiced

law and, until last Tuesday, had a husband who would be aware of her whereabouts, especially at night. That made off-island meetings unlikely. In the afternoons, there were too many people in and out of the house for a rendezvous there.

Max opened the door, wrinkled his nose at the musty smell. He stepped inside to dim light. A beefy-faced clerk looked up from a computer.

Annie worked hard, slicing open boxes, carefully easing out new titles, frowning at an occasional wrinkled edge to a book jacket. She soon had a stack of twenty Linda Fairsteins and thirty-five Randy Wayne Whites. Occasionally she checked the time. Was Billy talking to Elaine or to Tommy? Was Handler Jones representing Elaine or her nephew? If the spotlight was now on Tommy, Elaine had probably asked Jones to represent him. With every minute that passed, the time came nearer when Tommy Jamison would be taken into custody and charged with murder. Obviously, Max hadn't hit pay dirt or he would have called.

As if on cue, her cell phone rang.

She answered, hoping. "Max?"

"Nada, honey." He was philosophical. "I can affirm, attest, and swear that if Richard was screwing Cleo they were either invisible or off-island."

Annie felt as wilted as a day-old corsage. "I didn't have any luck either."

There was a silence. Then he said gently, "I'm sorry."

"You tried. We tried." She looked at the clock. Eleven. Had Tommy been arrested yet?

"Hey, Annie. Let's take *Lady* out."

Annie was tempted. *Island Lady* was Max's new 375 HP twenty-nine-foot speedboat. Max loved fast and faster and could reach a terrifying (to Annie) 70 mph, but when Annie was aboard he promised to keep her under forty. Yet she didn't feel comfortable seeking pleasure when she knew the grim prospect facing the Jamison family. Besides, it was Saturday and Ingrid deserved to have the owner at work. "Tomorrow. I promise." She looked toward the worktable. "I'm unpacking boxes. You go ahead." She dropped the cell phone into her pocket, returned to her task. She carried twelve Randy Wayne White books out of the stockroom. She placed six copies face out in the New Mystery section.

As she walked back toward the storeroom, she noted a Cat Truth poster at the end of the Romantic Suspense section. An elegant Havana Brown, its mahogany-colored coat thick and short, lifted its irregular muzzle to stare with large oval green eyes: *Are you paying homage yet?*

"Gorgeous," she murmured. She swerved toward the coffee bar. Only a few customers sat at the tables. A sunny Saturday morning was time to play golf or tennis, ride bikes, stroll on the beach, plunge into the ocean with a cautionary eye for jellyfish, feel the rush of the wind as a speedboat spanked across the bay.

Annie stepped behind the coffee bar. She poured Colombian Supremo into a mug emblazoned with *Dead End* by John Stephen Strange. That's where she was. Or caught between a rock and a hard place. The rock was Laura's view of the backyard. The hard place was Annie's disbelief in the guilt of the only person who could be guilty, according to what Laura claimed she had seen.

Annie drank deeply, but the wonderfully black and strong coffee didn't provide its usual boost. Her eyes narrowed in thought. Laura had waffled about her presence on the porch. Annie reached for the portable phone. She called Max's secretary and in a moment she had Laura's cell-phone number.

"Laura, Annie Dar—"

"You have a lot of nerve to call me." Laura's voice vibrated with anger. "Tommy's in big trouble and it's your fault. That policeman's talking to him. Elaine and that lawyer are with him."

Annie pictured the hard wooden bench in the anteroom of the police station. "Are you at the police station?"

"Where else would we be, thanks to you. Why didn't you let us alone?"

Annie was stung. "I was trying to help Elaine. I knew you saw someone. I thought you were protecting Kirk. When we found out he was wearing a madras shirt, I talked to Buddy Crawford. That's when I realized you must have seen Tommy when he came home to see your dad."

"They trapped me." Now Laura was crying. "They told me Kirk was wearing a plaid shirt and then they asked if the shirt I saw was blue. I was so glad it wasn't Kirk that I said yes. I wasn't thinking about Tommy. I didn't know he was wearing a blue shirt Tuesday morning."

"What did you see that morning?"

"I only caught a glimpse of a guy in blue coming onto the terrace. I thought it was Kirk. Then, in just a few minutes, I heard running feet and somebody raced from the terrace across the backyard. Again, I thought it was Kirk. I couldn't see Elaine's front door because of a willow. I'd have known it wasn't Kirk if I'd seen him go to the cottage. Tommy said he left his bike down by the garage."

Annie's voice was sharp. "Were you on the porch the entire morning?"

"I've told you and told the police. Yes. I was there."

"But once you said you'd gone inside for a few minutes."

"That's because you were badgering me and I didn't want to say I'd seen Kirk. I should have known it wasn't him, but I thought he was coming over to try and talk to Dad."

It was like hearing a cell door click.

"What difference does it make now?" Laura was querulous.

"If you were there the entire time and you saw only Tommy"—Annie drew a deep breath—"then there's no one else who could have shot your father."

The silence pulsed. "You mean . . . Oh, no, no, that can't be. Not Tommy. No, someone came through the front. That's what happened." There was huge relief in her voice.

Annie was brusque. "A telephone lineman was across the street. No one came in the front door until the police arrived."

"I don't understand."

"The murderer came across the backyard." Annie heard the sadness in her own voice.

"Oh. The guy could be wrong. And if he isn't"— the words came fast—"then I know the murderer must have come"—she struggled for breath—"when I went inside for a few minutes. I mean, I wasn't out there the whole time. Somebody could have come and I wouldn't have seen them. So it doesn't have to be Tommy. I'll tell them as soon as they let us talk to them again. Anybody can make a mistake. I wasn't thinking. I thought it didn't matter. See, I went inside and I went to the top of the stairs and I was going to go down and talk to Dad and"—a pause—"I heard a door close downstairs and I decided I'd wait and see him later. So there was time for someone else to come. Oh. I've got to go now."

The call ended.

Annie replaced the phone. Laura didn't lie particularly well. That didn't matter. Her response told Annie all she needed to know. Laura hadn't left the porch. She would be glad to claim that she'd left, if it would help Tommy. But Annie knew in her heart that Laura had been on the porch the entire morning. She had seen Darwyn. She had seen Tommy. She had not seen Elaine. She had seen Richard, but by that time Tommy had run to the cottage with the gun and the bloodied shirt, leaving his father dead in the study.

Annie poured the now lukewarm coffee in the sink. Her steps felt leaden as she moved across the coffee area. She and Max and Billy had tried hard to find the truth and now the truth seemed inescapable.

Laura had seen what she had seen.

She'd watched Darwyn, moving no doubt with his swagger and compelling maleness. Darwyn had tangled with the wrong person. He would never again be alive with lust in Jasmine Gardens. Somewhere on the island some woman knew him well. Now it didn't matter that she'd been impossible to find. There had been no one else in the Jamison backyard on that deadly Tuesday morning but Darwyn at work with the leaf blower and Tommy coming later, angry with his father, and in front of the house a telephone lineman with a clear view of the Jamison front porch.

Annie shook her head in confusion. Billy had emphasized the careful planning he thought he saw in the crimes. Was Tommy able to mount that kind of effort? Pat Merridew's death had been cunningly contrived. How would Tommy know she had pain pills? Would Pat serve Irish coffee to a teenager? Would a teenage boy think in terms of carefully washing and returning a crystal glass to a breakfront? Even if all of that were possible, would Tommy use his aunt's golf club for a third murder and hide her gardening gloves in a tree where they were sure to be found? And why would Darwyn calmly sit on the top step of the gazebo and permit someone he suspected of murder to step behind him in the dark?

Fragments of thoughts jostled in her mind. Tuesday morning . . . Laura sitting on the upper verandah . . . the leaf blower . . .

Annie paused in front of the fireplace. To her left, a Cat Truth poster was a little askew. She stepped forward, her hand out to straighten it, but she stopped and stared at the Bombay Tom, black as pitch, looking as satisfied as a gambler with a royal flush, bright yellow eyes gleaming, and on the floor a broken fishbowl: *Don't look at me. I was at the vet's.*

Don't look at me . . .

Everything shifted in her mind.

Billy had been right to emphasize planning. Now she understood why the gun had been hidden in the gazebo, the necessity for Glen to die on Tuesday morning, the function of the leaf blower, the deliberate use of Elaine's five iron, passion and lust, Kirk still a partner, Richard's decision to leave the island . . .

Annie darted into the storeroom, grabbed her purse. She reached for the door handle, then stopped. She turned and walked slowly to her desk, sank into the chair.

There was no proof.

All she had was an elegant theory.

Did her theory account for the quirks and oddities that had occurred since the key to the gun safe disappeared?

She pulled a pad close, began to write. When she finished, she nodded. Her conclusion was true. Everything fit. The design was clever, cruel, remorseless. Fingerprints? Slowly, Annie shook her head. There had been plenty of time to pull on plastic gloves, use a cloth damp with Windex to polish doorknobs, faucet handles, any and every spot likely to have been touched in the cabin at Jasmine Gardens. The execution would have been thorough, careful, patient. This murderer was never careless.

Fingerprints . . .

There might be a way . . . Billy must never know . . . So many things would have to play out the right way . . . Could she do it? Was she brave enough? She thought of Max. He had a lawyer's view of the law and her plan flouted the law big-time. If she succeeded in setting a trap, if everything broke her way, then she would call Max.

But not until then.

Annie pulled out her cell phone, punched the number. The phone rang six times, seven. *Please be home, please,* she willed.

"Hello." There was neither warmth nor rejection in the voice, there was only deep weariness.

Annie spoke briefly, listened, felt a flood of gladness. "Thank you. I'll come right now." Eyes narrowed in thought, she scrabbled in a catchall drawer, found a chisel. She slid the tool in a pocket. Frowning, almost stymied, she surveyed the storeroom, a table for packing and unpacking books, her computer, desk, a sink . . . She hurried across the room, picked up the long, narrow box of Saran wrap. She plucked a plastic sandwich bag from another box and dropped it into another pocket.

When she pulled up in front of Bella Mae Jack's well-kept frame house, Annie knew it wasn't too late to turn back. It took all of her determination to walk across the yard.

Bella Mae waited on the porch. She rose from the rocking chair, her face weary. "Here it is." She looked curiously at the key before she handed it to Annie. "Do you know what it's for?"

Annie didn't meet her eyes. "Yes."

There was a silence.

Bella Mae sighed. "I was always afraid . . ." She turned away. Her front door closed. The sharp click might have been the sound of a heart breaking.

Annie stared at the white panel, then whirled, ran down the steps and to the car. As she drove away, she thought about Tommy, scared, puzzled, accused, facing arrest.

Annie drove faster. She pulled into Pat Merridew's driveway, parked the car out of sight behind the house. She took plastic wrap and wound a thick strip around each hand. She tossed her purse into the trunk, dropped the car keys into her pocket. They clanked against the key given to her by Bella Mae Jack. She hurried to the opening into the woods.

On the trail, she stumbled once, her foot snagged by a vine. She was sweating profusely by the time she reached the end of the trail and the Jamison backyard. A crow cawed and flapped sturdy wings. Insects whirred, surrounding her in a cloud. She waved away no-see-'ums. Two cars were parked in the drive, a faded red Dodge and a black Mercedes. She would guess the Dodge belonged to Laura. The sleek Mercedes very likely was Glen's car. Kit's VW wasn't there or Elaine's Corolla. Annie felt certain Cleo would have taken her own car to the police station. Had Richard gone with her? But there should be another car if he had left his.

Annie stared at the house. There was no hint of occupancy, but a half-dozen people could be inside and she wouldn't know. She had to know. She pulled her cell phone from her pocket, punched numbers, the effort made awkward by the Saran wrap. This time the call was answered immediately.

"Broward's Rock Police."

Annie was relieved that Mavis had answered. Mavis was serious, solid, dependable. Would she step outside her comfort zone?

"Mavis, Annie Darling. Don't mention my name aloud. Please look as if you are taking an everyday kind of call. I know who killed Glen Jamison. I will tell Billy as soon as I obtain one more piece of information." This was not true, but if she succeeded in her plan, no one would ever know or care. "However, before I can make progress"—her stomach tightened at what lay ahead—"I have to know about the Jamisons. The last I heard, they were at the station. If they're sitting on the bench, don't look toward them. Don't give any indication that you are aware of them. When I mention a name, if that person is currently at the police station, don't say anything."

"All deliveries must be brought to the back door." Mavis sounded bored. "But I need to know more about the invoice. I need a clear description of the goods."

Annie smiled. Mavis wanted the lowdown on what Annie knew.

"I'll get to that." But not in this call, though this wasn't the moment to tell Mavis. "First, let me know about the Jamisons. Remember, no answer if the person named is there. Elaine Jamison?" Silence.

"Tommy Jamison." Silence. "Kit Jamison?" Silence. "Laura Jamison?" Silence. "Cleo Jamison?" Silence. "Richard Jamison?"

"No."

Annie felt a quiver of uneasiness. "Richard Jamison is not at the station?" She'd counted on all the Jamisons being present at the station.

"That's correct." Mavis continued to sound as if she might be discussing a shipment.

"All right." Possibly Annie was stymied before she began. But she would worry about that eventuality if it occurred.

"Please list the contents of the invoice." Now there was an edge to Mavis's voice.

"I can't go into detail right now. Tell Billy I know what happened and I will get back in touch as soon as I've set up a chance for an arrest. Until then, it is critically important that both Tommy Jamison and Elaine Jamison be kept at the station and the other Jamisons be told that Billy has just left for the mainland to speak with the circuit solicitor. That's essential. Do that for me. I'll call back as soon I can."

"Wait a min—"

The connection ended. Obviously Mavis wanted more information. She would alert Billy to Annie's call. Annie could not afford to have her cell phone ring, not for a good long while. She turned off the phone, dropped it into her pocket.

She moved out of the shadow of the woods into the Jamison backyard. She passed Elaine's cottage and the gazebo. She walked boldly to the back steps and climbed to the verandah. She knocked on the back door. If the door started to open, she would have time to remove the wrap from her hands.

There was no response.

Annie waited a moment, tried again. The door remained shut. The house was apparently empty.

Now she would set her plan in motion. If they ever knew, Billy—and Max—would be appalled. But she had made up her mind. The murderer of Glen Jamison had left no traces. Annie was certain she knew the identity of the shadowy figure behind three murders, but she had no proof. There would never be proof unless she succeeded in her scheme.

Getting into the Jamison house was the first essential step.

Annie opened the screen door, turned the handle of the back door. It was locked. Most island homes did not run to alarm systems and doors were often left unlocked during the day when residents were home. The locked door gave her a sense of reassurance that no one was in the house.

Annie moved down the verandah, trying the French doors. All were locked. Hurrying down the steps, she ran lightly to the end of the porch and came around to the west side of the house. The house was built on arches to avoid flooding by storm surges. She stopped at the first window. She stood on tiptoe and used the chisel to poke a hole about six inches up on the left side of the screen next to the frame. She edged the chisel inside, worked it back and forth to loosen the latch. She pulled the loose side out far enough to unsnap the other latch. Now she was able to unlatch the other side and stand between the loose screen and the sash. She pushed and the window slid up. She dropped the chisel into her pocket.

Annie felt a sweep of relief. If necessary, she would have found something in the garden, a brick, a small pottery decoration, to break a window. She had a fuzzy understanding of breaking and entering and hoped she would never have to understand the finer points. If she succeeded in slipping in and out of the Jamison house without leaving any evidence of her visit, she would be much better off. The small slit in the screen might escape notice, and certainly, if she relocked the screen, there wouldn't be a suggestion of forced entry.

An incorrigible optimist, Annie felt buoyed by the unlocked window. She pushed aside the interior shutters and scrambled to pull herself up and over the sill. It was only when she stood in the dim room, its silence broken by the tick of a stately grandfather clock, that she realized she was in Glen Jamison's study. The room was airless and still. The scrubbed patch on the Oriental carpet was a haunting reminder of violent death. Annie turned and pulled the screen shut. She latched it. As she pushed the window down, she felt trapped in a chamber of horrors.

She was breathing fast by the time she skirted the discolored rug and reached the door. She wanted to fling it open and be free of the study, but she carefully turned the knob, barely pulled the door ajar.

Silence.

She waited, listening over the quick rush of her breathing. There was no sound of life or occupancy. She slipped into the hall, again listened hard.

No one home. Thank heaven, no one home.

In a flash Annie was at the cross hall. She unlocked the door to the back verandah for her escape, then turned and hurried to the stairs. She eased up the steps, two at a time. In the shadowy upper hallway, she wanted to hurry, run and grab and be gone, but she forced herself to move stealthily.

She was close.

She tried one door after another. It didn't take long to find the room she sought. She stepped inside, noted the double bed with a canopy. She turned to her right and walked directly to a vanity in an alcove framed by velvet hangings. She opened a makeup kit, selected a smooth lipstick, a rich bronze. She held it delicately with her plastic-wrapped fingers. She pulled the plastic bag from her pocket, dropped the case inside, and tucked the bag in her pocket.

She hurried across the room, turned the knob, ready to step into the hall.

Distantly, unmistakably, she heard the slam of a door.

Max eased up on the throttle. Oh, man, did he like speed. What a fine and fabulous day. As the boat slowed, he turned the wheel. He was about ten miles offshore and could barely discern a faint hint of land. He glanced at his watch. Almost eleven-thirty. He had cheese and beer in the fridge. Annie, dutiful and dear, would stay at her post until closing time. But he could probably persuade her to take a lunch break. He needed to convince her that Tommy Jamison's problems were not of her making. Max shook his head. If Tommy shot his dad, surely Pat Merridew's death had to be classified as suicide. Henny swore that was wrong. But Tommy certainly couldn't have dropped ground-up pills in Pat's Irish coffee. Probably Annie right now was muddling about Death on Demand, trying to fit round pegs into square holes. He'd cheer her up. He whistled "Pretty Woman," but the tune was swept away by the breeze as he pulled on the throttle and headed home.

Fifteen

Treads creaked on the stairs.

Annie's heart thudded. She edged the bedroom door open just enough to peer down the hall. The doorway to the upper verandah was visible from the stair landing. She would be seen if she tried to reach the verandah. But there was no place to hide on the porch anyway. Her throat dry, she eased the door shut. If only she knew who was coming up the stairs. She had no assurance this room was not the destination.

Annie hurried back to the alcove, stepped within, pressed against the wall. She was hidden behind the red velvet hanging unless—oh, dear heaven—someone walked to the vanity.

The bedroom door opened.

Annie watched in the vanity mirror as the panel swung in. She shrank against the wall.

Richard Jamison stepped into the room. He didn't turn on the light. He stood with his head bent forward, his hands loose at his sides. He was big and formidable, muscular arms, large hands, knees slightly bent, as if he could spring forward, deal with any foe. He had the Jamison look, a narrow bony face, high cheekbones, thin lips. His gaze swung about the room. At one point, he stared directly toward the alcove, revealing his face in full in the vanity mirror. His eyes were intent. His lips pressed together, making a thin, grim line. Muscles bunched in his cheeks.

Finally, he turned away and moved toward the open door. He stepped into the hall, pulling the door shut with a slam.

Annie's chest ached. Her knees felt weak. She waited, her Saran-wrapped hands in tight balls. She wasn't sure how much time had passed. She felt a fury of impatience to escape the house, a terror of what she might face if she ventured into the hall. Finally, one hesitant step after another, she crossed the room, eased open the door.

She heard movement, the opening and closing of drawers, the thump of footsteps.

She had to leave before anyone else returned. Tommy may already have been arrested. If he were taken into custody, the other family members would surely return home. If she didn't leave soon, discovery was all but certain.

She crept down the hall, tiptoeing near the wall to avoid any creaks.

From an open door on the other side of the hall came the sounds of movement.

Annie crossed the hall, moved nearer the door. Carefully, she peeked into the room.

Richard was folding a polo shirt, adding it to a stack on the bed next to an open suitcase.

Silent as a wraith, Annie slipped past the open doorway, shoulders hunched, expecting a shout, pursuit.

Once past the opening, she moved faster, reached the top of the stairs. She picked her way down the stairs as delicately as a heron stepping into a marsh. She placed each foot carefully flush to the wall and in the center of the tread to avoid squeaks. She reached the hall below and with a feeling of enormous gratitude turned and ran lightly to the back door. She opened the door and the screen and stepped onto the verandah. Richard's room overlooked the front yard. She felt safe to slip down the steps and into the garden. She ran as if pursued, braced for shouts, a chase. As she plunged into the woods, she heard the sound of a car in the Jamison drive.

She ran on the trail, not pausing until she burst into Pat Merridew's backyard. She stopped there, one hand tight on the strands of a willow, gasping, trying to pull air into her burning lungs. Finally, feeling weak, she hurried to her car. In the driver's seat, she peeled the Saran wrap from her sweaty hands, compressed the plastic into tight little balls, dropped them into a drink holder. She turned on the motor.

Her journey was not yet at an end.

As Max nosed into the harbor, his cell phone rang. He expertly came alongside the slip and glanced at the caller ID. He answered without a qualm. Maybe something had broken in the search for Glen's murderer. "Yo, Billy."

"Where's Annie?" Billy Cameron's voice was crisp.

Max frowned. "At the store." Even as he spoke, he knew the police chief would have checked there.

"Ingrid says she raced out the back door without saying anything to her. Annie called Mavis on her cell, said she knew who killed Glen Jamison, that she'd be back in touch. Annie isn't answering her cell. Do you know what she's up to?"

Max felt like he'd been slammed hard against a wall. "I don't have any idea. I'll be right there."

Billy's voice was gruff. "She shouldn't take off on a harebrained scheme on her own. Obviously, she's up to something she shouldn't be doing. Damn fool. Look, she made some requests. I'm playing along. For now. Elaine Jamison and Tommy are having lunch in the break room courtesy of the county. The rest of the Jamisons have left. They're under the impression Elaine and Tommy are in custody and I've taken a cruiser over to the mainland to meet with the circuit solicitor. I don't like playing games, but I don't want your demented wife dead either."

Max's gut twisted.

"Long story short, part of Annie's deal is for me officially to be off-island. So I'm not here. Come in the back way."

The living room of Cabin Nine was dim, airless, stuffy, and hot. Jasmine Gardens didn't run the air-conditioning in vacant units. Annie pulled the small plastic bag from her pocket. She gazed around the room at the comfortable rattan furniture, then shook her head.

In three swift steps, she was in the bedroom. Again she studied the furnishings. Finally, she knelt near the desk. She held up the plastic bag, opened it. A tube of lipstick fell onto the carpet. The lipstick came to rest against the back leg of the desk, scarcely discernible.

She nodded in satisfaction. Everything was in place. She glanced at her watch. The next ferry to the mainland left in thirty-nine minutes.

She welcomed the fresh air as she walked to her car. She gave a decided nod after she slid into the driver's seat. She thought furiously as she drove, oblivious to sparkling sunshine and verdant greenery. It was a short drive from Jasmine Gardens to the harbor. Annie parked alongside the boardwalk. She stepped out of the car and a pleasant breeze stirred her hair. She walked to the railing, gazed out at the choppy water, then looked back at the park that sloped gradually upward.

The police station sat to the north on a slight rise. She gazed all around, saw no familiar cars or faces. It was unlikely any of the Jamisons would be strolling the boardwalk. If Billy had done as she had requested, the Jamisons thought Elaine and Tommy were being held for further questioning and the police chief had left for the mainland to consult with the circuit solicitor. Probably the remainder of the family—Cleo, Kit, and Laura—were now at the Jamison house, along with Richard, who was packing to leave.

It was essential that no Jamison see Annie approach the police station. She made one more careful survey, then pulled out her cell. *Blip blip*s informed her there were messages. She didn't doubt that Billy had been trying to get in touch. She punched the number of the police station. "Mavis, this is Annie Darling. I'm on the harbor boardwalk. I don't want to be seen arriving at the station. Please let me in the back door. I don't want anyone to know I'm at the police station. Tell Billy I need to talk to him without anyone knowing. Can you do that?"

Mavis Cameron was always calm and collected. "Will do. He wants to see you." Her crisp tone left no doubt that Billy Cameron definitely wanted to talk to Annie. The connection ended.

As Annie stepped into the corridor at the back of the station, where two holding cells were used for prisoners, she was startled when Max strode toward her, pulled her into his arms.

She clung to him, but only for a moment. "I'm fine." Time was speeding past. The ferry would leave on schedule.

But he held her tight, looked down with a face that mirrored incredible relief and enormous exasperation. "Why did you turn off your cell? I've been going nuts.

Billy called and said you'd figured out who killed Glen, then you disappeared. You've been out of contact for almost an hour."

"Just for a while." She didn't want to discuss that period of time. Some of it involved actions she hoped Billy would never learn about. She looked past Max.

Billy Cameron stood with folded arms in the corridor. "What have you been doing?" He was brusque.

Annie stepped away from Max and faced Billy. She talked as fast as she ever had in all her life. The incredulity in Billy's face faded as he listened.

Max watched with a growing frown. He knew her so well. He was anticipating what she might have in mind and the taut set of his features indicated a man determined to circumvent her.

She concluded, ". . . and that's why Glen was shot on Tuesday morning."

Billy's blue eyes were thoughtful. "How come it took you almost an hour to get here from Death on Demand?"

She didn't meet Billy's eyes, hoped he was not into reading body language, but she couldn't meet that demanding gaze. "I got the key to Cabin Nine at Jasmine Gardens from Darwyn's grandmother. I didn't want to take a chance the manager wasn't there. That's how I was able to find the lipstick."

Billy's heavy face was grim. "We searched."

"The lipstick was hard to see. It had rolled beneath a desk."

He made an indeterminate sound deep in his throat. "Yeah." He didn't say her claim was a crock, but there was no mistaking his disbelief. "I get the picture. But even if there's a tube of lipstick, even if we can prove the owner, that's not evidence of a murder."

"I have a plan."

Max took a step toward her. "You've done enough. Now Billy knows who to look for."

Annie looked straight at Billy. "There's no proof."

Billy took a deep breath, lines grooved in his face. Finally, reluctantly, he acceded. "There's no proof." His voice was heavy.

Annie glanced at her watch. "I can flush out the killer." Again she talked fast. "The ferry leaves in twenty-six minutes. Billy, let me try."

Max shook his head. "That's crazy. What if the killer has a gun?"

Annie flung out a hand in appeal. "You'll be there. The ferry can be full of police. Please, we don't have long. Let me call." She looked deep into Max's eyes. "If we don't try, Tommy Jamison will be arrested. The circuit solicitor will insist."

Max looked at Billy.

Billy's face furrowed. "She can have a tiny camcorder and we'll be close enough to protect her. The ferry's crowded on a summer Saturday. I'll have people everywhere. We'll have to move fast, but we can manage."

Annie touched Max's tense arm. "Tommy's just a kid, Max."

Max looked unhappy. "I don't suppose you'll be in danger if we're all around you." His face was grim. "All right. Make the call."

Annie pulled out her cell phone, punched a number. "This is Annie Darling. I'm so glad I caught you. So much has happened. You know they're going to arrest Tommy and maybe Elaine, too, but I've found a link to Darwyn Jack's girlfriend."

The voice was sharp. "Darwyn's girlfriend?"

"Yes. Apparently he was meeting her in a secluded cabin, someone I know saw him there. I'm sure Darwyn couldn't keep quiet about something as big as murder and what he saw Tuesday morning. It's too long a story for now, but I found her lipstick in the cabin. It looks expensive and I'll bet the police can trace it. Anyway, I don't have time to talk. I'm on my way to the ferry. It leaves in about fifteen minutes. The chief's gone to Chastain. I've tried to call him to tell him, but I can't get through. I'm going over on the ferry and I'll track him down and insist on speaking to him in person.

I'll let you know what happens." Annie clicked off the phone.

Annie felt queasy as she slid behind the wheel of her car. She may have set up a dandy trap, but the intelligence that had successfully warded off intervention by Pat Merridew and engineered Glen Jamison's death and coolly dispatched Darwyn Jack was formidable. Annie hoped she'd been convincing, dithery and excited enough to persuade her listener that she indeed was a threat but had no inkling of the grand design.

Annie glanced at her watch. In about ten minutes, she would turn the car and head for the line waiting to board the ferry. She watched in the rearview mirror, saw a battered station wagon she recognized as Mavis's pull into the line. Some vacationers in ball caps and shorts waited to buy tickets, with backpacks carelessly slung over a shoulder. Casual clothes would have been easy to come by, stashed in the officers' lockers. She wished she didn't feel a tiny frisson of terror. Surely everything would go as they'd planned. Her protectors would be armed and quick and fast. None of the cars in line was the one she sought. It was no more than a five-minute drive from the Jamison house to downtown. Surely she would soon see the car she expected.

Her cell phone rang.

Annie pulled the phone from her pocket, raised an eyebrow at the caller ID. "Hello."

A high, shrill, terrified voice cried, "You've got to come. Or I'll die. Don't hang up." Laura Jamison pleaded, her voice shaking, "If you hang up, I'm dead. Right now you have to start driving and you can't hang up. If you hang up and call for help, I'll be dead by the time you find me. Please, drive to Jasmine Gardens."

Sheer terror thinned Laura's voice. The words knocked against one another, uneven, desperate, unmistakably true. "Will you come? Please don't let me die."

"I'm coming." Annie started the car. Could she drive by the ferry line, honk, try to raise an alarm? "I'll be there in a few minutes." One hand on the wheel, the other holding the cell . . . Could she hold the cell between her cheek and shoulder? Annie tried and the phone slid away, bounced to the floor. She swiped frantically with her right hand, brought it up again. It was too small to hold in that fashion.

"It takes four minutes . . . to get to the cabin . . . from the harbor." Laura was obviously repeating the words of her captor. "The gun's pressed against my temple. Please, please . . ." She choked back a sob. Faintly, Annie heard her cry, "She's on the line. I swear she is. Oh God, here, listen."

The phone must have been held near the captor's ear.

Annie spoke sharply. "What's going on?" She turned the car, drove away from the harbor, saw the ferry in her rearview mirror until the road turned. "I'm coming. Don't hurt her." She didn't dare honk. That would be heard on the phone. If she drove erratically, someone might notice, but if a siren sounded, the next thing she heard might be the crack of a gun. Useless in her pocket was the small video cam in the shape of a package of gum.

A cool voice instructed. "Keep talking, Annie. You're very clever. I found the lipstick. I have it now. But I never dropped it and that means you brought it here. Clever. But stupid of you. Keep on driving. Speak up now!" The command was sharp, dangerous.

"I'm driving."

"Continue to talk or Laura dies. Tell me how you knew."

Annie talked. Richard Jamison's decision to leave the island. Kirk Brewster in his next to last week as a partner. The gun-safe key taken by a member of the household. Pat Merridew's fatal curiosity. Knowledge about Pat and pain pills. Sexy Darwyn Jack and luxurious Jasmine Gardens. The function of the leaf blower. What Darwyn saw. "How lucky for you that everyone focused on what Darwyn saw." The deliberate use of Elaine's five iron. "Tommy Jamison came home and found Glen and got blood on his shirt. That was another lucky break for you."

"I'm always lucky." The observation was almost amused.

Then, too soon—yes, the drive took only four minutes from the harbor—she was there. Annie turned onto the road that twisted around the secluded cabins of Jasmine Gardens. What could she do?

"When you get to the cabin, pull in behind Laura's car."

Annie curved around bamboo, the cell phone still clutched in her hand. There was the pittosporum hedge that screened the lanai of the cabin from view. A faded red Dodge was parked in the space. The car was empty. Laura, gun to her head, must be inside the cabin.

"Don't even think about it." The voice was steely. "I will count to five. If you are not inside by then, I'll pull the trigger. Keep talking."

A lawn-service truck rattled past. Annie heard the crunch of tires on oyster shells in the drive to the next cabin. If she screamed—

"One." A pause. "Two."

"I'm coming." Annie opened the car door, hurried around a trellis to the front steps. She grabbed the innocent-appearing gum package from her pocket, held the cell phone in her other hand.

"Three."

"I'm at the steps. I'm coming inside."

Annie never doubted that a finger was firm on the trigger. The gun would sound at five. But in the living room of the small cabin, there would be two against one. A gun could not be aimed at both of them at the same time. The scene had to be set for Annie to be shot and suicide staged for Laura. That would take maneuvering, afford her and Laura time. Surely somehow, between the two of them, they could disarm the murderer.

Annie clicked on the video cam, held the little device in her left hand, dropped her cell phone in her pocket, and used her right hand to open the cabin's front door.

Next door a leaf blower began its high scream. For an instant, her step checked. What bitter irony. A leaf blower would once again mask the sound of shots unless Annie and Laura managed to outwit a ruthless adversary.

Annie stepped inside.

Laura Jamison sagged, her tear-streaked face blanched, on the small sofa.

Cleo Jamison stood with her back to the bedroom door.

Annie turned her left hand slightly to afford the video cam a view of Cleo.

She held a black pistol in one hand. Her eyes burned as she stared at Annie. "What tipped you off?"

Annie felt cold and empty, knew that Death waited only a few feet away. "The gun in the gazebo. The police figured Elaine had taken the Colt and hidden it in the gazebo since she didn't live in the house. Instead, you put the gun out there for Darwyn."

"Darwyn?" Laura turned a shocked face toward Annie.

Annie glanced around the elegantly appointed living room, the beach-style furniture new and shining, the watercolors on the walls depicting a sailboat against a blazing sunset, pelicans flying in a V above gentle waves, a little girl digging in the sand.

Her eyes moved back to Cleo, who was no longer beautiful, despite her glossy dark hair and chiseled features. Her cheekbones jutted, full lips with bright red lipstick were drawn back in a grimace. She was a figure of fury, scarcely contained.

Annie picked her words carefully. "I suppose you started the affair with Darwyn for sheer pleasure. Your husband was old. Darwyn was young and sexy."

Behind Cleo, the bedroom door eased open perhaps a half inch.

Annie felt her eyes flare wide. She immediately tried to contain her expression, keep her face unchanging. She spoke more loudly. "You met Darwyn here. I imagine you planned trysts for the afternoons. You could slip away from the office, ostensibly to run an errand, and no one would be the wiser. How long had you been sleeping with him? A few months? Long enough, I suppose, to pick up on the coldness inside him. But Glen might still be alive if Richard Jamison hadn't come."

Behind Cleo the door continued to move, slowly, slowly.

Laura sat frozen on the sofa. She, too, watched, but her gaze appeared to be focused on Cleo.

Annie kept her eyes locked with Cleo's. "You wanted Richard, but Richard wasn't willing to have an affair with his cousin's wife. I'm sure you pretended to be stricken with nobility as well. But when Richard told you he was leaving the island, you made your plans. I don't know what you promised Darwyn, but he agreed and so the process began. You placed the gun in the gazebo. Pat Merridew had no liking for any of you by that time. She'd been fired. She must have enjoyed finding out something she could hold over your head. She saw you hide the towel and then checked and discovered the contents. She invited you for coffee to have a visit, but you went to her house earlier in the day, took her leftover pain pills."

Cleo's eyes burned. "She was a fool. Her back door was unlocked. I found the pills in a kitchen cabinet. She'd told us over and over about the pain in her wrist."

Annie spoke quietly. "You got the pills and ground them up and had them in a plastic bag in your purse. That evening at her house, did you ask for more honey for your Irish coffee? Something like that happened, I'm sure. When she went to the kitchen, you dropped the ground-up pills in her cup. When she began to get drowsy, you picked up the travel brochures, washed your own crystal mug, replaced it without fingerprints in the cabinet, discarded the prescription bottle in the trash, and left her to die. Now everything was on track for Glen's murder."

Annie was careful not to look beyond Cleo at the figure standing in the bedroom doorway.

"Glen had to die this week. You knew the information about the key man insurance would come out. That's why you arranged to be in Savannah for a deposition. No suspicion would attach to you. You weren't on the island. Moreover, Kirk was still a partner and he made a nice suspect for the police. And Glen had to die on Tuesday when Darwyn came to the house to work. Darwyn propped the leaf blower near the terrace. He left it running. He wore gardening gloves and he had the Colt. He opened the French door to the study and stepped inside.

"Glen must have stood up and walked toward him. Darwyn was a good shot. He had to be a good shot. Most shooters aim for the chest. There's less chance of missing. But arrogant, confident Darwyn shot Glen twice in the throat. I imagine he liked blood. Glen fell to the floor. Darwyn dropped the gun, slipped back outside, picked up the leaf blower, went back to work. Who did Darwyn see? Only Tommy. When I talked to Darwyn, he hinted at what he might have seen. He knew Elaine was a suspect and he made that threatening visit to her cottage. I don't know that he intended to ask for money. I think he was a bully and wanted to make her uncomfortable. Maybe he intended simply to widen the possibilities for the police, but it worked out very well for you. Everyone assumed Darwyn was killed because of what he had seen in the backyard. You asked him to meet you in the gazebo. You had already taken Elaine's five iron and hidden the club there."

A pulse throbbed in Cleo's throat. She lifted the gun.

Annie flung herself to one side as the man in the bedroom doorway plunged forward, strong and determined. He grabbed Cleo's wrist, twisted her arm.

The gun went off. The sound was huge in the small room.

Cleo sagged to her left. The gun clattered from her hand onto the floor.

Richard Jamison kicked the gun away.

Cleo moaned and rolled to one side, clutching at a welling flood of blood pumping from her upper leg. "Richard . . ." Her face worked. "Richard, I did it all for you."

Sixteen

Emma Clyde, the island's famous septuagenarian mystery author, lifted a coffee mug. Its inscription read: *Desperate Measures* by Dennis Wheatley. Emma's deep voice was admiring. "To Annie, brave and clever."

Max's blue eyes held remembered fear. "How about 'To Annie, reckless and demen—'" He paused. His face softened. "To Annie, champion of the lost and vulnerable. But"—his voice was imploring—"please don't ever do anything like that again. We were on the ferry and you didn't come."

"Not a good feeling." Billy Cameron shook his head. Comfortable in a polo and Levi's, his bulky frame made the rattan chair in Death on Demand's coffee area appear small.

Henny Brawley topped a cappuccino with a maraschino cherry. "Annie, why didn't you do something to alert everyone?"

Annie felt cold. "You didn't hear Laura's voice. I had to stay on the phone or Cleo would have shot her. Cleo knew how little time it took to drive to Jasmine Gardens. It took one hand to drive and one to talk on the phone. I had to keep talking. If I'd honked the horn or been late . . ."

She touched the red letters on her mug: *The Fatal Kiss Mystery.* "I kept thinking there would be two of us in the cabin, that I could do something . . ."

Billy shook his head. "Cleo was smart and ruthless. Fortunately for you and Laura, Richard Jamison was smart, too. He didn't want to believe Cleo was involved, but he saw her slip out into the garden Thursday night. He told me there was a look on her face that kept him from following her. He thought she was grieving for Glen. The next day Darwyn's body was found. She didn't say a word about having been in the backyard. That worried him. He tried to keep an eye on her after that. Saturday afternoon, he saw her come out of her room. He said, 'She had that look again.' He slipped down after her. She went into the study. She came out in a minute. Laura was sitting on the lower verandah. Cleo said something to her and in a minute they left in

Laura's car. Richard was worried. He said, 'Cleo was dangerous. I knew it. I didn't know what she'd said to Laura, but I thought I'd better follow. I didn't think I should use my car. She would recognize it.' He ran across the street, tossed his billfold to a guy working in the yard, yelled he'd bring the truck back in a few minutes, and jumped into the pickup. He followed Laura's car and said he could see Laura and he knew something awful was happening, Laura was crying into a cell phone. He thought about crashing into the back of the car, but he decided to keep following, find out what was going on. That's when he called us, but he didn't know where they were going. He kept after Laura's car into Jasmine Gardens and pulled into the drive at the next cabin. He was smart. He took a leaf blower, turned it on right behind Cabin Nine, and used the sound to mask the noise he made breaking in one of the bedroom windows."

Billy shook his head. "He did what was right, but now he blames himself for Cleo's death. I told him that she was the one with the gun in her hand, she was the one who fired, and it was her bad luck that she blew away a femoral artery."

"Bad luck? People make their own luck." Emma's crusty voice was didactic. "She took the wrong path. She married a man she didn't love, indulged her passion with a younger man, was drawn to yet another man, intended to profit from her husband's death, and killed sans merci."

There was a respectful silence. Emma nodded in self-approval at her sage pronouncement. She cleared her throat. "It's a shame I was so engaged in writing my new book." She stared grandly about. "The title is *Sans Merci*. Otherwise, I would likely have pinpointed the truth at once—a younger wife, the sexy gardener, and a great deal of money."

Laurel, elegant in a sky-blue chambray blouse and white skirt, smiled kindly at Emma, though her dark blue eyes danced with amusement. She said gently, "I'm proud of Annie that she"—there was the faintest emphasis on the pronoun—"saw the truth. No one but Annie realized that it didn't matter what the gardener saw." Laurel smoothed back a golden curl and lifted her mug in a salute. The inscription read: *Pattern of Murder* by Mignon Eberhart.

Annie came around the counter and slipped an arm around her mother-in-law's shoulders. "I owe the answer to you." She gave Laurel a swift hug, then crossed the floor and picked up the Cat Truth poster with the Bombay Tom: *Don't look at me. I was at the vet's.* "No one looked at Cleo because she was in Savannah. The murderer came from the backyard.

I knew that had to be true because of Laura on the upper verandah and the lineman across the street. If Glen wasn't shot by Tommy, the only other person in the backyard was Darwyn. Sexy, dangerous, wild Darwyn, who was meeting a woman in an exclusive cabin, the better to keep her identity hidden. Then I knew. But it was the poster that made everything clear. So, from now on, Cat Truth posters will be sold at Death on Demand."

Laurel was overcome with delight. "Oh my dear, how gracious of you. I have more posters in my car. I'll see about them right now." She popped down from a stool at the coffee bar, but paused to look up at the paintings. "Everything does seem to come out so well for me. And I am pleased"—she darted quick glances at Emma and Henny, spoke rapidly to forestall them— "to reveal the titles of this month's mystery paintings." She pointed at them in order: *"Murder at Madingley Grange* by Caroline Graham, *Miss Julia Renews Her Vows* by Ann Ross, *A Romantic Way to Die* by Bill Crider, *Dead Air* by Mary Kennedy, *Elvis and the Dearly Departed* by Peggy Webb."

Annie clapped in admiration and was joined, though reluctantly, by Henny and Emma. The two mystery experts bore a startling resemblance, in Annie's view, to yet another Cat Truth poster. A Colorpoint Persian with a short, cobby body and fluffy black legs and tail stood next to a fine-boned, long-haired Brown-Spotted Tabby-and-White Siberian. The two cats stared in reproof at a delicate, elegant Seal Tortie Tabby Point with one paw firmly planted on a mouse: *Don't think you're on our level. Obviously, it's beginner's luck.*

Was it Annie's imagination or did the Seal Point have a decidedly pleased expression?

Laurel certainly did.